THE ILL-MADE KNIGHT

T. H. White

CHAPTER I

In the castle of Benwick, the French boy was looking at his face in the polished surface of a kettle–hat. It flashed in the sunlight with the stubborn gleam of metal. It was practically the same as the steel helmet which soldiers still wear, and it did not make a good mirror, but it was the best he could get. He turned the hat in various directions, hoping to get an average idea of his face from the different distortions which the bulges made. He was trying to find out what he was, and he was afraid of what he would find.

The boy thought that there was something wrong with him. All through his life—even when he was a great man with the world at his feet—he was to feel this gap: something at the bottom of his heart of which he was aware, and ashamed, but which he did not understand. There is no need for us to try to understand it. We do not have to dabble in a place which he preferred to keep secret.

The Armoury, where the boy stood, was lined with weapons of war. For the last two hours he had been whirling a pair of dumbbells in the air—he called them "poises"—and singing to himself a song with no words and no tune. He was fifteen. He had just come back from England, where his father King Ban of Benwick had been helping the English King to quell a rebellion. You remember that Arthur wanted to catch his knights young, to train them for the Round Table, and that he had noticed Lancelot at the feast, because he was winning most of the games.

Lancelot, swinging his dumb–bells fiercely and making his wordless noise, had been thinking of King Arthur with all his might. He was in love with him. That was why he had been swinging the poises. He had been remembering all the words of the only conversation which he had held with his hero.

The King had called him over when they were embarking for France—after he had kissed King Ban good–bye—and they had gone alone into a corner of the ship. The heraldic sails of Ban's fleet, and the sailors in the rigging, and the armed turrets and archers and seagulls, like flake–white, had been a background to their conversation.

"Lance," the King had said, "come here a moment, will you?"

"Sir."

"I was watching you playing games at the feast."

"Sir."

"You seemed to win most of them."

Lancelot squinted down his nose.

"I want to get hold of a lot of people who are good at games, to help with an idea I have. It is for the time when I am a real King, and have got this kingdom settled. I was wondering whether you would care to help, when you are old enough?"

The boy had made a sort of wriggle, and had suddenly flashed his eyes at the speaker.

"It is about knights," Arthur had continued. "I want to have an Order of Chivalry, like the Order of the Garter, which goes about fighting against Might. Would you like to be one of those?"

"Yes."

The King had looked at him closely, unable to see whether he was pleased or frightened or merely being polite.

"Do you understand what I am talking about?"

Lancelot had taken the wind out of his sails.

"We call it Fort Mayne in France," he had explained. "The man with the strongest arm in a clan gets made the head of it, and does what he pleases. That is why we call it Fort Mayne. You want to put an end to the Strong Arm, by having a band of knights who believe in justice rather than strength. Yes, I would like to be one of those very much. I must grow up first. Thank you. Now I must say good–bye."

So they had sailed away from England—the boy standing in the front of the ship and refusing to look back, because he did not want to show his feelings. He had already fallen in love with Arthur on the night of the wedding feast, and he carried with him in his heart to France the picture of that bright northern king, at supper, flushed and glorious from his wars.

Behind the black eyes which were searching intently in the kettle–hat there was a dream which had come to him the previous night. Seven hundred years ago—or it may have been fifteen hundred according to Malory's notation—people took dreams as seriously as the psychiatrists do today, and Lancelot's had been a disturbing one. It was not disturbing because of anything it might mean—for he had not the least idea of its meaning—but because it had left him with a sense of loss. This was what it was.

Lancelot and his young brother, Ector Demaris, had been sitting in two chairs. They got out of these chairs and were mounted on two horses. Lancelot said: "Go we, and seek that which we shall not find." So they did. But a Man or a Power set upon Lancelot, and beat him and despoiled him, and clothed him in another array which was full of knots, and made him ride on an ass instead of on the horse. Then there was a beautiful well, with the fairest waters he had ever seen, and he got off his ass to drink out of it. It seemed to him that there could be nothing in the world more beautiful than to drink of this well. But as soon as he stooped his lips toward it, the water sank away. It went right down into the barrel of the well, sinking and sinking from him so that he could not get it. It made him feel desolate, to be abandoned by the water of the well.

Arthur and the well, and the dumb–bells which were to make him worthy of Arthur, and the ache in his tired arms from swinging them—all these were at the back of the boy's mind as he tilted the tin hat backward and forward between his fingers, but there was a more insistent thought in his head also. It was a thought about the face in the metal, and about the thing which must have gone wrong in the depths of his spirit to make a face like that. He was not a self–deceiver. He knew that whichever way he turned the morion, it would tell him the same story. He had already decided that when he was a grown knight he would give himself a melancholy title. He was the eldest son, so he was bound to be knighted, but he would not call himself Sir Lancelot. He would call himself the Chevalier Mal Fet—the Ill–Made Knight.

So far as he could see—and he felt that there must be some reason for it somewhere—the boy's face was as ugly as a monster's in the King's menagerie. He looked like an African ape.

CHAPTER II

Lancelot ended by being the greatest knight King Arthur had. He was a sort of Bradman, top of the battling averages. Tristram and Lamorak were second and third.

But you have to remember that people can't be good at cricket unless they teach themselves to be so, and that jousting was an art, just as cricket is. It was like cricket in many ways. There was a scorer's pavilion at a tournament, with a real scorer inside it, who made marks on the parchment just like the mark for one run which is made by the cricket scorer today. The people, walking round the ground in their best frocks, from Grand Stand to Refreshment Tent, must have found the fighting very like the game. It took a frightfully long time—Sir Lancelot's innings frequently lasted all day, if he were battling against a good knight—and the movements had a feeling of slow–motion, because of the weight of armour. When the sword–play had begun, the combatants stood opposite each other in the green acre like batsman and bowler—except that they stood closer together—and perhaps Sir Gawaine would start with an in–swinger, which Sir Lancelot would put away to leg with a beautiful leg–glide, and then Lancelot would reply with a yorker under Gawaine's guard —it was called "foining"—and all the people round the field would clap. King Arthur might turn to Guenever in the Pavilion, and remark that the great man's footwork was as lovely as ever. The knights had little curtains on the back of their helms, to keep the hot sun off the metal, like the handkerchiefs which cricketers will sometimes arrange behind their caps today.

Knightly exercise was as much an art as cricket is, and perhaps the only way in which Lancelot did not resemble Bradman was that he was more graceful. He did not have that crouching on the bat and hopping out to the pitch of the ball. He was more like Woolley. But you can't be like Woolley by simply sitting still and wanting to be so.

The Armoury, where the small boy who was later to be Sir Lancelot was standing with his morion, was the largest single room in the castle of Benwick. It was to be the room in which this boy was to spend most of his waking hours for the next three years.

The rooms of the main castle—which he could see from the windows—were mostly small, because people can't afford to build for luxury when they are making a fortification. Round the inner fort with its small rooms there was a wide byre, or shell–keep, into which the castle herds were driven during a siege. This was surrounded by a high wall with towers, and, on the inner side of this wall, the big rooms which were needed for stores, barns, barracks, and stables were built. The Armoury was one of these rooms. It stood between the stables, for fifty horses, and the cowsheds. The best family armour—the bits which were actually in use—was kept in a little room in the castle itself, and it was only the arms of the troops, and the spare parts of the family stuff, and the things which were needed for gymnastics, practice, or physical training, which reposed in the Armoury.

Under the raftered ceiling, and the nearest to it, there hung or leaned a collection of bannerettes and pennoncels, blazoned with the Ban charges—France Ancient, as they are now called—which would be needed on various occasions. Along the wall there were tilting lances, resting horizontally on nails so that they should not warp. These looked like bars for exercises in a gymnasium. In one corner a collection of old lances which had already warped or got injured in some way, but which might still be useful for something, were standing upright. A rack, running the whole length of the second main wall, held the infantry issue of mail habergeons with mittens, spears, morions, and Bordeaux swords. King Ban was fortunate in living at Benwick, for the Bordeaux swords were local and particularly good. Then there were harness–barrels, in which the armour was packed in hay for expeditions overseas—some of it was still packed from the last expedition, and a curious mixture it was. Uncle Dap, who looked after the Armoury, had been unpacking one of the barrels to make an inventory of its contents—and had gone away in despair on discovering ten pounds of dates and five loaves of sugar in it. It must have been some sort of honey sugar, unless it was loaf sugar brought back from the Crusades. He had left his list beside the barrel, and this recorded, among other articles: a salade garnessed with golde, iij peire gantelez, a vestment, a mesbooke, an auter cloth, a peir of brigandines, a pyssyng basin of silver, x schertes for my Lord, a jakete of leather, and a bagge of chessmen. Then, in an alcove formed by the harness–barrels, there was a set of shelves which formed the dispensary for sick armour. On the shelves there were huge bottles of olive oil—nowadays they prefer a mineral oil for armour, but they did not understand such niceties in Lancelot's time—together with boxes of fine sand for polishing, bags of brigandine nails at eleven shillings and eightpence the twenty thousand, rivets, spare rings for chain mail, leather skins for cutting new straps and bases for the knee harness, together with a thousand other details then fascinating, but now lost to us. There were gambesons like the pads which the goalkeeper wears in hockey, or like the quilted protections which Americans have at football. In various corners there were pushed, so as to leave a free space in the middle of the room, a collection of gymnastic apparatus such as quintains and so on, while Uncle Dap's desk stood near the door. On the desk there were splattering quill pens, blotting sand, sticks for beating Lancelot when he was stupid, and notes, in unutterable confusion, as to which jupons had lately been pawned—pawning was a great institution for valuable armour—and which helms had been brought up to date with a glancing surface, and whose vambrace stood in need of repair, and what had been paid to whom for fforbeshynge which when. Most of the accounts were wrongly added up.

Three years may seem a long time for a boy to spend in one room, if he only goes out of it to eat and sleep and to practise tilting in the field. It is even difficult to imagine a boy who would do it, unless you realize from the start that Lancelot was not romantic and debonair. Tennyson and the Pre–Raphaelites would have found it difficult to recognize this rather sullen and unsatisfactory child, with the ugly face, who did not disclose to anybody that he was living on dreams and prayers. They might have wondered what store of ferocity he had against himself, that could set him to break his own body so young. They might have wondered why he was so strange.

To begin with, he had to spend the weary months charging against Uncle Dap, with a blunt spear under his arm. Uncle Dap, armed cap–à–pie, would sit on a stool—and Lancelot, with the morne–headed spear, would charge and charge against him, learning the best lodges on armour for a point. Then there were lonely hours with poises, with many other hours out of doors—before he was even allowed to touch real arms—in which he learned various kinds of throwing, casting with the sling–stick or the casting spear, and tossing the bar. After that, after a year of toil, there was his promotion to the pel–quintain. It was a stake driven upright in the ground, and he had to fight against it with sword and shield—rather like shadow–boxing, or using a punch–ball. He had to use arms for this exercise which weighed twice as much as the ordinary sword and shield. Sixty pounds was considered a good weight for the arms used on the pel–quintain—so that, when he did come at length to the usual weapons, he would wield them featly. They would seem light by comparison. The final stage of breaking to the cricket standard was by mock combats. In these at last; and after all the bitter setbacks of discipline, he was allowed to fight battles which were nearly real ones, against his brother and cousins. The combats were held under strict rules. They might begin with a cast of the spear blunted, followed by seven strokes with the sword, point and edge rebated, "without close, or griping one another with the handes, upon paine of punishment as the judges for the time being shall thinke requisite." It was not lawful in these matches to foin—that is, to make a thrust of the point. Finally there was swashbuckling. The now vigorous boy might go at his companions harum–scarum, with sword and buckler.

If you have been down in one of the old–fashioned diving suits which used to be standard in the Royal Navy before frogmen and free diving came along, you will know why divers move slowly. A diver has forty pounds of lead on each foot and two plaques of lead—each weighing fifty pounds—one on his back and one on his chest. These are apart from the weight of the suit and the helmet. Except when he is in the sea, he weighs twice as much as a man. When he has to step over a rope or an air–tube on deck, it is hard work—like climbing a wall. If you push him from in front, the weight behind him tends to take over, so that he might fall backwards. The same thing happens vice versa. Practised divers become adept at dealing with these handicaps, and can hoist those forty pound feet up and down the ship's ladder fairly nimbly—but an amateur half kills himself with the mere toil of movement. Lancelot, like the diver, had to learn to be nimble against the force of gravity.

Knights–in–armour were like divers in more ways than one.

Apart from their helmets and encumbrances and the difficulty of breathing, they had to be dressed in their suits by kind and careful assistants. They had to rely on these assistants to do it properly. A diver puts his life in the hands of the ratings who are dressing him. These young men, like pages or squires, mother him with great tenderness and concentration and with a sort of protective respect. They always address him by his title, not by his name. They say, "Sit down, diver," or "Now the left foot, diver," or "Diver

Two, can you hear me on the inter–com?"

It is good to put your life in other people's hands.

Three years of it. The other boys did not worry, for they had other things to think about—but for the ugly one it was the whole of an obscure and mystic life. He had to perfect himself for Arthur as somebody who was good at games, and he had to think about the theories of chivalry even when he was in bed at night. He had to teach himself to possess a sound opinion on hundreds of disputed points—on the proper length of weapons, or the cut of a mantling, or the articulation of a pauldron, or whether cedar–wood was better than ash for spears, as Chaucer seems to have believed.

Here is a short example of the problems of chivalry, which he thought about in his early times. There was a knight once called Reynaud de Roy, who had a tilting match with another one called John de Holland. Reynaud purposely fastened his tilting helm—the huge straw–padded drum which sometimes fitted over the helmet proper—so that it was loose. When John of Holland's spear point struck it, it simply fell off. This meant that the helm came off Reynaud, instead of Reynaud coming off his horse. An effective trick, but a dangerous one—the whole of chivalry argued about it for a long time, some saying that it was unsporting, some that it was fair but too risky, and some that it was a good idea.

Three years of discipline made Lancelot, not a merry heart and a capacity for singing tirra–lirra. Out of a lifetime which at his age must have seemed to stretch little more than a week ahead, he gave thirty–six months to another man's idea because he was in love with it. He supported himself meanwhile on daydreams. He wanted to be the best knight in the world, so that Arthur would love him in return, and he wanted one other thing which was still possible in those days. He wanted, through his purity and excellence, to be able to perform some ordinary miracle—to heal a blind man or something like that, for instance.

CHAPTER III

There was a feature about the great families which centred round the doom of Arthur. All three had a resident genius of the family, half–way between a tutor and a confidant, who affected the characters of the children in each. At Sir Ector's castle there had been Merlyn, who was the main influence in Arthur's life. In lonely and distant Lothian there had been St. Toirdealbhach, whose warlike philosophy must have had something to do with the clannishness of Gawaine and his brothers. In King Ban's castle there was an uncle of Lancelot's, whose name was Gwenbors. Actually he was the old man we have met, known to everybody as Uncle Dap, but his given name was Gwenbors. In those days you generally named your children in the same way as we name foxhounds and foals today. If you happened to be Queen Morgause and had four children, you put a G in all their names (Gawaine, Agravaine, Gaheris, and Gareth)—and, naturally if your brothers happened to be called Ban and Bors, you were doomed to be called Gwenbors yourself. It made it easier to remember who you were.

Uncle Dap was the only one in the family who took Lancelot seriously, and Lancelot was the one who was serious about Uncle Dap. It was easy not to be serious about the old fellow, for he was that peculiar creation which ignorant people laugh at—a genuine maestro. His branch of learning was chivalry. There was not a piece of armour proofed in Europe but what Uncle Dap had a theory about it. He was furious with the new Gothic style, with its ridges and scallop–patterns and fluting. He considered it ridiculous to wear armour like the ropework on a Nelson sideboard, for it was obvious that every groove would be liable to hold a point. The whole object of good armour, he said, was to throw the point off—and, when he thought of the people in Germany making their horrible furrows, he nearly went frantic. There was nothing in Heraldry which he did not know. If anybody committed any of the grosser errors—such as putting metal on metal or colour on colour—he became electrified with passion. His long white moustaches quivered at their tips like antennae, the ends of his fingers came together in gestures of the wildest passion, and he waved his arms and jumped up and down and wagged his eyebrows and almost fizzed. Nobody can be a maestro without being subject to these excitements, so Lancelot seldom minded when he got his face slapped in a mêlée about shields cut *à bouche* or about whether it was a good idea to have a guige on your shield or not. Sometimes Uncle Dap was tantalized into beating him, but he bore that also. In those days they did.

One reason for not minding Uncle Dap's transports was that everything the boy wanted could be learned from him. He was not only a distinguished clerk and authority on his own subjects—he was also one of the finest swordsmen in France. It was for this, really, that the boy had attached himself. It was in order to rase and trace and foin under the brutal tuition of genius—in order to hold out a heavy sword at arm's length in a lunge until he felt he would split in half—only to have Uncle Dap catch hold of his point and pull him into a crueller stretch.

Ever since he could remember, there had been the excited man with the eyes of blue steel, jumping up and down, and snapping his fingers, and shouting out as if life itself depended on it: "Doublez! Dedoublez! Degagez! Un! Deux!"

One fine day in late summer, Lancelot was sitting in the Armoury with his uncle. In the big room there was a lot of dust dancing in the sunbeams, dust which they had themselves been stirring up a moment before, and round the walls there were the ranks of polished armour, and the racks of spears, and helms and morions hanging on pegs. There were misericordes and harness and the various banners and pennoncels, blazoned with the Ban chargers. The two fencers had sat down to rest after an exciting bout, and Uncle Dap was blown. Lancelot was eighteen now. He was a better fencer than his maestro—though Uncle Dap would not admit it, and his pupil tactfully pretended that he was not.

A page came in while they were still panting, and told him that he was wanted by his mother.

"Why?"

The page said that a gentleman had arrived who wanted to see him, and the Queen had said that he was to come at once.

Queen Elaine was sitting in the solar, where she had been doing tapestry work, and her two guests were sitting on either side of her. She was not the Elaine who had been one of the Cornwall sisters. It was a popular name in those days and several women in the Morte d'Arthur had it, particularly as some of its manuscript sources have got mixed up. The three grown–ups at the long table looked like a row of examiners in the dim room. One of the guests was an elderly gentleman with a white beard and pointed hat, and the other was a handsome minx with an olive complexion and plucked eyebrows. They all three looked at Lancelot, and the old gentleman spoke first.

"Hum!"

They waited.

"You called him Galahad," said the old gentleman.

"His first name was Galahad," he added, "and now he is Lancelot, since he was confirmed."

"However did you know?"

"It can't be helped," said Merlyn. "It is one of the things one does know, and there's an end on't. Now, let me see, what are the other things I was supposed to tell you?"

The young lady with the plucked eyebrows put her hand before her mouth and yawned gracefully, like a cat.

"He will get the hope of his heart thirty years from now, and he will be the best knight in the world."

"Shall I live to see it?" asked Queen Elaine.

Merlyn scratched his head, gave it a bump on the top with his knuckles, and replied:

"Yes."

"Well," said the Queen, "it is all very wonderful, I must say. Do you hear that, Lance? You are to be the best knight in the world!"

The boy asked: "Have you come from the court of King Arthur?"

"Yes."

"Is everything well?"

"Yes. He sent you his love."

"Is the King happy?"

"Very happy. Guenever sent her love too."

"Who is Guenever?"

"Good gracious!" exclaimed the magician. "Didn't you know about that? No, of course not. I have been getting bejingled in my brains."

Here he glanced at the beautiful lady, as if she might be responsible for the jingling—which she was. She was Nimue, and he had fallen in love with her at last.

"Guenever," said Nimue, "is Arthur's new queen. They have been married for some time."

"Her father is King Leodegrance," explained Merlyn. "He gave Arthur a present of a round table when they were married, and a hundred knights to go with it. There is room at the table for a hundred and fifty."

Lancelot said: "Oh!"

"The King meant to tell you," said Merlyn. "Perhaps the messenger got drowned on the way over. There may have been a storm. He really did mean to tell you."

"Oh," said the boy, for the second time.

Merlyn began to talk quickly, because he saw that it was a difficult situation. From Lancelot's face he could not tell whether he was hurt or whether it was like that always.

"He has only managed to fill in twenty–nine of the seats so far," he said. "There is room for twenty–one more. Plenty of room. All the knights' names are written on them in gold."

There was a pause, during which nobody knew what to say. Then Lancelot cleared his throat.

"There was a boy," he said, "when I was in England. His name was Gawaine. Has he been made one of the knights of the table?"

Merlyn looked guilty, and nodded his head.

"He was created on the day Arthur was married."

"I see."

There was another long pause.

"This lady," said Merlyn, feeling that he had better fill in the silence, "is called Nimue. I am in love with her. We are having a sort of honeymoon together—only it is a magical one—and now we shall have to be off to Cornwall. I am sorry we could not visit you for longer."

"My dear Merlyn," exclaimed the Queen, "but surely you will stay the night?"

"No, no. Thank you. Thank you very much. We are in a hurry just now."

"You will have a glass of something before you leave?"

"No, thank you. It is very kind of you, but really, we must be off. We have some magic to attend to in Cornwall."

"Such a short visit—" began the Queen.

Merlyn cut her short by standing up and taking Nimue's hand in his.

"Good–bye now," he said with determination—and in a couple of spins they were both gone.

Their bodies were gone, but the magician's voice remained in the air.

"That's that," they could hear him saying in a relieved tone. "Now then, my angel, what about that place I was telling you of in Cornwall, the one with the magical cave in it?"

Lancelot went back to Uncle Dap in the Armoury, with slow steps. He stood in front of his uncle, and bit his lip.

"I am going to England," he said.

Uncle Dap looked at him in amazement, but said nothing.

"I shall start this evening."

"It seems sudden," said Uncle Dap. "Your mother does not usually make up her mind so quickly."

"My mother does not know."

"Do you mean that you are going to run away?"

"If I told my mother and father, there would only be a fuss," he said. "It is not that I am running away. I shall come back again. But I must go to England as quick as I can."

"Do you expect me not to tell your mother?"

"Yes, I do."

Uncle Dap gnawed the ends of his moustache, and wrung his hands.

"If they get to know that I could have prevented it," he said, "Ban will cut off my head."

"They will not know," said the boy indifferently, and he went away to arrange about his packing.

A week later, Lancelot and Uncle Dap were sitting in a peculiar boat in the middle of the English Channel. The boat had a sort of castle at each end. There was another castle half–way up the single mast, which gave it the appearance of a dovecote. It had flags fore and aft. The one gay sail had a Cross Potent on it, while an enormous streamer floated from the top of the mast. There were eight oars, and the two passengers were seasick.

CHAPTER IV

The hero–worshipper rode towards Camelot with a bitter heart. It was hard for him at eighteen to have given his life to a king, only to be forgotten—hard to have spent those sorrowful hours with the heavy arms in the dust of the Armoury, only to see Sir Gawaine knighted first—hardest of all to have broken his body for the older man's ideal, only to find this mincing wife stepping in at the end of it to snatch away his love at no cost at all. Lancelot was jealous of Guenever, and he was ashamed of himself for being so.

Uncle Dap rode behind the grieving boy in silence. He knew a thing which the other was still too green to know—that he had taught the finest knight in Europe. Like an excited tit which had nursed a cuckoo, Uncle Dap fluttered along behind his prodigy. He was carrying the fighting harness, which was strapped up in apple–pie order according to his own dodges and wrinkles—for, from now on, he was Lancelot's squire.

They came to a clearing in the wood, and a little stream ran through the middle. There was a ford here and the stream ran tinkling over the clean stones, only a few inches deep. The sun shone down into the clearing. Some wood–pigeons sang drowsily their Take Two Cows Taffy, and, on the other side of the musical water, there was an enormous knight in black armour with his tilting helm in position. He sat motionless on a black charger, and his shield was still in its canvas case. It was impossible to read his blazon. Being so still, so portly in his iron sheath, and having the great blind helm over his head so that he had no proper face, he had a look of danger about him. You did not know what he was thinking, nor what action he might be going to take. He was a menace.

Lancelot halted, and so did Uncle Dap. The black knight walked his horse into the shallow water, and drew rein in front of them. He raised his lance in a gesture of salute, then pointed with it to a place behind Lancelot's back. Either he was telling him to go home again, or else he was pointing out a good position from which they could start their charges. Whichever the case might be, Lancelot saluted with his gauntlet and turned round to go to the place. He took one of his spears from Uncle Dap, pulled his tilting helm round in front of him—it had been hanging behind on a chain—and lifted the steel turret into position on his head. He laced it on. Now he too had become a man without an expression.

The two knights faced each other from opposite ends of the little glade. Then, although neither of them had so far spoken a word, they fewtered their spears, put spurs to their horses, and began to charge. Uncle Dap, drawn up safely behind a near–by tree, could hardly contain his delight. He knew what was going to happen to the black knight, although Lancelot did not know, and he began to snap his fingers.

The first time you do a thing, it is often exciting. To go alone in an airplane for the first time used to be so exciting that it nearly choked you. Lancelot had never ridden a serious joust before—and, although he had charged at hundreds of quintains and thousands of rings, he had never taken his life in his hands in earnest. In the first moment of the charge, he felt to himself: "Well, now I am off. Nothing can help me now." In the second moment he settled down to behave automatically, in the same way as he had always behaved with the quintain and the rings.

The point of his spear took the black knight under the rim of his shoulder–harness at exactly the right place. His mount was in full gallop, and the black knight's was still in a canter. The black knight and his horse revolved rapidly toward their sinister side, left the ground together in a handsome parabola, and came down again with a clash. As Lancelot rode by, he could see them sprawling on the ground together, with the knight's broken lance between the horse's legs and one flashing horse–shoe tearing the canvas from the fallen shield. The man and the horse were mixed together. Each was afraid of the other, and each was kicking against the other in the effort to be parted. Then the horse got up on its forelegs, its haunches heaved upright, and the knight sat up, lifting one steel gauntlet, as if to rub his head. Lancelot reined in and rode back to him.

Generally, when one knight had given another a fall with the lance, the fallen one used to lose his temper, blame the fall on his horse, and insist upon fighting it out with swords on foot. The usual excuse was to say: "The son of a mare hath failed me, but I wote well my father's sword never shall."

The black knight, however, did not do the usual thing. He was evidently a more cheerful kind of person than the colour of his armour would suggest, for he sat up and blew through the split of his helm, making a note of surprise and admiration. Then he took off the helm and mopped his brow. The shield, whose cover the horse's hoof had torn, bore, *or, a dragon rampant gules.*

Lancelot threw his spear into a bush, got off his horse very quickly, and knelt down beside the knight. All his love was back again inside him. It was typical of Arthur not to lose his temper, typical of him to sit on the ground making noises of admiration when he had just been given a great fall.

"Sir," said Lancelot, taking off his own helm with a humble gesture; and he bowed his head in the French fashion.

The King began scrambling to his feet in great excitement.

"Lancelot!" he exclaimed. "Why, it's the boy Lancelot! You are the king's son of Benwick. I remember seeing you when he came over for the Battle of Bedegraine. What a fall! I never saw anything like it. Where did you learn to do this? It was terrific! Were you coming to my Court? How is King Ban? How is your charming mother? Really, my dear chap, this is magnificent!"

Lancelot looked up at the breathless King, who held out both hands to help him to his feet, and his jealousy and grief were over.

They caught their horses and jogged off toward the palace side by side, forgetting Uncle Dap. They had so much to say to each other that they both talked all the time. Lancelot gave imaginary messages from King Ban or from Queen Elaine, and Arthur talked about how Gawaine had killed a lady. He told how King Pellinore had got so courageous since his marriage that he had killed King Lot of Orkney by mistake in a tournament, and how the Round Table was going as well as could be expected, but very slowly, and how, now that Lancelot had arrived, everything would come right before they knew where they were.

He was knighted the first day—he might have been knighted at any time during the past two years, but he had refused to be done by anybody except Arthur—and he was introduced to Guenever the same evening. There is a story that her hair was yellow, but it was not. It was so black that it was startling, and her blue eyes, deep and clear, had a sort of fearlessness which was startling too. She was surprised by the young man's twisted face, but not frightened.

"Now," said the King, putting their hands together. "This is Lancelot, the one I told you about. He is going to be the best knight I have. I never saw such a fall as he gave me. I want you to be kind to him, Gwen. His father is one of my oldest friends."

He kissed the Queen's hand coldly.

He did not notice anything particular about her, because his mind was filled with previous pictures which he had made for himself. There was no room for pictures of what she was really like. He thought of her only as the person who had robbed him, and, since robbers are deceitful, designing, and heartless people, he thought of her as these.

"How do you do?" asked the Queen.

Arthur said: "We shall have to tell him what has been happening since he went away. What a lot of things to tell! Where can we begin?"

"Begin with the Table," said Lancelot.

"Oh dear!"

The Queen laughed and smiled at the new knight.

"Arthur thinks about it all the time," she said. "He even dreams about it at night. He won't be able to tell you unless he talks for a week."

"It is not going badly," said the King. "You can't expect a thing like that to go smoothly the whole time. The idea is there, and people are beginning to understand it, and that is the great thing. I am sure it will work."

"What about the Orkney faction?"

"They will come round in time."

"Is that Gawaine?" inquired Lancelot. "What is the matter with the Orkney faction?"

The King looked uncomfortable. He said: "The real matter with them is

Morgause, their mother. She brought them up with so little love or security that they find it difficult to understand warm–hearted people themselves. They are suspicious and frightened. They don't get hold of the idea as I wanted them to do. We have three of them here—Gawaine, Gaheris and Agravaine. It is not their fault."

"Arthur had his first Pentecost feast the year we were married," explained Guenever, "and sent everybody out looking for good adventures, to see how the idea would work. When they came back, Gawaine had cut a lady's head off, and even dear old Pellinore had failed to rescue a damsel in distress. Arthur was furious about it."

"It is not Gawaine's fault," said the King. "He is a nice fellow. I like him. It is the fault of that woman."

"I hope things have got better since then?"

"Yes. It is slow work, of course, but I am sure we could say that things have got better."

"Did Pellinore repent?"

Arthur said: "Pellinore repented, yes. There was not much to repent. It was one of his muddles. But the trouble is that he has got so valiant since he married the Queen's daughter of Flanders that he has taken to jousting in earnest, and quite often wins. I was telling you how he killed King Lot one day, when they were having a practice. It has created a great deal of ill–feeling. The Orkney children have sworn to revenge their father's death, and they are out on the warpath for poor old Pellinore's blood. I am having difficulty in making them behave."

"Lancelot will help you," said the Queen. "It will be nice to have an old friend to help."

"Yes, it will be nice. Now, Lance, I expect you will want to see your room."

It was the second half of summer, and the amateur falconers in Camelot were bringing their peregrines to the last stages of their training. If you are a clever falconer, you get your hawk on the wing quickly. If you are not, you are apt to make mistakes, and the result is that the hawk does not finish her training for some time. So all the falconers in Camelot were trying to show that they were clever ones—by getting their hawks entered as quickly as possible—and, in all directions, if you went for a walk in the fields, there were atrabilious hawk–masters stretching out their creances and quarrelling with their assistants. Hawking, as James the First pointed out, is an extreme stirrer up of passions. It is because the hawks themselves are furious creatures, and the people who associate with them catch it.

Arthur presented Sir Lancelot with an inter–mewed jerfalcon, with which to keep himself amused. This was a great compliment, for jerfalcons were only supposed to be used by kings. At any rate that is what the Abbess Juliana Berners tell us—perhaps incorrectly. An emperor was allowed an eagle, a king could have a jerfalcon, and after that there was the peregrine for an earl, the merlin for a lady, the goshawk for a yeoman, the sparrow hawk for a priest, and the musket for a holy–water clerk. Lancelot was pleased with his present, and settled down busily in competition with the other angry falconers, who were hard at work criticizing each other's methods and sending each other messages of sugary venom and getting yellow about the eyeballs.

The jerfalcon which had been given to Lancelot was not properly through her moult. Like Hamlet, she was fat and scant of breath. Her long confinement in the mews, while she moulted, had got her into a sulky and temperamental state. So Lancelot had to fly her on the creance for several days before he could be sure that she was safe to the lure.

If you have ever flown a hawk on a creance, which is a long line tied to the hawk's jesses so that she cannot fly away, you know what a nuisance the thing can be. Nowadays people use a fishing reel, which makes it easier to stretch it out and to wind it up—but in Lancelot's day there were no good reels, and you simply had to wind your creance into a ball, like string. There were two main horrors to which it was subject, the first of which was the horror peculiar to all balls of string—that they invariably became tangles instead of balls. The second was that if you flew the hawk in any field which had not been carefully mowed, the string became wound round thistles or tufts of grass, thus checking the hawk and doing damage to its training. So Lancelot, and all the other angry men, went circling round Camelot in a bitter atmosphere of knots and competition and bating hawks.

King Arthur had asked his wife to be kind to the young man. She was fond of her husband, and she realized that she had come between him and his friend. She was not such a fool as to try to atone to Lancelot for this, but she had taken a fancy for him as himself. She liked his broken face, however hideous it was, and Arthur had asked her to be kind. There was a shortage of assistants in Camelot for the hawking, because there were so many people at it. So Guenever began going with Lancelot to help him with the balls of string.

He did not take much notice of the woman. "Here comes that woman," he would remark to himself, or "There goes that woman." He was already deep in the hawking atmosphere, which was only partly an affair for females, and he seldom thought of her more than that. He had grown into a beautifully polite youth, in spite of his ugliness, and he was too self–conscious to allow himself to have petty thoughts for long. His jealousy had turned into unconsciousness of her existence. He went on with his hawk–mastery, thanking her politely for her help and accepting it with courtesy.

One day there was particular trouble with a thistle, and he had miscalculated the amount of food which ought to have been given the day before. The jerfalcon was in a foul temper, and Lancelot caught its mood. Guenever, who was not particularly good with hawks and had no special interest in them, was frightened by his frowning brow, and, because she was frightened, she became clumsy. She was sweetly trying her best to help, but she knew that she was not clever at falconry, and there was confusion in her mind. Very carefully and kindly, and with the best intentions, she wound the creance up quite wrong.

He took the wretched ball away from her with a gesture which was almost rough.

"That's no good," he said, and he began to unwind her hopeful work with angry fingers. His eyebrows made a horrible scowl.

There was a moment in which everything stood still. Guenever stood, hurt in her heart. Lancelot, sensing her stillness, stood also. The hawk stopped bating and the leaves did not rustle.

The young man knew, in this moment, that he had hurt a real person, of his own age. He saw in her eyes that she thought he was hateful, and that he had surprised her badly. She had been giving kindness, and he had returned it with unkindness. But the main thing was that she was a real person. She was not a minx, not deceitful, not designing and heartless. She was pretty Jenny, who could think and feel.

CHAPTER V

The first two people to notice that Lancelot and Guenever were falling in love with each other were Uncle Dap and King Arthur himself. Arthur had been warned about this by Merlyn—who was now safely locked up in his cave by the fickle Nimue—and he had been fearing it subconsciously. But he always hated knowing the future and had managed to dismiss it from his mind. Uncle Dap's reaction was to give his pupil a lecture, as they stood in the mews with the chastened jer.

"God's Feet!" said Uncle Dap, with other exclamations of the same kind. "What is this? What are you doing? Is the finest knight in Europe to throw away everything I have taught him for the sake of a lady's beautiful eyes? And a married lady too!"

"I don't know what you are talking about."

"Don't know! Won't know! Holy Mother!" shouted Uncle Dap. "Is it Guenever I am talking about, or is it not? Glory be to God for evermore!"

Lancelot took the old gentleman by the shoulders and sat him down on a chest.

"Look, Uncle," he said with determination. "I have been wanting to talk to you. Isn't it time you went back to Benwick?"

"Benwick!" cried his uncle, as if he had been stabbed to the heart.

"Yes, Benwick. You can't go on pretending to be my squire for ever. For one thing, you are the brother of two kings, and for another thing, you are three times as old as I am. It would be against the laws of arms."

"Laws of arms!" shouted the old man. "Pouf!"

"Well, it is no good saying Pouf."

"And me that has taught you everything you know! Me to go back to

Benwick without having seen you prove yourself at all! Why, you have not even used your sword in front of me, not used Joyeux! It is ingratitude, perfidy, treachery! Sorrow to the grave! My faith! By the Blue!"

And the agitated old fellow went off into a long string of Gallic remarks, including the so–called William the Conqueror's oath of *Per Splendorem Dei,* and the *Pasque Dieu* which was the imaginary King Louis the Eleventh's idea of a joke. Inspired by the royal train of thought he added the exclamations of Rufus, Henry the First, John, and Henry the Third, which were, in that order, By the Holy Face of Lucca, By God's Death, By God's Teeth, and By God's Head. The jerfalcon, seeming to appreciate the display, roused his feathers heartily, like a housemaid shaking a mop out of the window.

"Well, if you won't go, you won't," said Lancelot. "But please don't talk to me about the Queen. I can't help it if we are fond of each other, and there is nothing wrong in being fond of people, is there? It is not as if the Queen and I were villains. When you begin lecturing me about her, you are making it seem as if there was something wrong between us. It is as if you thought ill of me, or did not believe in my honour. Please do not mention the subject again."

Uncle Dap rolled his eyes, disarranged his hair, cracked his knuckles, kissed his finger–tips, and made other gestures calculated to express his point of view. But he did not refer to the love affair afterwards.

Arthur's reaction to the problem was complicated. Merlyn's warning about his lady and his best friend had contained within itself the seeds of its own contradiction, for your friend can hardly be your friend if he is also going to be your betrayer. Arthur adored his rose–petalled Guenever for her dash, and had an instinctive respect for Lancelot, which was soon to become affection. This made it difficult either to suspect them or not to suspect.

The conclusion which he came to was that it would be best to solve the problem by taking Lancelot with him to the Roman war. That, at any rate, would separate the boy from Guenever, and it would be pleasant to have his disciple with him—a fine soldier—whether Merlyn's warning were true or not.

The Roman war was a complicated business which had been brewing for years. It need not concern us long. It was in its way the logical consequence of Bedegraine—the continuation of that battle on a European scale. The feudal idea of war for ransom had been squashed in Britain, but not abroad, and now the foreign ransom–hunters were after the newly settled King. A gentleman called Lucius, who was the Dictator of Rome—and it is strange to reflect that Dictator is the very word which Malory uses—had sent an embassy asking for tribute from Arthur—it was called a tribute before a battle and a ransom afterwards—to which the King, after consulting his parliament, had returned a message that no tribute was due. So the Dictator Lucius had declared war. He had also sent his messengers, like Lars Porsena in Macaulay, to all the points of the compass to gather allies. He had no less than sixteen kings marching with him from Rome into High Germany, on their way to do battle with the English. He had allies from Ambage, Arrage, Alisandrie, Inde, Hermonie, Euphrates, Affrike, Europe the Large, Ertaine, Elamie, Arabic, Egypt, Damaske, Damiete, Gayer, Gapadoce, Tarce, Turkey, Pounce, Pampoille, Surrie and Galacie, beside others from Greece, Cyprus, Macedone, Calabre, Cateland, Portingale, and many thousands of Spaniards.

During the first weeks of Lancelot's infatuation for Guenever, it became time for Arthur to cross the Channel to meet his enemy in France—and it was on this war that he decided to carry the young man with him. Lancelot, of course, was not at that time recognized as the chief knight of the Round Table, or he would have been taken in any case. At the present period of his life he had only fought one joust with Arthur himself, and the accepted captain of the knights was Gawaine.

Lancelot was angry at being taken from Guenever, because he felt that it implied a lack of trust. Besides, he knew that Sir Tristram had been left with King Mark's wife of Cornwall on a similar occasion. He did not see why he should not be left with Guenever in the same way.

There is no need to go into the whole story of the Roman campaign, although it lasted several years. It was the usual sort of war, with a great deal of shoving and shouting on both sides, great strokes smitten, many men overthrown, and great valiances, prowesses, and feats of arms shown every day. It was Bedegraine enlarged—with the same refusal on Arthur's part to regard it as a sporting or commercial enterprise—although it did have its characteristic touches. Redheaded Gawaine lost his temper when sent on an embassy and killed a man in the middle of the negotiations. Sir

Lancelot led a terrific battle in which his men were outnumbered by three to one. He slew the King Lyly and three great lords called Alakuke, Herawd, and Heringdale. During the campaign three notorious giants were accounted for—two of them by Arthur himself. Finally, in the last engagement, Arthur gave the Emperor Lucius such a blow on the head that Excalibur stinted not till it came to his breast, and it was discovered that the Sowdan of Surrie and the King of Egypt and the King of Ethiope—an ancestor of Haile Selassie—together with seventeen other kings of diverse regions and sixty senators of Rome, were among the slain. Arthur put their bodies into sumptuous coffins—not sarcastically—and sent them to the Lord Mayor of Rome, instead of the tribute which had been demanded. This induced the Lord Mayor and nearly the whole of Europe to accept him as overlord. The lands of Pleasance, Pavia, Petersaint, and the Port of Tremble yielded him homage. The feudal convention of battle was broken for good, on the Continent as well as in England.

During this warfare Arthur became genuinely fond of Lancelot, and, by the time they came home, he no longer believed in Merlyn's prophecy at all. He had put it at the back of his mind. Lancelot was acknowledged to be the greatest fighter in the army. Both of them were determined that Guenever could not come between them, and the first few years were safely past.

CHAPTER VI

What sort of picture do people have of Sir Lancelot from this end of time? Perhaps they only think of him as an ugly young man who was good at games. But he was more than this. He was a knight with a medieval respect for honour.

There is a phrase which you sometimes come across in country districts even nowadays, which sums up a good deal of what he might have tried to say. Farmers use it in Ireland, as praise or compliment, saying, "So–and–so has a Word. He will do what he promised."

Lancelot tried to have a Word. He considered it, as the ignorant country people still consider it, to be the most valuable of possessions.

But the curious thing was that under the king–post of keeping faith with himself and with others, he had a contradictory nature which was far from holy. His Word was valuable to him not only because he was good, but also because he was bad. It is the bad people who need to have principles to restrain them. For one thing, he liked to hurt people. It was for the strange reason that he was cruel, that the poor fellow never killed a man who asked for mercy, or committed a cruel action which he could have prevented. One reason why he fell in love with Guenever was because the first thing he had done was to hurt her. He might never have noticed her as a person, if he had not seen the pain in her eyes.

People have odd reasons for ending up as saints. A man who was not afflicted by ambitions of decency in his mind might simply have run away with his hero's wife, and then perhaps the tragedy of Arthur would never have happened. An ordinary fellow, who did not spend half his life torturing himself by trying to discover what was right so as to conquer his inclination towards what was wrong, might have cut the knot which brought their ruin.

When the two friends arrived in England from the Roman war, the fleet landed at Sandwich. It was a grey September day, with the blue and copper butterflies flitting in the after–grass, the partridges calling like crickets, the blackberries colouring, and the hazel nuts still nursing their tasteless little kernels in cradles of cotton wool. Queen Guenever was on the beach to meet them, and the first thing Lancelot knew after she had kissed the King, was that she was able to come between them after all. He made a movement as if his entrails were tying themselves in knots, saluted the Queen, went off to bed in the nearest inn at once, and lay awake all night. In the morning, he asked leave of absence from the court.

"But you have hardly been at court at all," said Arthur. "Why do you want to go away so soon?"

"I ought to go away."

"Ought to go away?" asked the King. "What do you mean, you ought to go away?"

Lancelot clenched his fist until the knuckles stood out, and said, "I want to go on a quest. I want to find an adventure."

"But, Lance—"

"It is what the Round Table is for, isn't it?" shouted the young man. "The knights are to go on quests, aren't they, to fight against Might? What are you trying to stop me for? It's the whole point of the idea."

"Oh, come," said the King. "You needn't get excited about it. If you want to go, of course you can do whatever you like. I only thought it would be nice to have you with us for a little. Don't be cross, Lance. I don't know what has come over you."

"Come back soon," said the Queen.

Chapter VII

This was the beginning of the famous quests. They were not made to win him fame or recreation. They were an attempt to escape from Guenever. They were his struggles to save his honour, not to establish it.

We shall have to describe one of the quests in detail—so as to show the way in which he tried to distract himself, and the way in which this famous honour of his worked. Also it will give a picture of the state of England, which forced King Arthur to work for his theory of justice. It was not that Arthur was a prig—it was that his country of Gramarye lay in such a toil of anarchy in the early days that some idea like the Round Table was needed to make the place survive. The warfare of people like Lot had been suppressed, but not the unbiddable baronage who lived like gangsters on their own estates. Barons were pulling teeth out of Jews to get their money, or roasting bishops who contradicted them. The villeins who belonged to bad masters were being basted over slow fires, or sprinkled with molten lead, or impaled, or left to die with their eyes gouged out, or else they were crawling along the roads on hands and knees, because they had been hamstrung. Petty feuds were raging to the destruction of the poor and helpless, and, if a knight did happen to be dragged from his horse in a battle, he was so well screwed up that only an expert could do him harm. Philip Augustus of France, for instance, was dismounted and surrounded at the legendary battle of Bouvines: yet, as the unfortunate infantry were quite unable to puncture him, he was rescued soon after, and continued to fight all the better because he had lost his temper. But the story of Lancelot's first quest must speak for their troubled age of Might in its own way.

There were two knights on the borders of Wales called Sir Carados and Sir Turquine. They were of Celtic stock. These two conservative barons had never yielded to Arthur, and they did not believe in any form of government except the rule of force. They had strong castles and wicked retainers, who found more opportunity for wickedness under their leadership than they would have found in a settled state of society. They existed like eagles, to prey on weaker brethren. It is unfair to compare them with eagles, for many of these birds are noble creatures, while Sir Turquine at any rate was not noble. If he had lived now he might even have been locked in a lunatic hospital, and his friends would certainly have urged him to be psycho–analysed.

One day, when Sir Lancelot had been riding on his adventure for about a month—and all the time going away from where he wanted to be, so that every pace of his horse was a torment—there appeared a knight in armour riding a great mare, with another bound knight thrown across the saddlebow. The bound knight had fainted. He was bloody and bedraggled, and his head, which hung by the mare's shoulders, had red hair. The riding knight who had captured him was a man of enormous stature, and Lancelot recognized him by his blazon as Sir Carados.

"Who is your prisoner?"

The big knight lifted the prisoner's shield, which was hanging behind him, and showed *or, a chevron gules, between three thistles vert.*

"What are you doing with Sir Gawaine?"

"Mind your own business," said Sir Carados.

Gawaine must have come to his senses when the mare halted, for his voice now said, coming from upside down: "Is that you, man, Sir Lancelot?"

"What cheer, Gawaine. How stands it with you?"

"Never so hard," said Sir Gawaine, "unless that ye help me, for without ye rescue me, I know nae knight that may."

He was speaking formally in the High Language of Chivalry—for in those days there were two kinds of speech like High and Low Dutch or Norman French and Saxon English.

Lancelot looked at Sir Carados, and said in the vernacular: "Will you put that fellow down, and fight with me instead?"

"You are a fool," said Sir Carados. "I shall only serve you in the same way."

Then they put Gawaine on the ground, tied up so that he could not get away, and prepared for battle. Sir Carados had a squire to give him his spear, but Lancelot had insisted on leaving Uncle Dap at home. He had to serve himself alone.

The fight was different from the one with Arthur. For one thing, the knights were more evenly matched, and, in the tilt with which it began, neither of them was unhorsed. They broke their ashwood spears to splinters, but both stayed in the saddle, and the horses stood the shock. In the sword–play which followed, Lancelot proved to be the better of the two. After little more than an hour's fighting he managed to give Sir Carados such a buffet on the helm that it pierced his brain–pan—and then, while the dead man was still swaying in the saddle, he caught him by the collar, pulled him under his horse's feet, dismounted in the same instant, and struck off his head. He liberated Sir Gawaine, who thanked him heartily, and rode on again into the wild ways of England, without giving Carados another thought. He fell in with a young cousin of his own, Sir Lionel, and they rode together in search of wrongs to redress. But it was unwise of them to have forgotten Sir Carados.

One day, when they had been riding for some time, they came to a forest during a sultry noon, and Lancelot was so worn out by the struggle inside him about the Queen, and by the weather as well, that he felt he could not go further. Lionel felt sleepy also, so they decided to lie down under an apple tree in a hedge, after tying their horses to sundry branches. Lancelot went to sleep at once—but the buzzing of the flies kept Sir Lionel awake, and while he was awake a curious sight came by.

The sight was of three knights fully armed, galloping for their lives, with a single knight in pursuit of them. The horses' hoofs thundered on the ground and shook it—so that it was peculiar that Lancelot did not wake up —until, one by one, the huge pursuer ran his quarries down, unhorsed them, and bound them prisoners.

Lionel was an ambitious boy. He thought that he would steal a march on his famous cousin. He got up quietly, put his armour to rights, and rode off to challenge the victor. In less than a minute he too was lying on the ground, trussed so that he could not move, and before Lancelot woke the whole pageant had disappeared. The mysterious conqueror in these four battles was Sir Turquine, a brother to the Carados whom Lancelot had lately killed. His habit was to take his captives into his grimly castle, where he took off all their clothes and whacked them to his heart's content, as a hobby.

Lancelot was still asleep when a new pageant came prancing by. In the middle of it there was a green silk canopy borne on four spears by four knights gorgeously apparelled. Under the canopy there rode four middle–aged queens on white mules, looking picturesque. They were passing the apple tree, when Lancelot's charger gave a brassy neigh.

Queen Morgan le Fay, who was the senior queen of the four—all witches —halted the procession and rode over to Sir Lancelot. He looked dangerous as he lay there in full armour of war, among the long grasses.

"It is Sir Lancelot!"

Nothing travels quicker than scandal, especially among supernatural people, so the four queens knew that he was in love with Guenever. They also knew that he was now recognized as the strongest knight in the world. They were jealous of Guenever on this account. They were delighted by the opportunity which they saw before them. They began to quarrel among themselves, about which of them should have him for her magic.

"We need not quarrel," said Morgan le Fay. "I will put an enchantment on him so that he does not wake for six hours. When we have got him safely into my castle, he can choose which of us he will have, himself."

This was done. The sleeping champion was carried on his shield, between two knights, into the Castle Chariot. The castle no longer had its fairy appearance as a castle of food, but its everyday aspect of an ordinary fortress. There he was put into a cold, bare chamber, fast asleep, and left until the enchantment wore off.

When Lancelot woke, he did not know where he was. The room was dark, and seemed to be made of stone like a dungeon. He lay in the dark wondering what would happen next. Later he began to think about Queen Guenever.

The thing which did happen, was that a young damsel came in with his dinner and asked him what cheer?

"How are you, Sir Lancelot?"

"I don't know, fair damsel. I don't know how I got here, so I don't rightly know how I am."

"No need to be frightened," she said. "If you are as great a man as you are supposed to be, I may be able to help you tomorrow morning."

"Thank you. Whether you can help me or not, I should like you to think kindly of me."

So the fair maid went away.

In the morning there was banging of bolts and creaking of rusty locks and several retainers in chain mail came into the dungeon. They lined up on either side of the door, and the magic queens came in behind them, all dressed in their best clothes. Each of the queens made a stately curtsey to Sir Lancelot. He stood up politely and bowed gravely to each of the queens. Morgan le Fay introduced them as the queens of Gore, Northgalis, Eastland, and the Out Isles.

"Now," said Morgan le Fay, "we know about you, so you need not think we don't. You are Sir Lancelot Dulac, and you are having a love affair with Queen Guenever. You are supposed to be the best knight in the world, and that is why the woman is fond of you. Well, that is all over now. We four queens have you in our power, and you have to choose which of us you will have for your mistress. It would be no good unless you chose for yourself, obviously—but one of us you must have. Which is it to be?"

Lancelot said: "How can I possibly answer a thing like that?"

"You have to answer."

"In the first place," he said, "what you say about me and the King's wife of Britain is untrue. Guenever is the truest lady unto her lord living. If I were free, or had my armour, I would fight any champion you liked to put forward, to prove that. And in the second place, I certainly will not have any of you for my mistress. I am sorry if this is discourteous, but it is all I can say."

"Oh!" said Morgan le Fay.

"Yes," said Lancelot.

"That is all?"

"Yes."

The four queens curtsied with frigid dignity, and marched out of the room. The sentries made smart about–turns, their mail ringing on the stone floor. The light went out of the door. The door slammed, and the key creaked, and the bolts rumbled into their sockets.

When the fair damsel came in with the next meal, she showed signs of wanting to talk to him. Lancelot noticed that she was a bold creature, who was probably fond of getting her own way.

"You said you might be able to help me?"

The girl looked suspiciously at him and said: "I can help you if you are who you are supposed to be. Are you really Sir Lancelot?"

"I am afraid I am."

"I will help you," she said, "if you will help me."

Then she burst into tears.

While the damsel is weeping, which she did in a charming and determined way, we had better explain about the tournaments which used to take place in Gramarye in the early days. A real tournament was distinct from a joust. In a joust the knights tilted or fenced with each other singly, for a prize. But a tournament was more like a free fight. A body of knights would pick sides, so that there were twenty or thirty on either side, and then they would rush together harum–scarum. These mass battles were considered to be important—for instance, once you had paid your green fee for the tournament, you were admitted on the same ticket to fight in the jousts— but if you had only paid the jousting fee, you were not allowed to fight in the tourney. People were liable to be dangerously injured in the mêlées. They were not bad things altogether, provided they were properly controlled. Unfortunately, in the early days, they were seldom controlled at all.

Merry England in Pendragon's time was a little like Poor Ould Ireland in O'Connell's. There were factions. The knights of one county, or the inhabitants of one district, or the retainers of one nobleman, might get themselves into a state in which they felt a hatred for the faction which lived next door. This hatred would become a feud, and then the king or leader of the one place would challenge the leader of the other one to a tourney—and both factions would go to the meeting with full intent to do each other mischief. It was the same in the days of Papist and Protestant, or Stuart and Orangeman, who would meet together with shillelaghs in their hands and murder in their hearts.

"Why are you crying?" asked Sir Lancelot.

"Oh dear," sobbed the damsel. "That horrid King of Northgalis has challenged my father to a tournament next Tuesday, and he has got three knights of King Arthur's on his side, and my poor father is bound to lose. I am afraid he will get hurt."

"I see. And what is your father's name?"

"He is King Bagdemagus."

Sir Lancelot got up and kissed her politely on the forehead. He saw at once what he was expected to do.

"Very well," he said. "If you can rescue me out of this prison, I will fight in the faction of King Bagdemagus next Tuesday."

"Oh, thank you," said the maiden, wringing out her handkerchief. "Now I must go, I am afraid, or they will miss me downstairs."

Naturally she was not going to help the magic Queen of Northgalis to keep Lancelot in prison—when it was the King of Northgalis himself who was going to fight her father.

In the morning, before the people of the castle had got up, Lancelot heard the heavy door opening quietly. A soft hand was put in his, and he was led out in the darkness. They went through twelve magic doors, until they reached the armoury, and there was all his armour bright and ready. When he had put it on, they went to the stables, and there was his charger scratching on the cobbles with a sparkling shoe.

"Remember."

"Of course," he said. And he rode out over the drawbridge into the morning light.

While they had crept through the corridors of Castle Chariot, they had made a plan about meeting King Bagdemagus. Lancelot was to ride to an abbey of white friars which was situated near by, and there he was to meet the damsel—who would, of course, be forced to flee from Queen Morgan because of her treachery in letting him escape. At this abbey they were to wait until King Bagdemagus could be brought over, and then the arrangements for the tournament were to be made. Unfortunately, the Castle Chariot was in the Forest Sauvage, and Lancelot now lost his way to the abbey. He and his horse wandered about all day, bumping against branches, getting tangled in blackberry bushes, and rapidly losing their tempers. In the evening they stumbled on a pavilion of red sendal, with nobody inside.

He got off his horse and looked at the pavilion. There was something queer about it—luxurious as it was in the rooky wood, and without anybody in sight.

"This is a strange pavilion," he thought sadly, for his mind was full of Guenever, "but I suppose I may as well stay in it for the night. Either it is here for some adventure or other, in which case I ought to try the adventure, or else the owners have gone away on holiday, and in that case they will not mind my taking shelter for one evening. Anyway, I am lost, and there is nothing else I can do."

He unharnessed the horse and spancelled him. Then he took off his own armour and hung it neatly on a nearby tree with the shield on top. After this he ate some bread which the girl had given him, drinking water from a stream which ran beside the pavilion, stretched his arms out until the elbows went click, yawned, hit his front teeth with his fist three times, and went to bed. The bed was a sumptuous one with a coverlet of red sendal, to match the tent. Lancelot rolled himself in it, pressed his nose into the silk pillow, kissed it for Guenever, and was fast asleep.

It was moonlight when he woke, and a naked man was sitting on his left foot, trimming his finger–nails.

Lancelot, who had been woken from his love sleep with a start, moved suddenly in the bed when he felt the man. The man, equally surprised at feeling a movement, jumped up and snatched his sword. Lancelot jumped out on the other side of the bed and ran for his own arms, where they were hanging in the tree. The man came after him, waving his blade and trying to get a cut at him from behind. Lancelot reached the tree in safety and swung round with his weapon in his hand. They looked strange and terrible in the moonlight, both stark naked, with their silver steel glancing under the harvest moon.

"Now," cried the man, and he aimed a furious swipe at Lancelot's legs. The next minute he had dropped his sword and was holding his stomach with both hands, doubled up and whistling. The cut which Lancelot had given welled over with blood which looked black in the moonlight, and you could see some of the insides of the stomach with their secret life laid open.

"Don't hit me," cried the man. "Mercy. Don't hit me again. You have killed me."

"I am sorry," said Lancelot. "You did not even wait till I had a sword."

The man went on wailing: "Mercy! Mercy!"

Lancelot stuck his blade in the ground and went over to examine the wound.

"I am not going to hurt you," he said. "It's all right. Let me see."

"You have cut open my liver," said the man accusingly.

"Well, I can't do more than say I am sorry, even if I have. I don't know what we were fighting about anyway. Lean on my shoulder and we will get you into bed."

When he had got the man to bed, and stopped his bleeding, and discovered that the wound was not a mortal one, a beautiful lady appeared in the opening of the tent. They had lit a rush light, so that she saw what had happened in a flash, and immediately she began screaming at the top of her voice. She rushed over to comfort the wounded man, and accused Lancelot of being a murderer, and carried on a great deal.

"Do stop howling," said the man. "He is not a murderer. We just made a mistake."

"I was in bed," said Lancelot, "when he came and sat on me, and we were both so startled that we had a fight. I am sorry that I hurt him."

"But it was our bed," cried the lady, like one of the Three Bears. "What were you doing in our bed?"

"Really," he said, "I am sorry. There was nobody in the pavilion when I found it, and I was lost and tired, so I thought it would not matter if I took a night's lodging."

"Nor did it matter," said the man. "You are welcome to a night's lodging, and I don't think the wound is going to be a bad one after all. May I inquire your name?"

"Lancelot."

"Well!" exclaimed the man. "There now, my dear, look who I have been fighting. No wonder I got a bit of a chip. I was wondering why my life was spared so easily."

So they insisted that Lancelot should stay the night, and in the morning they put him on the correct road for the abbey of white friars.

Nothing much came of this encounter in the main story, except that the knight, whose name was Belleus, was introduced to the Round Table by Lancelot as soon as he was well again. He was the kind of generous fellow that Arthur needed, and Lancelot tried to make up for the trouble which he had caused by getting him a seat at the Table.

At the abbey of white friars the fair damsel was waiting in a state of excitement. She was afraid that he might have let her down. His horse's hoofs, however, had no sooner clattered on the cobbles than she came flying from her tower room to welcome him with delight.

"Father will be here this evening," she cried. "Oh, I am so glad you came! I was afraid you might have forgotten."

Lancelot's twisted mouth grinned at the word she had chosen to use. Then he changed into civilian dress, had a bath, and waited for King Bagdemagus.

"It is a puzzling life in Gramarye," he said to himself, trying to keep his mind off the young Queen. "Things happen so quickly. One hardly knows where one is half the time, and there is that cousin of mine who vanished under the apple tree, who has still to be accounted for. What with magic queens and faction tournaments and people getting into bed with you at night, and half the family vanishing without trace, it is difficult to keep in line."

Then he brushed his hair, smoothed his gown, and went down to meet King Bagdemagus.

There is no need to give a long description of the tourney. Malory gives it. Lancelot picked three knights who were recommended by the young damsel to go with him, and he arranged that all four of them should bear the vergescu. This was the white shield carried by unfledged knights, and Lancelot insisted on this arrangement because he knew that three of his own brethren of the Round Table were going to fight on the other side. He did not want them to recognize him, because it might cause ill–feeling at court. On the other hand, he felt that it was his duty to fight against them because of the promise which he had given to the damsel. The King of Northgalis, who was the leader of the opposite side, had one hundred and sixty knights in his faction, and King Bagdemagus only had eighty. Lancelot went for the first knight of the Round Table, and put his shoulder out of joint. He went for the second one so hard that the unlucky fellow was carried over his horse's tail and buried his helm several inches in the ground. He hit the third knight on the head so hard that his nose bled, and his horse ran away with him. By the time he had broken the thigh of the King of Northgalis, everybody could see that to all intents and purposes the tournament was over.

The next thing that happened was that our hero set out to discover what had become of Lionel. He was free to do so, for the first time—for, since the disappearance of his cousin, he had either been imprisoned by the malignant queens or else he had been discharging his obligations to the girl who had rescued him from them. King Bagdemagus got the prize at the tournament before he left, and the damsel was almost tearfully grateful. Everybody said that they would be friends for ever, and that they had only to send each other word if there was anything that anybody could do for anybody in return. Then Lancelot mounted his horse, got his bearings by asking several peasants where he was, and rode off toward the forest of the apple tree where he had lost his cousin. He thought that by making an all–round–the–hat cast at the place where he had last seen his cousin, he might be able to pick up the scent once more, although it was cold.

In the forest of the apple tree, indeed at the very foot of the tree itself, he came across a lady riding a white palfrey. The tree was thought to be a magic one, which was the reason why such a lot of traffic went on round it.

"Lady," said he, "do you know of any adventures in this forest?"

"Plenty," she said, "if you are man enough to take them on."

"I could try."

"You look a strong man," said the lady. "You have a bold look, too, in spite of your ears which stick out so frightfully. If you like, I will take you where the fiercest baron in the world lives, but he is sure to kill you."

"Never mind."

"I will only take you if you tell me your name. It would be murder to take you unless you are a famous knight."

"My name is Lancelot."

"I thought it was," said the lady. "Well, it is lucky it is. According to the things which people are saying about you, you are probably the only knight in the world who can beat the man I am taking you to. His name is Sir Turquine."

"Good."

"Some say he is a madman. He has sixty–four knights in prison, whom he has captured in single combat, and he spends the time beating them with thorns. If he captures you, he will beat you too, all naked."

"He sounds an exciting man to fight."

"It is a sort of concentration camp."

"That is what I have been getting ready for," said Sir Lancelot. "It is what Arthur invented the Round Table to prevent."

"If I take you to him, you must promise to do something for me afterwards —that is, if you win."

"What sort of thing?" he asked cautiously.

"You need not be afraid," said the lady. "It is only to vanquish another knight I know of, who is distressing some damsels."

"I will promise that gladly."

"Well," said the lady, "God, He knows how you will get on. Anyway, I will say a prayer for you while you are fighting."

When they had been riding for some time, they came to a ford like the one at which he had fought the first fight with King Arthur. On the trees round the ford there were hanging rusty helms and melancholy shields—sixty–four of them, with their bends and chevrons and luces hauriant and merles and eagles displayed and lions passant guardant looking desolate and abandoned. The leather of their guiges was green and mildewy. It looked like a gamekeeper's gallows.

In the middle of the glade, on the chief tree, there hung an enormous copper basin, triumphing over the beaten shields. The latest shield under it was Lionel's—argent, a bend gules distinguished with some sort of label of cadency.

Lancelot knew what he had to do with this basin, and he did it. He put his helm in position, rode through the dripping leaves to the basin, and beat on it with the butt of his spear until the bottom fell out. Then he and the lady stood still in the forest, which was as if it had been shocked silent by the hideous noise.

Nobody came.

"His castle is beyond," said the lady.

They went to the castle gates in silence, and rode up and down in front of them for half an hour. He took off his helm and gauntlets, and frowned, and bit his finger–nails from anxiety.

After the half–hour was over, a gigantic knight came riding through the forest. He looked so like Sir Carados—the knight who had been slain at the rescue of Gawaine—that Lancelot was startled. Not only was he of the same build, but he also had a bound knight thrown across the saddlebow of his mare. Most peculiar of all, the bound knight's shield carried the three thistles and the chevron, with a red canton. In fact, the second of the big knights had captured Gaheris—Gawaine's brother. Lancelot watched him with a critical eye.

It may not be amiss to mention that a good judge of style could often recognize a knight in armour, even if he was disguised and bearing the vergescu. In later life Lancelot sometimes had to fight disguised, because otherwise nobody would fight him. Yet Arthur and others generally guessed him by his riding. People nowadays can recognize cricketers, even when their faces are too far away to be seen, and so it was then.

Lancelot was a good judge of style, because of his long practice. As soon as he had watched Sir Turquine for a moment or two, he noticed that there was a slight weakness in his seat. He remarked to the lady that unless Turquine sat better, he thought he would be able to rescue the prisoners. As it turned out, Turquine did sit better when it came to the tilt, so that this particular criticism came to nothing—but it throws a sidelight on jousting and may have been worth mentioning.

The riding was the whole thing. If a man had the courage to throw himself into the fullest gallop at the moment of impact, he generally won. Most men faltered a little, so that they were not at their best momentum. This was why Lancelot constantly gained his tilts. He had what Uncle Dap called the *élan*. Sometimes, when he was in disguise, he would ride clumsily on purpose, showing daylight at his seat. But at the last moment there was always the true dash—so that the onlookers, and frequently his wretched opponent, could exclaim, "Ah, Lancelot!" even before the lance drove home.

"Fair knight," he said, "put down that wounded man and let him rest a little. Then we two can prove our strengths."

Sir Turquine rode up to him, and said through his teeth: "If you are a knight of the Round Table, it will give me great pleasure to knock you down first and whack you afterwards. I could do that to you, and your whole table with you."

"It seems a tall order."

Then they retreated in the usual way, fewtered their spears, and charged together like thunder. Lancelot, at the last moment, noticed that he was wrong about Turquine's seat. In the last flash he realized that Turquine was the finest tilter he had met, that he was coming with a hurl as great as his own, and that his aim was sure.

The knights ducked and drew themselves together; the spears struck at the same moment; the horses, checked in mid–career, reared up and fell over backward; the spears burst and went sailing high in the air, turning over and over gracefully like the results of high explosive; and the lady on the palfrey looked away. When she looked again, both horses were down with their backs broken, and the knights lay still.

Two hours later, Lancelot and Turquine were still fighting with their swords.

"Stop," said Turquine. "I want to speak to you."

Lancelot stopped.

"Who are you?" asked Sir Turquine. "You are the finest knight I ever fought with. I never saw a man with such good wind. Listen, I have sixty–four prisoners in my castle, and I have killed or maimed hundreds of others, but none were as good as you. If you will have peace, and be my friend, I will loose my prisoners."

"It is kind of you."

"I will do this for you, if you are anybody except one person. If you are he, I must fight you to the death."

"Who is this person?"

"Lancelot," said Sir Turquine. "If you are Lancelot, I must never yield or make friends. He killed my brother Carados."

"I am that man."

Sir Turquine made a hissing through his helm and struck craftily, before his enemy was ready.

"Ah, would you?" said Lancelot. "I only had to pretend I was not myself, and I could have had the prisoners safe. But you try to kill me without warning."

Sir Turquine continued to hiss.

"I am sorry about Carados," said Lancelot. "He was killed in fair fight and never offered to yield. I never had him at mercy. He was killed in the middle of the fight."

They fought for two more hours. The blade was not the only weapon used by knights in armour. Sometimes they struck each other with the edges of their shields, sometimes they clubbed each other with the pommels of their swords. The grass all round was speckled with their blood—little spots like those on trout, but with a kind of tail on each spot, like a tadpole. Sometimes, because of their weight, they fell over each other. The heavy, straw–stuffed helms of chivalry had such small holes to breathe through that they felt like suffocating. Their shields hung wearily, not covering them properly.

It was over in a second. Neither of them spoke. Lancelot dropped his sword at a moment of opportunity and caught Turquine by the snout of his helm. They fell over, and the helm came off. They drew their misericordes for the close work. Turquine bounced and shuddered and was dead.

Later, while Gaheris and the lady were giving him some water, Lancelot said: "Whatever was wrong with him, he was game. I am sorry he would not yield."

"But think of the maimed knights and the beating."

"He was the old school," he said. "It is what we have to stop. But he was a credit to the old school as a fighter, all the same."

"He was a brute," said the lady.

"Whatever he was, he was fond of his brother. Look, Gaheris, will you lend me your horse? I want to go on, and my own is dead, poor creature. If you could lend me yours, you could go forward and let Lionel and the others out of the castle. Tell Lionel to go back to court and not to be a silly fellow. I have to ride with this lady. Will you do that?"

"You can have my horse, certainly," said Gaheris. "You have saved him and me as well. How you keep on saving the Orkneys! Last time it was Gawaine. And Agravaine is in that castle at this minute. Of course you can have my horse, Lancelot, of course you can."

CHAPTER VIII

Lancelot had several other adventures during his first quest—it lasted a year—but perhaps only two are worth repeating in detail. They were both mixed up with the conservative ethics of Force Majeur against which the King had started his crusade. It was the old school, the Norman baronial attitude, which provided the adventures at this period—for few people can hate so bitterly and so self–righteously as the members of a ruling caste which is being dispossessed. The knights of the Round Table were sent out as a measure against Fort Mayne, and the choleric barons who lived by Fort Mayne took up the cudgels with the ferocity of despair. They would have written to *The Times* about it, if there had been such a paper. The best of them convinced themselves that Arthur was newfangled, and that his knights were degenerate from the standards of their fathers. The worst of them made up uglier names than Bolshevist even, and allowed the brutal side of their natures to dwell on imaginary enormities which they attributed to the knights. The situation became divorced from common sense, so that atrocity stories were accepted by the atrocious people. Many of the barons whom Lancelot had to put down had worked themselves into such a state about him, through fear of losing their ancient powers, that they believed him to be a sort of poison–gas man. They fought him with as much unscrupulousness and hatred as if he had been an antichrist, and they truly believed themselves to be defending the right. It became a civil war of ideologies.

One day in the fine summer, he was riding through the park land of a castle which was strange to him. The trees grew dispersedly about the sward—great elms and oaks and beeches—and Lancelot was thinking about Guenever with a heavy heart. Before he had parted from the lady who led him to Sir Turquine—and he had done the thing for her which he had promised—they had started a conversation about marriage, which had upset him. The lady had said that he ought either to have a wife or a mistress, and Lancelot had been angry. "I can't stop people from saying things if they want to," he had said, "but circumstances make it impossible for me to marry, while I consider that having a mistress is no good." They argued about it for some time, and then parted. Now, although he had passed several adventures in between, he was still thinking of the lady's advice and feeling wretched.

There was the sound of bells in the air—and he looked up immediately.

A fine peregrine falcon, with her music jingling in the whistling wind als clear, and her creance trailing behind her, was beating along above his head toward the top of one of the elms. She was in a temper. As soon as she reached the top of the elm she sat down in it, looking about her with raging eye and panting beak. The creance wrapped itself three times round the nearest bough. When she noticed Sir Lancelot riding toward her, she tried to fly away again in fury. The creance caught her. She hung upside down, bating with her wings. His heart came into his mouth for fear that she would break some feathers. In a few moments she ceased to flap, and hung upside down, revolving slowly, looking ignoble and indignant and ridiculous, holding her head the right way up like a snake's.

"Oh, Sir Lancelot, Sir Lancelot!" cried an unknown gentlewoman, riding toward him at full speed and evidently trying to wring her hands in spite of the reins. "Oh, Sir Lancelot! I have lost my falcon."

"There she is," he said, "in that tree."

"Oh, dear! Oh, dear!" cried the lady. "I was only trying to call her in cranes, and the string broke! My husband will kill me if I do not catch her again. He is so hasty and such a keen falconer."

"But surely he will not kill you?"

"Oh, he will! He will not mean it, but he will do it! He is such a hasty man."

"Perhaps I could stop him?"

"Oh, no," said the gentlewoman. "That would not do at all. You might hurt him. I would not like you to hurt my dear husband. Don't you think you could climb up the tree and catch the hawk instead?"

Lancelot looked at the gentlewoman and at the tree. Then he heaved a deep sigh and remarked, as Malory reports him: "Well, fair lady, since that ye know my name, and require me of my knighthood to help you, I will do what I may to get your hawk; and yet truly I am an ill climber, and the tree is passing high, and few boughs to help me withal."

He had spent his childhood learning to be a fighter. It had left him no time for birds'–nesting like other boys. The lady's request, which would have given no trouble to people brought up like Arthur or Gawaine, really was an upset for him.

Lancelot took off his armour sadly, with an occasional crooked glance at the horrible tree, until he was dressed in his shirt and breeches. Then he assaulted the first boughs manfully, while the gentlewoman ran about underneath, talking about hawks and husbands and the nice weather they were having.

"All right," he said, with his eyes full of bark and a hideous scowl on his face. "All right. All right."

At the top of the tree, the falcon was in such a tangle with her creance— she had wound it round her neck and wings, as usual, and was under the impression that it was assaulting her—that Lancelot had to let her stand on his bare hand. This she gripped with the fury of hysteria, but he patiently disentangled her without minding the stabs. Falconers seldom fuss when their hawks hurt them. They are too interested.

When the hawk was safely rescued from the branches, he realized that he would not be able to climb down again with one hand.

He shouted to the lady, who seemed small at the foot of the tree: "Look out, I am going to tie her jesses to a heavy branch, if I can break one off, and then throw her down. I will get one that is not too heavy, so that she comes gently. I shall have to throw her out a bit, so that she is clear of the boughs."

"Oh, do be careful!" cried the lady.

When Lancelot had done what he said, he began to make his way down again with care. There were some bad bits on the way, where he had to rely on balance alone. He was about twenty feet from the ground when a fat knight in full armour came galloping up.

"Ha, Sir Lancelot!" shouted the fat knight. "Now I have you where I want you."

The lady picked up the falcon and began to go away.

"Lady!" said Lancelot, wondering how everybody came to know his name.

The fat man screamed out: "You leave her alone, you assassin. That is my wife, that is. She has only been doing what I told her. It was a trick. Ha! Ha! Now I have got you without any of your famous armour on, and I am going to kill you, like drowning a kitten."

"It is not very knightly," said Lancelot, with a grimace. "You might at least let me arm and fight fair."

"Let you arm, you puppy! Whatever do you take me for? I don't want any of this newfangled nonsense. When I catch a man who eats human children roasted, I kill him like the vermin he is."

"But really—"

"Come down, come down! I can't wait about all day. Come down and take your medicine like a man, if you are a man."

"I assure you that I do not roast children."

The fat knight grew quite purple in the face and shouted: "Liar! Liar! Devil! Come down at once."

Lancelot sat on a branch and dangled his feet and bit his fingernails.

"Do you mean to say," he asked, "that you loosed that falcon on purpose, with her cranes on, so as to be able to murder me when I was naked?"

"Come down!"

"If I come down, I shall do my best to kill you."

"Buffoon!" cried the fat knight.

"Well," said Lancelot, "it is your own fault. You should not play dirty tricks. For the last time, will you let me arm like a gentleman?"

"Certainly not."

Lancelot broke off a bough of rotten wood, and jumped down on the other side of his horse, so that the horse was between them. The fat knight rode at him, and tried to swipe off his head, leaning across the horse between. Lancelot parried the stroke with his bough, and the knight's sword stuck in the wood. Then he took the sword away from its owner and slit his throat.

"Go away," said Lancelot to the gentlewoman. "Stop howling. Your husband was a fool and you are a bore. I am not sorry I killed him."

But he was sorry.

The last adventure was also concerned with treachery and a lady. The young man was riding mournfully through the fen country—which had not been drained in those days and was probably the wildest part of England. It was all secret ways through the marshes, which were known only to the Saxon marsh men who had been conquered by Uther Pendragon, and the whole sea–smelling plain was one vast quack under the low sky. The bitterns boomed and the marsh harriers skimmed over the reeds and millions of widgeon and mallard and tufted ducks flew about in various wedges, looking like champagne bottles balanced on a nimbus of wings. On the salt marshes the geese from Spitzbergen walked and nibbled, with their necks bent into their peculiar loop, and the fen men stalked them with nets and engines. The fen people had spotted bellies and their toes were webbed—at any rate that was the belief in the rest of England. They generally killed foreigners.

While Lancelot was riding along a straight road which seemed to lead nowhere, he saw two people galloping towards him from the other end. They turned out to be a knight and his lady. The lady was in front, going like mad, and the knight was after her. His sword flashed against the dull sky.

"Here! Here!" cried Lancelot, riding at them.

"Help!" screamed the lady. "Oh, save me! He is trying to cut my head off."

"Leave her alone! Get out!" shouted the knight. "She is my wife, and she has been committing adultery!"

"I never did," wailed the lady. "Oh, sir, save me from him. He is a cruel, beastly brute. Just because I am fond of my cousin german, he is jealous. Why should I not be fond of my cousin german?"

"Scarlet woman!" exclaimed the knight, and he tried to get at her.

Lancelot rode between them and said: "Really, you must not go for a woman like that. I don't care whose fault it is, but you can't kill women."

"Since when?"

"Since King Arthur was king."

"She is my wife," said the knight. "She is nothing to do with you. Get out! And she is an adulteress, whatever she says."

"Oh no, I am not," said the lady. "But you are a bully. And you drink."

"Who made me drink, then? And, besides, it is no worse to drink than be an adulteress."

"Be quiet," said Lancelot, "both of you. This is a nuisance. I shall have to ride between you until you cool off. I suppose you would not care to have a fight with me, sir, instead of killing this lady?"

"Certainly not," said the knight. "I know by your argent, a bend gules, that you are Lancelot; and I would not be such a fool as to fight you, especially for a bitch like this. What the devil has it got to do with you?"

"I will go," said Lancelot, "as soon as you promise on your knighthood not to kill women."

"Well, I won't promise."

"You wouldn't," said the lady. "Anyway, you would not keep your promise, if you did."

"There are some marsh soldiers," said the knight, "cantering after us. Look behind. They are armed cap–à–pie."

Lancelot reined his horse and looked over his shoulder. At the same moment the knight leaned over to his near side and swapped off the lady's head. When Lancelot looked back again, without seeing any soldiers, he found the lady sitting beside him with no head on. She slowly began to sag to the left, throbbing horribly, and fell in the dust. There was blood all over his horse.

Lancelot grew white about the nostrils.

He said, "I shall kill you for that."

The knight immediately jumped off his horse and lay on the ground.

"Don't kill me!" he said. "Mercy! She was an adulteress."

Lancelot dismounted also and drew his sword.

"Get up," he said. "Get up and fight, you, you—"

The knight scrambled along the ground toward him, and threw his arms round his thighs. By being close to the avenger, he made it difficult for him to swing the sword. "Mercy!" His abjection made Lancelot feel horrible.

"Get up," he said. "Get up and fight. Look, I will take my armour off and fight you with my sword only."

But "Mercy, mercy!" was all the knight would say.

Lancelot began to shudder, not at the knight but at the cruelty in himself. He held his sword loathingly, and pushed the knight away.

"Look at all the blood," he said.

"Don't kill me," said the knight. "I yield. I yield. You can't kill a man at mercy."

Lancelot put up his sword and went back from the knight, as if he were going back from his own soul. He felt in his heart cruelty and cowardice, the things which made him brave and kind.

"Get up," he said. "I won't hurt you. Get up, go."

The knight looked at him, on all fours like a dog, and stood up, crouching uncertainly.

Lancelot went away and was sick.

At the feast of Pentecost it was customary for the knights who had been on
Table quests to gather again at Carlion so as to relate their adventures.
Arthur had found that this made people keener on fighting in the new way
of Right, if they had to tell about it afterwards. Most of them preferred to
bring their prisoners with them, as witnesses to their stories. It was as if
some Inspector General of Police in a very distant part of Africa were to
send out his superintendents into the jungle, asking them to come back
next Christmas with all the savage chiefs whom they had brought to
righteousness. For one thing, it impressed the savage chiefs to see the great
court, and they often went home reformed.

The Pentecost next after Lancelot's first quest was almost a fiasco. A few
seedy giants of the Strong Arm, who had been captured by the Orkney
faction, turned up and said their homage, but the Lancelot contingent was a
spate. "Whose man are you?" "Lancelot's." "And whose are you, my good
fellow?" "Lancelot's." After a bit the whole table began shouting the
answers. Arthur would say: "You are welcome to Carlion, Sir Belleus, and
may I ask which of my knights you have yielded to?" "Lancelot," the
Table would shout in chorus. And Sir Belleus, blushing rather and
wondering whether the laughter was at him, would say in a small voice:
"Yes, I yielded to Sir Lancelot."

Sir Bedivere came and admitted how he had swapped off his adulterous
wife's head. He had brought it with him, and was told to take it to the Pope
as a penance—he became very holy after that. Gawaine came gruffly and
told in Scottish English how he had been rescued from Sir Carados.
Gaheris, at the head of a deputation of sixty–four knights with rusty
shields, related his rescue from Sir Turquine. The daughter of King
Bagdemagus arrived in an enthusiastic state and told about the tournament
with the King of Northgalis. Besides these, there were many people from
adventures which we have left out—mainly knights who had yielded to Sir
Lancelot when he was disguised as Sir Kay. You may remember from the
first book that Kay was inclined to throw his tongue a bit too much, and he
had got himself unpopular on account of this. Lancelot had been
compelled during the quest to rescue him from three knights who were
pursuing him. Then, so that Kay could get home to court unmolested,
Lancelot had changed armour with him one night while he was asleep—

and thereafter the knights who went for Lancelot under the impression that he was Kay had gotten the surprise of their lives, while the knights who met Kay in Lancelot's armour had given him a wide berth. Knights yielded under this category included Gawaine, Uwaine, Sagramour, Ector de Maris, and three others. Also there came a knight called Sir Meliot de Logres, who had been rescued under supernatural circumstances.

All these people gave themselves up, not to King Arthur, but to Guenever. Lancelot had kept himself away for a whole year, but there was a limit to his endurance. Thinking of her all the time and longing to be back with her, he had allowed himself this one indulgence. He had sent his captives to kneel at her feet. It was a fatal course of action.

CHAPTER IX

It is difficult to explain about Guenever, unless it is possible to love two people at the same time. Probably it is not possible to love two people in the same way, but there are different kinds of love. Women love their children and their husbands at the same time—and men often feel a lusty thought for one woman while they are feeling a love of the heart for another. In some way such as this Guenever did come to love the Frenchman without losing her affection for Arthur. She and Lancelot were hardly more than children when it began, and the King was about eight years their senior. At twenty–two, the age of thirty seems to be the verge of senility. The marriage between her and Arthur had been what they call a "made" marriage. That is to say, it had been fixed by treaty with King Leodegrance, without consulting her. It had been a successful union, as "made" marriages generally are, and before Lancelot came on the scene the young girl had adored her famous husband, even if he was so old. She had felt respect for him, with gratitude, kindness, love, and a sense of protection. She had felt more than this—you might say that she had felt everything except the passion of romance.

And then the captives arrived. A blushing queen of little more than twenty summers on her throne, and the whole flame–lit hall filling with noble knights on bended knee. "Whose prisoner are you?" "I am the Queen's prisoner, to live or die, sent by Sir Lancelot." "Whose you?" "The Queen's, by Lancelot's arm." Sir Lancelot—the name on everybody's lips: the best knight in the world, top of the averages, even above Tristram: the courtly, the merciful, the ugly, the invincible: and he had sent them all to her. It was like a birthday party, so many presents. It was like the story books.

Guenever sat straight and bowed royally to her prisoners. She pardoned them all. Her eyes were brighter than her crown.

Lancelot came last. There was a stir among the torchbearers near the door, and a sound went round the hall. The clatter of knives and plates and tankards, the noise of friendly shouting which had sounded a moment before like a meeting of seabirds on St. Kilda, the yells for more mutton or a pint of mead were stilled—and the blurs of white faces turned toward the door. There was Lancelot, no longer in armour but dressed in a magnificent velvet robe, scalloped and diapered. He hesitated in the dark frame, hideous and friendly, wondering why the silence was—and the lights showed him up. Then the faces turned back again, the seabird meeting started once more, and Lancelot came forward to kiss the King's hand.

It was the moment. Perhaps it is better than trying to explain.

"Well, Lance," said Arthur cheerfully, "these are some high jinks, and no mistake about it. Jenny can hardly sit still, with all her captives."

"They were for her," said Lancelot. The Queen and he did not look at each other. They had done so with the click of two magnets coming together, the moment that he crossed the threshold.

"I can't help thinking they were for me too," said the King. "The result ought to be that you have made me a present of about three counties."

Lancelot felt a need to prevent silence. He began talking too quickly.

"Three counties is not much," he said, "for the Emperor of all Europe. You speak as if you had never conquered the Dictator of Rome. How are your dominions getting on?"

"They are getting on as you make them, Lance. It was no good conquering the Dictator, unless you and the others do the civilizing part. What is the use of being the Emperor of Europe, if the whole place is fighting mad?"

Guenever supported her hero in the effort against silence. It was their first partnership.

"You are a strange man," she said, "Arthur dear. You fight all the time, and conquer countries and win battles, and then you say that fighting is a bad thing."

"So it is a bad thing. It is the worst thing in the world. Oh, God, we needn't explain it again."

"No."

"How is the Orkney faction?" asked the younger man hastily. "How is your famous civilization going? Might for Right? You mustn't forget I have been away a year."

The King put his head in his hands and looked miserably at the table between his elbows. He was a kind, conscientious, peace–loving fellow, who had been afflicted in his youth by a tutor of genius. Between the two of them they had worked out their theory that killing people, and being a tyrant over them, was wrong. To stop this sort of thing, they had invented the idea of the Table—a vague idea like democracy, or sportsmanship, or morals—and now, in the effort to impose a world of peace, he found himself up to the elbows in blood. When he was feeling healthy he did not grieve much, because he knew the dilemma was inevitable—but in weak moments he was persecuted by shame and indecision. He was one of the first Nordic men who had invented civilization, or who had desired to do otherwise than Attila the Hun had done, and the battle against chaos sometimes did not seem to be worth fighting. He often thought that it might have been better for all his dead soldiers to be alive—even if they had lived under tyranny and madness—rather than be quite dead.

"The Orkney faction is bad," he said. "So is civilization, except for the bit which you have just brought in. Before you came, I was thinking that I was the Emperor of nothing—now I feel as if I were the Emperor of three counties."

"What is wrong with the Orkney faction?"

"Oh, God, must we talk about it when we were feeling happy because you had come back? I suppose we must."

"It is Morgause," said the Queen.

"Partly. Morgause is having love affairs with anybody she can get hold of, now that Lot is dead. How I wish King Pellinore had not had that unfortunate accident when he killed him! It is having a bad effect on her children."

"How do you mean?"

The King scratched on the table and stated: "I wish you had not conquered Gawaine, that time when you were disguised as Kay. I almost wish you had not made such brilliant successes in rescuing him and his brothers from Carados and Turquine."

"Why not?"

"This Round Table," said the older man slowly, "was a good thing when we thought of it. It was necessary to invent a way for the fighting men to express themselves without doing harm. I can't see how we could have done it otherwise than by starting a fashion, like children. To get them in, we had to have a gang, as kids have in schools. Then the gang had to swear a darksome oath that they would only fight for our ideas. You could call it for civilization. What I meant by civilization when I invented it, was simply that people ought not to take advantage of weakness—not violate maidens, and rob widows, and kill a man when he was down. People ought to be civil. But it has turned into sportsmanship. Merlin always said that sportsmanship was the curse of the world, and so it is. My scheme is going wrong. All these knights now are making a fetish of it. They are turning it into a competitive thing. Merlin used to call it Games–Mania. Everybody gossips and nags and hints and speculates about who unseated whom last, and who has rescued most virgins, and who is the best knight of the Table. I made it a round table to prevent that very thing, but it has not prevented it. The Orkney faction have got the craze worst. I suppose their sense of insecurity over their mother makes it necessary for them to be sure of a safe place at the top of the list. They have to excel, to make up for her. That is why I wish you had not beaten Gawaine. He is a decent chap, but he will hold it against you inside himself. You have hurt him in his tilting average—it is a part of their make–up which has now become more important to my knights than their souls. If you are not careful, you will have the Orkney faction after your blood, as well as after poor Pellinore's. It's a foul position. People will do the basest things on account of their so–called honour. I wish I had never invented honour, or sportsmanship, or civilization."

"What a speech!" said Lancelot. "Cheer up. The faction won't hurt me, even if it does come after my blood. As for your scheme going wrong, that is nonsense. The Round Table is the best thing that ever happened."

Arthur, whose head was still in his hands, raised his eyes. He saw that his friend and his wife were looking at each other with the wide pupils of madness, so he quickly attended to his plate.

CHAPTER X

Uncle Dap said, turning the helm round in his hands: "Your mantling is cut and torn. We shall have to get another. It is honourable to have the mantling slashed, but dishonourable to keep it so when there is an opportunity to replace it. Such a course of action would be boastful."

They were talking in a little closet with a north window, cold and grey, and the blue light lay like frozen oil upon the steel.

"Yes."

"How did Joyeux go? Is he sharp still? Did you like his balance?"

Joyeux had been made by Galand, the greatest swordsmith of the Middle Ages.

"Yes."

"Yes! Yes!" cried Uncle Dap. "Can you say nothing but Yes? Death of my soul, Lancelot, but one asks if you are dumb! What in the world is this that has come over you, in the end?"

Lancelot had been smoothing the panache of feathers which was used as a distinguishing mark on the helm in Uncle Dap's hands. It was detachable. People have got it into their heads, through the cinema and the comic advertisements, that knights in armour generally wore ostrich plumes, nodding like stalks of pampas grass. This was not the case. Kay's panache, for instance, was shaped like a rigid, flat fan, with its edges pointing fore and aft. It was carefully arranged out of the eyes of peacock feathers, exactly as if a stiff peacock fan had been erected endwise on his head. It was not a tuft of plumes, and it did not nod. It was rather like the adipose fin of a fish, but gaudy. Lancelot, who did not care for gaudy things, wore a few heron's hackles bound with silver thread, which suited the argent of his shield. He had been stroking them. Now he threw them violently into a corner and stood up. He began walking the narrow room in a jerky way.

"Uncle Dap," he said, "do you remember how I asked you not to talk about something?"

"I do."

"Is Guenever in love with me?"

"You should ask her," replied his uncle, with French logic.

"What must I do?" he cried. "What must I do?"

If it is difficult to explain about Guenever's love for two men at the same time, it is almost impossible to explain about Lancelot. At least it would be impossible nowadays, when everybody is so free from superstitions and prejudice that it is only necessary for all of us to do as we please. Why did not Lancelot make love to Guenever, or run away with his hero's wife altogether, as any enlightened man would do today?

One reason for his dilemma was that he was a Christian. The modern world is apt to forget that several people were Christians in the remote past, and in Lancelot's time there were no Protestants—except John Scotus Erigena. His Church, in which he had been brought up—and it is difficult to escape from your upbringing—directly forbade him to seduce his best friend's wife. Another stumbling block to doing as he pleased was the very idea of chivalry or of civilization which Arthur had first invented and then introduced into his own young mind. Perhaps a bad baron who believed in the Strong Arm might have gone off with Guenever, even in the face of his Church's councils, because taking your neighbour's wife was really a form of Fort Mayne. It was a matter of the stronger bull winning. But Lancelot had spent his childhood between knightly exercises and thinking out King Arthur's theory for himself. He believed as firmly as Arthur did, as firmly as the benighted Christian, that there was such a thing as Right. Finally, there was the impediment of his nature. In the secret parts of his peculiar brain, those unhappy and inextricable tangles which he felt at the roots, the boy was disabled by something which we cannot explain. He could not have explained either, and for us it is all too long ago. He loved Arthur and he loved Guenever and he hated himself. The best knight of the world: everybody envied the self–esteem which must surely be his. But Lancelot never believed he was good or nice. Under the grotesque, magnificent shell with a face like Quasimodo's, there was shame and self–loathing which had been planted there when he was tiny, by something which it is now too late to trace. It is so fatally easy to make young children believe that they are horrible.

"It seems to me," said Uncle Dap, "that it depends very largely on what the Queen wants to do."

CHAPTER XI

Lancelot stayed at the court for several weeks this time, and each week made it more difficult to go away. On top of the more or less social tangle in which he found himself, there was a personal puzzle—for he put a higher value on chastity than is fashionable in our century. He believed, like the man in Lord Tennyson, that people could only have the strength often on account of their hearts being pure. It so happened that his strength was as the strength of ten, and such was the medieval explanation which had been discovered for it. As a corollary to this belief, he supposed that if he gave in to the Queen he would lose his tenfold might. So, for this reason, as well as for the other ones, he fought against her with the courage of despair. It was not pleasant for Guenever either.

One day Uncle Dap said: "You had better go away. You have lost nearly two stone in weight. If you go away something will either snap or not snap. It is better to get it over quickly."

Lancelot said: "I cannot go."

Arthur said: "Please stay."

Guenever said: "Go."

The second quest which he embarked upon was the turning–point of his life. There had been a good deal of talk in Camelot about a certain King Pelles, who was lame and lived in the haunted castle of Corbin. He was supposed to be slightly mad, because he believed himself to be a relation of Joseph of Arimathea. He was the sort of man who would become a British Israelite nowadays, and spend the rest of his life prophesying the end of the world by measuring the passages in the Great Pyramid. However, King Pelles was only slightly mad, and his castle was certainly haunted. It had a haunted room in it, with innumerable doors out of which things came and fought you in the night. Arthur thought it was worth sending Lancelot to investigate the place.

On the way to Corbin Lancelot had a strange adventure, which he remembered for many years with awful grief. He was to look back on it as the last adventure of his virginity, and to believe, day by day for the next twenty years, that before it had happened he had been God's man, while, after it, he had become a lie.

There was a village under the castle of Corbin, which seemed a prosperous one. It had cobbled streets and stone houses and old bridges. The castle stood on a hill to one side of the valley, and there was a handsome pele tower on the hill of the other side. All the people of the village were in the street, as if they were waiting for him, and there was a dreamlike quality in the air, as if a shower of gold dust had come from the sun. Lancelot felt peculiar. His blood might have had too much oxygen in it, from the way he was conscious of every stone in every wall, and all the colours in the valley, and the joyful stepping of his horse. The people of the enchanted village knew his name.

"Welcome, Sir Lancelot Dulac," they cried, "the flower of all knighthood! By thee we shall be holpen out of danger."

He reined his horse and spoke to them.

"Why do you call out to me?" he asked, thinking of other things. "How do you know my name? What is the matter?"

They answered in chorus, speaking together solemnly and without difficulty.

"Ah, fair knight," they said. "Do you see that tower on the hill? There is a dolorous lady in it, who has been kept boiling in scalding water for many winters by magic, and nobody can get her out except the best knight in the world. Sir Gawaine was here last week, but he could not do it."

"If Sir Gawaine could not do it," he said, "I am sure that I can't."

He did not like this sort of competition. The danger about being the best knight in the world was that if you were always being tested about it, the day was bound to come when you would fail to retain the title.

"I think I had better ride on," he said, and he gave his reins a shake.

"No, no," said the people gravely. "You are Sir Lancelot and we know it.

You will get our lady out of the boiling water."

"I must go."

"She is in pain."

Lancelot leaned on the withers of his horse, lifted his right leg over the crupper, and found himself on the ground.

"Tell me what I must do," he said.

The people formed in a procession round him, and the mayor of the village took him by the hand. They walked together silently up the hill to the pele tower, except that the mayor explained the situation as they went.

"Our lady of the manor," said the mayor, "used to be the most beautiful girl in the country. So Queen Morgan le Fay and the Queen of Northgalis grew jealous of her, and they have put her in this magic for revenge. It is terrible how it hurts her, and she has been boiling for five years. Only the best knight in the world can get her out."

When they came to the tower gate, another strange thing happened. It was heavily bolted and barred in the old–fashioned way. The masonry of the doorway was constructed with deep slots in it, in which heavy beams ran to and fro—heavy enough to withstand a battering ram. Now these beams withdrew into the wall of their own accord, and the iron locks turned their own wards with a grinding noise. The door quietly opened.

"Go in," said the mayor, and the people stood still outside, waiting for what was to happen.

On the first floor of the tower there was the furnace which kept the magic water hot. Lancelot could not enter there. On the second floor there was a room full of steam, so that he could not see across it. He went into this room, holding his hands joined together in front of him, as blind people do, until he heard a squeak. A clearing in the steam, caused by the draught from the door so long unopened, showed him the lady who had given the squeak. She was sitting shyly in the bath looking at him, a charming little lady, who was—as Malory puts it—as naked as a needle.

"Well!" said he.

The girl blushed, so far as she could blush when she was boiled, and said in a small voice: "Please give me your hand." She knew how the magic had to be undone.

Lancelot gave her his hand, and she stood up, and got out of the bath, and all the people outside began cheering, as though they knew exactly what was happening. They had brought a dress with them, and the proper underwear, and the ladies of the village formed a circle in the gateway while the pink girl was dressed.

"Oh, it does feel lovely to be dressed!" she said.

"My popsy!" cried a fat old woman who had evidently been her nurse when she was small, weeping tears of joy.

"Sir Lancelot done it," shouted the villagers. "Three cheers for Sir Lancelot!"

When the cheering had died away, the boiled girl came to him and put her hand in his.

"Thank you," she said. "Ought we to go to church now, and thank God as well as you?"

"Certainly we must."

So they went to the clean little chapel in the village and thanked God for His mercies. They kneeled between the frescoed walls, where some important–looking saints with blue haloes were standing on tiptoe to avoid foreshortening, and the gay paints of the stained–glass window poured upon their heads. They were cobalt blue, purple from manganese, yellow from copper, red, and a green which was also got from copper. The whole inside of the place was a tankful of colour. It was half–way through the service before he realized that he had been allowed to do a miracle, just as he had always wanted.

King Pelles limped down from his castle on the other side of the valley, to find out what the excitement was about. He looked at Lancelot's shield, kissed the boiled child absent–mindedly, leaning over like an obedient stork to have his cheek pecked, and remarked: "Dear me, you are Sir Lancelot! And I see you have fetched my daughter out of that kettle arrangement. How kind of you! It was prophesied long ago. I am King Pelles, near cousin to Joseph of Arimathea—and you, of course, are but the eighth degree from Our Lord Jesus Christ."

"Good gracious!"

"Indeed, indeed," said King Pelles. "It is all written down arithmetically in the stones at Stonehenge, and I have some sort of holy dish in my castle at Carbonek, together with a dove which flies about in various directions holding a censer of gold in its beak. Still, it was extremely kind of you to fetch my daughter out of the kettle."

"Daddy," said the girl. "We ought to be introduced."

King Pelles waved his hand as if he were trying to scare away the midges.

"Elaine," he said. It was another one with the same name. "This is my daughter, Elaine. How do you do? And this is Sir Lancelot Dulac. How do you do? All written in the stones."

Lancelot, perhaps slightly biased by having first met her with no clothes on, thought that Elaine was the most beautiful girl he had seen, except Guenever. He felt shy too.

"You must come and stay with me," said the King. "That is in the stones also. Show you the holy dish some day, and all that. Teach you arithmetic. Nice weather. Don't have daughters unboiled every day. I think dinner will be ready."

Chapter XII

Lancelot stayed at the castle of Corbin for days. Its haunted rooms were up to expectation and there was nothing else to do. He felt such feelings in his breast because of Guenever—the frightful pang of hopeless love—that he was drained of effort. He could not summon the energy to go elsewhere. At the beginning of his love for her there had been restlessness, so that he had felt that if only he kept moving and doing new things every moment there might be a hope of escape. Now his power to be busy was gone. He felt that he might as well be in one place as another, if he was only waiting to see whether his heart would break or not. He was too simple to see that if the finest knight in the world rescued you out of a kettle of boiling water, with no clothes on, you would be likely to fall in love with him—if you were only eighteen.

One evening, when Pelles had been particularly tiresome about religious family trees, and when the gnawing in the boy's heart had made it impossible for him to eat properly or even to sit still at dinner, the butler took the situation in hand. He had served the Pelles family for forty years, was married to the nurse who had greeted Elaine with tears of joy, and he approved of love. He also understood about young men like Lancelot— young men who might still be undergraduates or jet–pilots if they were in England today. He would have made an excellent college butler.

"More wine, sir?" asked the butler.

"No, thank you."

The butler bowed politely and poured another horn, which Lancelot drained without looking at it.

"A nice vintage, sir," said the butler. "His Majesty takes great trouble with his cellar."

King Pelles had gone to the library to work out some prognostications, and his guest was left gloomily in the hall.

"Yes."

There was a rustling outside the buttery door, and the butler went over to it while Lancelot was drinking another measure.

"Now this is a fine wine, sir," said the butler. "His Majesty sets great store by this wine, and my wife has just fetched up a fresh bottle from the cellar. Observe the crust, sir. It is a wine which I am sure you will appreciate."

"All wines are the same to me."

"You modest young gentleman," said the butler, substituting a larger horn. "If I may say so, sir, you will have your little joke. But it is easy to recognize a judge of wine when you come across him."

He was bothering Lancelot, who wanted to be alone with his misery, and Lancelot realized that he was being bothered. For this reason he automatically wondered whether he had not perhaps been discourteous to the butler in his distraction. Perhaps the butler was really keen on the wine, and had troubles of his own. He politely drank it up.

"Very nice," he said encouragingly. "A splendid vintage."

"I am glad to hear you praise it, sir."

"Have you ever," asked Lancelot, putting the question which all young men are always asking, and without noticing that it had anything to do with the drink, "have you ever been in love?"

The butler smiled discreetly and poured another bumper.

By midnight Lancelot and the butler were sitting on opposite sides of the table, both looking red in the face. They had a brew of piment between them—a mixture of red wine, honey, spices, and whatever else the butler's wife had added.

"So I tell you," said Lancelot, glaring like an ape. "Wouldn't tell everybody, but you are a nice chap. Understanding chap. Pleasure to tell anything. Have another drink."

"Good health," said the butler.

"What am I to do?" he cried. "What am I to do?"

He put his horrible head between his arms on the table, and began to weep.

"Courage!" said the butler. "Do or die!"

He made a rapping on the table with one hand, looking at the buttery door, and with the other poured out another bumper.

"Drink," he said. "Drink hearty. Be a man, sir, if I may make so bold. You will have good news in a minute, that you will, and you want to seize the unforgiving minute, as the bard says."

"Good chap," said Lancelot. "Damned if I wouldn't, if I could."

"Jack is as good as his master."

"Certainly is," said the young man, winking in a way which he was afraid must look most beastly. "Better, in fact, eh, butler?"

He began to grin like an ass.

"Ah," said the butler, "and there is my wife Brisen at the buttery door, holding a message. I dare say it might be for you.

"What does it say?" asked the butler, watching the boy who sat staring at the paper.

"Nothing," he said, throwing the paper on the table and walking unsteadily to the door.

The butler read the paper.

"It says that Queen Guenever is at the castle of Case, five miles from here, and she wants you. It says the King is not with her. There are some kisses on it."

"Well?"

"You dare not go," said the butler.

"Dare not?" shouted Sir Lancelot, and he went into the darkness staggering, laughing like a caricature, and calling for his horse.

In the morning he woke suddenly in a strange room. It was quite dark, with tapestry over the windows, and he had no headache because his constitution was good. He jumped out of bed and went to the window, to draw the curtain. He was fully aware, in the suddenness of a second, of all that had happened on the previous night—aware of the butler and of the drink and of the love–potion which had perhaps been put in it, of the message from Guenever, and of the dark, solid, cool–fired body in the bed which he had just got out of. He drew the curtain and leaned his forehead against the cold stone of the mullion. He was miserable.

"Jenny," he said, after minutes which seemed to be hours.

There was no answer from the bed.

He turned round and found himself looking at the boiled girl, Elaine. She lay in the bed, her small bare arms holding the bedclothes to her sides, with her violet eyes fixed on his.

Lancelot was always a martyr to his feelings, never any good at disguising them. When he saw Elaine his head went back. Then his ugly face took on a look of profound and outraged sorrow, so simple and truthful that his nakedness in the window–light was dignity. He began to tremble.

Elaine did not move, but only looked upon him with her quick eyes, like a mouse.

Lancelot went over to the chest where his sword was lying.

"I shall kill you."

She only looked. She was eighteen, pitifully small in the big bed, and she was frightened.

"Why did you do it?" he cried. "What have you done? Why have you betrayed me?"

"I had to."

"But it was treachery!"

He could not believe it of her.

"It was treachery! You have betrayed me."

"Why?"

"You have made me—taken from me—stolen—"

He threw his sword into a corner and sat down on the chest. When he began to cry, the gross lines of his face screwed themselves up fantastically. The thing which Elaine had stolen from him was his might. She had stolen his strength of ten. Children believe such things to this day, and think that they will only be able to bowl well in the cricket match tomorrow, provided that they are good today.

Lancelot stopped crying, and spoke with his eyes on the floor.

"When I was little," he said, "I prayed to God that he would let me work a miracle. Only virgins can work miracles. I wanted to be the best knight in the world. I was ugly and lonely. The people of your village said that I was the best knight of the world, and I did work my Miracle when I got you out of the water. I did not know it would be my last as well as my first."

Elaine said: "Oh, Lancelot, you will work plenty more."

"Never. You have stolen my miracles. You have stolen my being the best knight. Elaine, why did you do it?"

She began to cry.

He got up, wrapped himself in a towel, and went over to the bed.

"Never mind," he said. "It was my fault for getting drunk. I was miserable, and I got drunk. I wonder if that butler tried to make me? It was not very fair if he did. Don't cry, Elaine. It was not your fault."

"It was. It was."

"Probably your father made you do it, so as to have the eighth degree from Our Lord in the family. Or else it was that enchantress Brisen, the butler's wife. Don't be sorry about it, Elaine. It is over now. Look, I will give you a kiss."

"Lancelot!" cried Elaine. "It was because I loved you. Haven't I given something too? I was a maiden, Lancelot. I didn't rob you. Oh, Lancelot— it was my fault. I ought to be killed. Why didn't you kill me with your sword? But it was because I loved you, and I couldn't help it."

"There, there."

"Lancelot, suppose I have a baby?"

He stopped comforting her and went to the window again, as if he were going mad.

"I want to have your baby," said Elaine. "I shall call him Galahad, like your first name."

She still held the coverlet to her sides with the small, bare arms. Lancelot turned upon her in fury.

"Elaine," he said, "if you have a baby, it is your baby. It is unfair to bind me with pity. I am going straight away now, and I hope I shall never see you again."

Chapter XIII

Guenever was doing some petit point in the gloomy room, which she hated doing. It was for a shield–cover for Arthur, and had the dragon rampant gules. Elaine was only eighteen, and it is fairly easy to explain the feelings of a child—but Guenever was twenty–two. She had grown to have some of the nature of an individual, stamped on the simple feelings of the child–queen who had once received her present of captives.

There is a thing called knowledge of the world, which people do not have until they are middle–aged. It is something which cannot be taught to younger people, because it is not logical and does not obey laws which are constant. It has no rules. Only, in the long years which bring women to the middle of life, a sense of balance develops. You can't teach a baby to walk by explaining the matter to her logically—she has to learn the strange poise of walking by experience. In some way like that, you cannot teach a young woman to have knowledge of the world. She has to be left to the experience of the years. And then, when she is beginning to hate her used body, she suddenly finds that she can do it. She can go on living—not by principle, not by deduction, not by knowledge of good and evil, but simply by a peculiar and shifting sense of balance which defies each of these things often. She no longer hopes to live by seeking the truth—if women ever do hope this—but continues henceforth under the guidance of a seventh sense. Balance was the sixth sense, which she won when she first learned to walk, and now she has the seventh one—knowledge of the world.

The slow discovery of the seventh sense, by which both men and women contrive to ride the waves of a world in which there is war, adultery, compromise, fear, stultification and hypocrisy—this discovery is not a matter for triumph. The baby, perhaps, cries out triumphantly: I have balance! But the seventh sense is recognized without a cry. We only carry on with our famous knowledge of the world, riding the queer waves in a habitual, petrifying way, because we have reached a stage of deadlock in which we can think of nothing else to do.

And at this stage we begin to forget that there ever was a time when we lacked the seventh sense. We begin to forget, as we go stolidly balancing along, that there could have been a time when we were young bodies flaming with the impetus of life. It is hardly consoling to remember such a feeling, and so it deadens in our minds.

But there was a time when each of us stood naked before the world, confronting life as a serious problem with which we were intimately and passionately concerned. There was a time when it was of vital interest to us to find out whether there was a God or not. Obviously the existence or otherwise of a future life must be of the very first importance to somebody who is going to live her present one, because her manner of living it must hinge on the problem. There was a time when Free Love versus Catholic Morality was a question of as much importance to our hot bodies as if a pistol had been clapped to our heads.

Further back, there were times when we wondered with all our souls what the world was, what love was, what we were ourselves.

All these problems and feelings fade away when we get the seventh sense. Middle–aged people can balance between believing in God and breaking all the commandments, without difficulty. The seventh sense, indeed, slowly kills all the other ones, so that at last there is no trouble about the commandments. We cannot see any more, or feel, or hear about them. The bodies which we loved, the truths which we sought, the Gods whom we questioned: we are deaf and blind to them now, safely and automatically balancing along toward the inevitable grave, under the protection of our last sense. "Thank God for the aged," sings the poet:

> Thank God for the aged
> And for age itself, and illness and the grave.
> When we are old and ill, and particularly in the coffin,
> It is no trouble to behave.

Guenever was twenty–two as she sat at her petit point and thought of Lancelot. She was not half–way to her coffin, not ill even, and she only had six senses. It is difficult to imagine her.

A chaos of the mind and body—a time for weeping at sunsets and at the glamour of moonlight—a confusion and profusion of beliefs and hopes, in God, in Truth, in Love, and in Eternity—an ability to be transported by the beauty of physical objects—a heart to ache or swell—a joy so joyful and a sorrow so sorrowful that oceans could lie between them: then, as a counterpoise to these attractive features, outcrops of selfishness indecently exposed—restlessness or inability to settle down and stop bothering the middle–aged—pert argument on abstract subjects like Beauty, as if they were of any interest to the middle–aged—lack of experience as to when truth should be suppressed in deference to the middle–aged—general effervescence and nuisance and unfittingness to the set patterns of the seventh sense—these must have been some of Guenever's characteristics at twenty–two, because they are everybody's. But on top of them there were the broad and yet uncertain lines of her personal character—lines which made her different from the innocent Elaine, lines of less pathos perhaps but more reality, lines of power which made her into the individual Jenny that Lancelot loved.

"Oh, Lancelot," she sang as she stitched at the shield–crown. "Oh, Lance, come back soon. Come back with your crooked smile, or with your own way of walking which shows whether you are angry or puzzled—come back to tell me that it does not matter whether love is a sin or not. Come back to say that it is enough that I should be Jenny and you should be Lance, whatever may happen to anybody."

The startling thing was that he came. Straight from Elaine, straight from her robbery, Lancelot came like an arrow to the heart of love. He had slept with Guenever already in deceit, already had been cheated of his tenfold might. He was a lie now, in God's eyes as he saw them, so he felt that he might as well be a lie in earnest. No more to be the best knight in the world, no more to work miracles against magic, no more to have compensation for ugliness and emptiness in his soul, the young man sped to his sweetheart for consolation. There was the clatter of his iron–shod horse on the cobbles, which made the Queen drop her needlework to see whether it was Arthur back from his hunting—the ring of his chain–mail feet upon the stairs, going chink–chink like spurs against the stone—and then, before she was quite certain of what had happened, Guenever was laughing or weeping, unfaithful to her husband, as she had always known she would be.

CHAPTER XIV

Arthur said: "Here is a letter from your father, Lance. He says he is being attacked by King Claudas. I promised to help him against Claudas, if it was necessary, in exchange for his help at Bedegraine. I shall have to go."

"I see."

"What do you want to do?"

"How do you mean, what do I want to do?"

"Well, do you want to come with me or to stay here?"

Lancelot cleared his throat and said: "I want to do whatever you think best."

"It will be difficult for you," said Arthur. "I hate to ask you. But would you mind if I asked you to stay?"

Lancelot could not think of the safe words, so the King mistook his silence for disappointment.

"Of course, you have a right to see your father and mother," he said. "I don't want you to stay, if it hurts too much. Probably we can manage it another way."

"Why did you want to leave me in England?"

"There ought to be somebody here to look after the factions. I should feel safer in France if I knew there was a strong man left behind. There is going to be trouble in Cornwall soon, between Tristram and Mark, and there is the Orkney feud. You know the difficulties. And it would be nice to think there was somebody looking after Gwen."

"Perhaps," said Lancelot, choosing the words with pain, "it would be better to trust somebody else."

"Don't be absurd. How could I trust anybody more? You would only have to show that mug of yours outside the dog kennel and all the thieves would run away at once."

"It is not a very handsome one."

"Cut–throat!" exclaimed the King affectionately, and he thumped his friend on the back. He went off to arrange about the expedition.

They had a year of joy, twelve months of the strange heaven which the salmon know on beds of river shingle, under the gin–clear water. For twenty–four years they were guilty, but this first year was the only one which seemed like happiness. Looking back on it, when they were old, they did not remember that in this year it had ever rained or frozen. The four seasons were coloured like the edge of a rose petal for them.

"I don't understand," said Lancelot, "why you should love me. Are you sure you do? Is there some mistake about it?"

"My Lance."

"But my face," he said. "I am so horrible. Now I can believe that God might love the world, whatever it was like, because of himself."

At other times, they were in a terror which came from him. Guenever did not feel remorse on her own account, but she caught it from her lover.

"I dare not think. Don't think. Kiss me, Jenny."

"Why think?"

"I can't help thinking."

"Dear Lance!"

Then there were different times when they quarrelled about nothing—but even the quarrels were those of lovers, which seemed sweet when they remembered them afterwards.

"Your toes are like the little pigs which went to market."

"I wish you would not say things like that. It is not respectful."

"Respectful!"

"Yes, respectful. Why shouldn't you be respectful? I am the Queen, after all."

"Do you seriously mean to tell me that I am supposed to treat you with respect? I suppose I am to kneel on one knee all the time and kiss your hand?"

"Why not?"

"I wish you wouldn't be so selfish. If there is one thing I can't stand, it is being treated like a possession."

"Selfish, indeed!"

And the Queen would stamp her foot, or perhaps sulk for a day. But she forgave him when he had made a proper act of contrition.

One day, when they were at the stage of telling each other their private feelings, with a sort of innocent amazement when they corresponded, Lancelot gave the Queen his secret.

"Jenny, when I was little I hated myself. I don't know why. I was ashamed. I was a very holy little boy."

"You are not very holy now," she said, laughing. She did not understand what she was being told.

"One day my brother asked me to lend him an arrow. I had two or three specially straight ones, which I was very careful of, and his were a bit warped. I pretended that I had lost my straight arrows, and said I couldn't lend them to him."

"Little liar!"

"I know I was. Afterwards I had the most dreadful remorse for having told him the lie, and I thought I had been untrue to God. So I went out to a bed of stinging nettles that was on the moat, and put my arrow arm into them, as a punishment. I rolled up my sleeve and put it right in."

"Poor Lance! What an innocent you must have been."

"But, Jenny, they didn't sting me! I am sure I am right in remembering that they didn't sting me."

"Do you mean there was a miracle?"

"I don't know. It is difficult to be sure. I was such a dreamy boy, always living in a make–up world where I was Arthur's greatest knight. I may have made it up about the nettles. But I think I can remember the shock when they didn't sting."

"I am sure it was a miracle," said the Queen decidedly.

"Jenny, all my life I have wanted to do miracles. I have wanted to be holy. I suppose it was ambition or pride or some other unworthy thing. It was not enough for me to conquer the world—I wanted to conquer heaven too. I was so grasping that it was not enough to be the strongest knight—I had to be the best as well. That is the worst of making day–dreams. It is why I tried to keep away from you. I knew that if I was not pure, I could never do miracles. And I did do a miracle, too: a splendid one. I got a girl out of some boiling water, who was enchanted into it. She was called Elaine. Then I lost my power. Now that we are together, I shall never be able to do my miracles any more."

He did not like to tell her the full truth about Elaine, for he thought that it would hurt her feelings to know that he had come to her as the second.

"Why not?"

"Because we are wicked."

"Personally I have never done a miracle," said the Queen, rather coldly. "So I have less to regret."

"But, Jenny, I am not regretting anything. You are my miracle, and I would throw them overboard all over again for the sake of you. I was only trying to tell you about the things I felt when I was small."

"Well, I can't say I understand."

"Can't you understand wanting to be good at things? No, I can see that you would not have to. It is only people who are lacking, or bad, or inferior, who have to be good at things. You have always been full and perfect, so you had nothing to make up for. But I have always been making up. I feel dreadful sometimes, even now, with you, when I know that I can't be the best knight any longer."

"Then we had better stop, and you can make a good confession, and do some more miracles."

"You know we can't stop."

"The whole thing seems fanciful to me," said the Queen. "I don't understand it. It seems unpractical and selfish."

"I know I am selfish. I can't help it. I try not to be. But how can I help being what I was made? Oh, can't you understand what I am telling you? I was lonely when I was small, and I worked hard at my exercises. I used to tell myself that I would be a great explorer, and cross the Chorasmian Waste: or I would be a great king, like Alexander or St. Louis: or a great healer: I would find out a balsam which cured wounds and give it away free: perhaps I would be a saint, and salve wounds just by touching them, or I would find something important—a relic of the True Cross, or the Holy Grail, or something like that. These were my dreams, Jenny. I am only telling you what I used to day–dream about. They are what I mean by my miracles, which are lost now. I have given you my hopes, Jenny, as a present from my love."

CHAPTER XV

The year of their happiness ended with Arthur's return—and almost immediately collapsed in ruin, but not on account of the King. The evening after his home–coming, while he was still giving them details of the defeat of Claudas as they happened to come into his memory, there was a disturbance at the Porter's Lodge, and Sir Bors was ushered into the Great Hall at dinner. He was Lancelot's cousin, and had been spending a holiday at the castle of Corbin, investigating the hauntings. He had some news for Lancelot, which he told him in a whisper after dinner—but unfortunately he was a misogynist, and, like most people of that sort, he had the female failing of indiscretion. He told the news to some of his bosom friends as well. Soon it was all over the court. The news was that Elaine of Corbin had given birth to a fine son, whom she had christened Galahad—which was Lancelot's first name, as you remember.

"So this," said Guenever, when she next saw her lover alone, "so this is why you lost your miracles. It was all lies about your giving them to me."

"What do you mean?"

Guenever began to breathe through her nose. She was feeling as if there were two red thumbs behind her eyeballs, trying to push them out, and she did not want to look at him. She was trying not to make a scene, and she dreaded her heart. She had shame and hatred of what she might say, but she could not help saying it. She was like a person swimming in a rough sea.

"You know what I mean," she said bitterly, looking away.

"Jenny, I wanted to tell you, but it was too difficult to explain."

"I can understand the difficulty."

"It is not what you think."

"What I think!" she cried. "How do you know what I think? I think what everybody would think—that you are a mean seducer, just a liar, you and your miracles. And I was fool enough to believe you."

Lancelot turned his head at each of her stabs, as if he were trying to let them glance off him. He looked on the ground, to hide his eyes. He had wide eyes, which generally gave him an expression of fear or surprise.

"Elaine means nothing to me," he said.

"Then she ought to do. How can you say that she means nothing to you when she is the mother of your child? When you tried to keep her secret? No, don't touch me, go away."

"I can't go away, when it is like this."

"If you touch me I shall go to the King."

"Guenever, I was made drunk at Corbin. Then they told me that you were waiting for me at Case, and they took me to a dark room with Elaine in it. I came away next morning."

"A clumsy lie."

"It is true."

"A baby wouldn't believe it."

"I can't make you believe it, if you don't want to. I drew my sword to kill Elaine, when I found out."

"I will have her killed."

"It was not her fault."

The Queen began plucking at the neck of her dress, as if it were too tight for her.

"You are standing up for her," she said. "You are in love with her, and deceiving me. I thought so all along."

"I swear I am telling the truth."

She suddenly gave up and began to cry.

"Why didn't you tell me before?" she asked. "Why didn't you tell me you had a baby? Why have you lied to me all the time? I suppose she was your famous miracle, which you were so proud of."

Lancelot, who also suffered from violent emotions, began to cry in turn. He put his arms round her.

"I didn't know I had one," he said. "I didn't want one. It was not my seeking."

"If you had told me the truth, I could have believed you."

"I wanted to tell you, but I couldn't. I was afraid you would be hurt."

"It has hurt me worse like this."

"I know it has."

The Queen dried her tears and looked at him, smiling like a spring shower. In a minute they were kissing, feeling like the green earth refreshed by rain. They thought that they understood each other once more—but their doubt had been planted. Now, in their love, which was stronger, there were the seeds of hatred and fear and confusion growing at the same time: for love can exist with hatred, each preying on the other, and this is what gives it its greatest fury.

CHAPTER XVI

In the castle of Corbin, the child Elaine was making ready for her journey. She was coming to capture Lancelot from Guenever, an expedition of which everybody except herself could feel the pathos. She had no weapons to fight with, and did not know how to fight. She was quite without character. Lancelot did not love her. And she was in the yet more hopeless position of loving him. She had nothing to oppose against the Queen's maturity except her own immaturity and humble love, nothing except the fat baby which she was carrying to its father—a baby which was to him only the symbol of a cruel trick. It was an expedition like that of an army without weapons against an impregnable fortress, an army which at the same time had its hands tied behind its back. Elaine, with an artlessness which could only be explained by the fact that she had spent most of her life in the seclusion of her magic cauldron, had decided to meet Guenever on her own ground. She had ordered gowns of the utmost magnificence and sophistication—and in these, which would only make her look all the more stupid and provincial, she was going to Camelot to fight her battle with the English Queen.

If Elaine had not been Elaine, she might have taken Galahad as her weapon. Pathos and proprietorship, rightly applied to a nature like Lancelot's, might have been successful in binding him. But Elaine was not clever, did not understand the attempt to bind her hero. She took Galahad because she adored him. She took him only because she did not want to be parted from her baby, and because she wanted to show him off to his father, and partly because she wanted to compare the faces. It was a year since she had set eyes on the man for whom her child–mind lived.

Lancelot, while Elaine was planning his capture, remained with the Queen at court. But he now remained without the temporary peace of heart which he had been able to invent for himself while the King was away. In the King's absence he had been able to drown himself in the passing minute— but Arthur was perpetually at his elbow now, as a comment on his treachery. He had not buried his love for Arthur in his passion for Guenever, but still felt for him. To a medieval nature like Lancelot's, with its fatal weakness for loving the highest when he saw it, this was a position of pain. He could not bear to be made to feel that his sentiment for Guenever was an ignoble sentiment, for it was the profound feeling of his life—yet every circumstance now conspired to make it seem ignoble. The hasty moments together, the locked doors and base contrivances, the guilty manoeuvres which the husband's presence forced on the lovers—these had the effect of soiling what had no excuse unless it was beautiful. On top of this stain there was the torture of knowing that Arthur was kind, simple and upright—of knowing that he was always on the edge of hurting Arthur dreadfully, although he loved him. Then there was pain about Guenever herself, the tiny plant of bitterness which they had sown, or seen sown, in each other's eyes, on the occasion of their first quarrel of suspicion. It was a pain to him to be in love with a jealous and suspicious woman. She had given him a mortal blow by not believing his explanation about Elaine instantly. Yet he was unable not to love her. Finally there were the revolted elements of his own character—his strange desire for purity and honour and spiritual excellence. All these things, working together with the unconscious dread of Elaine's arrival with his son, broke his happiness without allowing him to escape. He seldom sat down, but strayed about with nervous movements, picking things up and setting them down without looking at them, walking to windows and looking out but seeing nothing.

For Guenever the dread of Elaine's arrival was not unconscious. She had known from the first moment that Elaine was bound to come. For her, however, as for all women, the dreads were in advance of the male horizon. Men often accuse women of driving them to unfaithfulness by senseless jealousy, before there has been any thought of unfaithfulness on their own part. Yet the thought was probably there, unconscious and undetectable except to women. The great Anna Karenina, for instance, forced Vronsky into a certain position by the causeless jealousy of a maniac—yet that position was the only real solution to their problem, and it was the inevitable solution. Seeing so much further into the future than he did, she pressed towards it with passionate tread, wrecking the present because the future was bound to be a wreck.

So with Guenever. Probably she was not over–strained by Elaine's immediate problem. Probably she had no real suspicion against that side of Lancelot. Yet, with her prescience, she was aware of dooms and sorrows outside her lover's purview. It would not be accurate to say that she was aware of them in a logical sense, but they were present in her deeper mind. It is a pity that language is such a clumsy weapon that we cannot say that a mother was "unconscious" of her baby crying in the next room—with the meaning that the mother somehow, unconsciously, knew that it was crying. Facts of which Guenever was subconscious, in this sense, included the whole of the Arthur–Lancelot situation, most of the future tragedy at court, and the grievous fact of her own childlessness—which was never to be remedied.

She said to herself that Lancelot had betrayed her, that she was the victim of Elaine's cunning, that her lover was sure to betray her again. She tormented herself with a thousand words of the same sort. But what she felt to herself, in the uncharted regions of her heart, was a different matter. Perhaps she was actually jealous, not of Elaine, but of the baby. Perhaps it was Lancelot's love for Arthur that she feared. Or it may have been a fear of the whole position, of its instability and the nemesis inherent in it. Women know, far better than men, that God's laws are not mocked. They have more cause to know it.

Whatever the explanation of Guenever's attitude, the fruits of it were pain for her lover. She became as restless as he was, more unreasonable, and much more cruel.

Arthur's feelings completed the misery of the court. He, unfortunately for himself, had been beautifully brought up. His teacher had educated him as the child is educated in the womb, where it lives the history of man from fish to mammal—and, like the child in the womb, he had been protected with love meanwhile. The effect of such an education was that he had grown up without any of the useful accomplishments for living—without malice, vanity, suspicion, cruelty, and the commoner forms of selfishness. Jealousy seemed to him the most ignoble of vices. He was sadly unfitted for hating his best friend or for torturing his wife. He had been given too much love and trust to be good at these things.

Arthur was not one of those interesting characters whose subtle motives can be dissected. He was only a simple and affectionate man, because Merlyn had believed that love and simplicity were worth having.

Now, with a situation developing before his eyes which has always been notoriously difficult of solution—so difficult that it has been given a label and called the Eternal Triangle, as if it were a geometrical problem like the

Pons Asinorum in Euclid—Arthur was only able to retreat. It is generally the trustful and optimistic people who can afford to retreat. The loveless and faithless ones are compelled by their pessimism to attack. Arthur was strong and gentle enough to hope that, if he trusted Lancelot and Guenever, things would come right in the end. It seemed to him that this was better than trying to bring them right at once by such courses as, for instance, by cutting off the lovers' heads for treason.

Arthur did not know that Lancelot and Guenever were lovers. He had never actually found them together or unearthed proofs of their guilt. It was in the nature of his bold mind to hope, in these circumstances, that he would not find them together—rather than to lay a trap by which to wreck the situation. This is not to say that he was a conniving husband. It is simply that he was hoping to weather the trouble by refusing to become conscious of it. Unconsciously, of course, he knew perfectly well that they were sleeping together—knew too, unconsciously, that if he were to ask his wife, she would admit it. Her three great virtues were courage, generosity and honesty. So he could not ask her.

Such an attitude to the position did not make it easier for the King to be happy. He became, not excitable like Guenever nor restless like Lancelot, but reserved. He moved about his own palace like a mouse. Yet he made one effort to grasp the nettle.

"Lancelot," said the King, finding him one afternoon in the rose garden, "you have been looking wretched lately. Is there anything the matter?"

Lancelot had snapped off one of the roses, and was pinching the sepals. These ancient roses, it has lately been asserted, were so constructed that the five sepals did actually stick out beyond the petals—just as they are represented to do in the heraldic rose.

"Is it anything," asked the King, hoping against hope, "about this girl who is said to have had your baby?"

If Arthur had left him alone with the first question, and a silence to answer it in, perhaps they would have had the matter out. But Arthur was afraid of what might come in the silence, and, once he had given the lead of the second question, the chance was gone.

"Yes," said Lancelot.

"You could not bring yourself to marry her, I suppose?"

"I don't love her."

"Well, you know your own business best."

Lancelot, with an uncontrollable desire to get some of his misery off his chest by telling about it—and yet unable to tell the true story to this particular listener—began a long rigmarole about Elaine. He began telling Arthur half the truth: how he was ashamed and had lost his miracles. But he was forced to make Elaine the central figure of this confession, and, after half an hour, he had unwittingly presented the King with a story to believe in—a story with which Arthur could content himself if he did not want to be conscious of the true tale. This half–truth was of great use to the poor fellow, who learned to substitute it for the real trouble in later years. We civilized people, who would immediately fly to divorce courts and alimony and other forms of attrition in such circumstances, can afford to look with proper contempt upon the spineless cuckold. But Arthur was only a medieval savage. He did not understand our civilization, and knew no better than to try to be too decent for the degradation of jealousy.

Guenever was the next person to find Lancelot in the rose garden. She was all sweetness and reason.

"Lance, have you heard the news? A messenger has just arrived to say that this girl who is persecuting you is on her way to court, bringing the baby. She will be here this evening."

"I knew she would come."

"We shall have to do our best for her, of course. Poor child, I expect she is unhappy."

"It is not my fault if she is unhappy."

"No, of course it isn't. But people get made unhappy by the world, and we must help them when we can."

"Jenny, it is sweet of you to be kind about it."

He turned towards her, and made a movement to catch her hand. Her words had made him hope that all would be well. But Jenny took her hand away.

"No, dear," she said. "I don't want you to make love to me until she has gone. I want you to be quite free."

"Free?"

"She is the mother of your baby, and she is unmarried. We two can't ever be married. I want you to be able to marry her if you would like it, because that is the only thing which can be done."

"But, Jenny—"

"No, Lance. We must be sensible. I want you to keep away from me while she is here, and to find out whether you could love her after all. It is the least that I can do for you."

Chapter XVII

Elaine arrived at the yawning barbican, and Guenever kissed her coolly. "You are welcome to Camelot," she said. "Five thousand welcomes."

"Thank you," said Elaine.

They looked at each other with hostile, smiling faces.

"Lancelot will be delighted to see you."

"Oh!"

"Everybody knows about the baby, dear. There is nothing to be shy about. The King and I are quite excited to see whether he will be like his father."

"It is kind of you," said Elaine uncomfortably.

"You must let me be the first to see him. You have called him Galahad, have you not? Is he strong? Does he notice things?"

"He weighs fifteen pounds," the girl announced with pride. "You can see him now, if you like."

Guenever took hold of herself with an effort which was hardly noticeable, and began fussing with Elaine's wraps.

"No, dear," she said. "I must not be so selfish as that. You must rest after your long journey, and probably Baby will have to be settled down. I can come to see him this evening, when he has had a sleep. There will be plenty of time."

But she had to see the baby in the end.

When Lancelot next met the Queen, her sweetness and reason were gone. She was cold and proud, and spoke as if she were addressing a meeting.

"Lancelot," she said, "I think you ought to go to your son. Elaine is grieving because you have not been to see him."

"Have you seen him?"

"Yes."

"Is he ugly?"

"He takes after Elaine."

"Thank God. I will go at once."

The Queen called him back.

"Lancelot," she said, taking a breath through her nose, "I am trusting you not to make love to Elaine under my roof. If you and I are to keep apart until it is settled, it is only fair that you should keep away from her."

"I don't want to make love to Elaine."

"You must say that, of course. And I will believe you. But if you break your word this time, it will be finished between us. Absolutely finished."

"I have said all I can say."

"Lancelot, you have deceived me once, so how can I be sure? I have put Elaine in the next room to mine, and I shall see if you go to it. I want you to keep in your own room."

"If you like."

"I shall send for you some time tonight, if I can get away from Arthur. I will not tell you when. If you are not in your room when I send for you, I shall know that you are with Elaine."

The girl was weeping in her chamber, while Dame Brisen arranged the cradle for the little boy.

"I saw him in the archery butts, and he saw me too. But he looked away. He made an excuse and went out. He has not even seen our baby."

"There, there," said Dame Brisen. "Lawks a mussy."

"I ought not to have come. It has only made me more miserable, and him too."

"'Tis that there Queen."

"She is beautiful, isn't she?"

The Dame said darkly: "Handsome is as handsome does."

Elaine began to sob helplessly. She looked repulsive, with her red nose, as people do when they abdicate their dignity.

"I wanted him to be pleased."

There was a knock on the door, and Lancelot came in—which made her quickly dry the eyes. They greeted each other with constraint.

"I am glad you have come to Camelot," he said. "I hope you are well?"

"Yes, thank you."

"How is—the baby?"

"Your lordship's son," said Dame Brisen with emphasis.

She turned the cradle towards him, and moved back so that he could see.

"My son."

They stood looking down at the fresh thing, helpless and only half alive. They were strong, as the poet sings, and it was weak—one day they would be weak, and it strong.

"Galahad," said Elaine, and she leaned over the wrappings, making the foolish gestures and meaningless sounds which mothers delight to use when their babies are beginning to pay attention. Galahad clenched his fist and hit himself in the eye with it, an achievement which seemed to give pleasure to the women. Lancelot watched them in amazement. "My son," he thought. "It is a part of me, yet it is fair. It does not seem to be ugly. How can you tell with babies?" He held out his right finger to Galahad, putting it inside the fat palm of his hand, which clutched it. The hand looked as if it had been fitted to the arm by a cunning doll maker. There was a deep crease round the wrist.

"Oh, Lancelot!" cried Elaine.

She tried to throw herself into his arms, but he pushed her off. He looked at Brisen over her shoulder with fear and exasperation. He made a wild, senseless sound—and rushed out of the room. Elaine, unsupported, sank down beside the bed and began to sob more than ever. Brisen, standing rigid, as she had stood to bear Sir Lancelot's glare, looked at the closed door with an inscrutable expression.

Chapter XVIII

In the morning he and Elaine were summoned to the Queen's chamber. He, for his part, went with a kind of happiness. He was remembering how Guenever must have pleaded illness on the previous evening, so as to leave the King's room. Her lover had been sent for in the darkness. The usual conniving hand had led him by the finger on tiptoe to the chosen bed. In the silence forced on them by being next to Arthur's chamber, but in passionate tenderness, they had done their best to make it up. Lancelot was happier today than he had been since the story of Elaine started. He felt that if he could only persuade his Guenever to make a clean break with the King, so that everything was in the open, there might still be a possibility of honour.

Guenever was stiff, as if she were in a rigor, and her face was drained white—except that there was a red spot on either side of her nostrils. She looked as if she had been seasick. She was alone.

"So," said the Queen.

Elaine looked straight in her blue eyes, but Lancelot stopped as if he had been shot.

"So."

They stood, waiting for Guenever to speak or die.

"Where did you go last night?"

"I—"

"Don't tell me," shouted the Queen, moving her hand so that they could see a ball of handkerchief in it, which she had torn to pieces. "Traitor! Traitor! Get out of my castle with your strumpet."

"Last night—" said Lancelot. His head was whirling with a desperation which neither of the women noticed.

"Don't speak to me. Don't lie to me. Go!"

Elaine said calmly: "Sir Lancelot was in my room last night. My woman Brisen brought him in the dark."

The Queen began pointing at the door. She made stabbing movements at it with her finger, and, in her trembling, her hair began to come down. She looked hideous.

"Get out! Get out! And you go too, you animal! How dare you speak so in my castle? How dare you admit it to me? Take your fancy man and go!"

Lancelot was breathing heavily and looking upon the Queen with a fixed stare. He might have been unconscious.

"He thought he was coming to you," said Elaine. She had her hands folded together, and watched the Queen passively.

"The old lie!"

"It is not a lie," said Elaine. "I could not live without him. Brisen helped me to pretend."

Guenever ran up to her with tottering steps. She wanted to hit Elaine in the mouth, but the girl did not move. It was as if she was hoping that Guenever would hit her.

"Liar!" screamed the Queen.

She ran back to Lancelot, where he had sat down on a chest and was staring blankly at the floor, with his head between his hands. She caught hold of his mantle and began pushing or heaving him toward the door, but he would not move.

"So you taught her the story! Why couldn't you think of a new one? You might have given me something interesting. I suppose you thought the old, stale stuff would do?"

"Jenny—" he said, without looking up.

The Queen tried to spit on him, but she had never practised spitting.

"How dare you call me Jenny? You are reeking of her still. I am the Queen, the Queen of England! I am not your trull!"

"Jenny—"

"Get out of my castle," screamed the Queen at the top of her voice. "Never show your face in it again. Your evil, ugly, beastlike face."

Lancelot suddenly said to the floor, in a loud voice: "Galahad!"

Then he took down his hands from his head and looked up, so that they could see the face she spoke of. It had a surprised look, and one of the eyes had begun to squint.

He said, more quietly: "Jenny." But he looked like a blind man.

The Queen opened her mouth to say something, though nothing came out.

"Arthur," he said. Then he gave a loud shriek, and jumped straight out of the window, which was on the first floor. They could hear him crash into some bushes, with a crump and crackle of boughs, and then he was running off through the trees and shrubbery with a loud sort of warbling cry, like hounds hunting. The hullabaloo faded into the distance, and there was silence in the chamber with the women.

Elaine, who was now as white as the Queen had been but still held herself proud and upright, said: "You have driven him mad. His wits must have been weak."

Guenever said nothing.

"Why have you driven him mad?" asked Elaine. "You have a fine husband of your own, the greatest in the land. You are a Queen, with honour and happiness and a home. I had no home, and no husband, and my honour was gone too. Why would you not let me have him?"

The Queen was silent.

"I loved him," said Elaine. "I bore a fine son for him, who will be the best knight of the world."

"Elaine," said Guenever, "go away from my court."

"I am going."

Guenever suddenly caught her by the skirt.

"Don't tell anybody," she said quickly. "Don't say anything about what happened. It will be his death if you do."

Elaine freed the skirt.

"Did you expect I would?"

"But what are we to do?" cried the Queen. "Is he mad? Will he get better? What will happen? Ought we to do something? What are we to say?"

Elaine would not stay to talk with her. At the door, however, she turned with a trembling lip.

"Yes, he is mad," she said. "You have won him, and you have broken him. What will you do with him next?"

When the door was closed, Guenever sat down. She dropped her tattered handkerchief. Then—slowly, deeply, primitively—she began to cry. She put her face in her hands and throbbed with sorrow. (Sir Bors, who did not care for the Queen, once said to her: "Fie on your weeping, for ye weep never but when there is no boot.")

Chapter XIX

King Pelles was sitting in the solar with Sir Bliant two years later. It was a fine winter morning with the fields frosted, no wind, and a light fog which was not enough to confuse the pigeons. Sir Bliant, who had been staying the night, was dressed in scarlet furred with miniver. His horse and squire were in the courtyard, ready to take him back to Castle Bliant, but the two men were having their elevenses before he started. Sitting with their hands spread to the splendid log fire, they sipped their mulled wine, nibbled pastry, and talked about the Wild Man.

"I am sure he must have been a gentleman," said Sir Bliant. "He kept doing things which nobody but a gentleman would do. He had a natural leaning to arms."

"Where is he now?" asked King Pelles.

"God He knows. He vanished one morning when the hounds were at Castle Bliant. But I am sure he was a gentleman."

They sipped and gazed into the flames.

"If you want to have my opinion," added Sir Bliant, lowering his voice, "I believe he was Sir Lancelot."

"Nonsense," said the King.

"He was tall and strong."

"Sir Lancelot is dead," said the King. "God be good to him. Everybody knows that."

"It was not proved."

"If he had been Sir Lancelot, you could not have mistaken him. He was the ugliest man I have ever seen."

"I never met him," said Sir Bliant.

"It was proved that Lancelot ran mad in his shirt and breeches, until he got gored by a wild boar and died in a hermitage."

"When was that?"

"Last Christmas."

"It was about the same time that my Wild Man ran away with the hunt. Ours was a boar hunt too."

"Well," said King Pelles, "they *may* have been the same person. If they were, it is interesting. How did your fellow arrive?"

"It was during the summer questing, the year before last. I had my pavilion pitched in a fair meadow, in the usual way, and I was inside it, waiting for something to turn up. I was playing chess, I remember. Then there was a frightful row outside, and I went out, and there was this naked lunatic lashing on my shield. My dwarf was sitting on the ground, rubbing his neck—the maniac had half broken it—and he was calling out for help. I went to the fellow and said: 'Look here, my good man, you don't want to be fighting me. Come now, you lay down that sword and be a good chap.' He had got hold of one of my own swords, you know, and I could see that he was mad straightway. I said: 'You ought not to be fighting, old boy. I can see that what you need is a good sleep and something to eat.' And, really, he did look dreadful. He was like a man who had been watching a passager for three nights. His eyeballs were bright red."

"What did he say?"

"He just said: 'As for that, come not too nigh: for, an thou do, wit thou well I will slay thee.'"

"Strange."

"Yes, it was strange, wasn't it? That he should have known the high language, I mean."

"What did you do?"

"Well, I was only in my gown, and the man looked dangerous. I went back into the pavilion and did on my armour."

King Pelles handed him another pasty, which Sir Bliant accepted with a nod.

"When I was armed," he went on, with his mouth full, "I went out with a spare sword to disarm the chap. I did not intend to strike him, or anything like that, but he was a homicidal maniac and there was no other way of getting the sword from him. I went up to him like you do to a dog, holding out my hand and saying: 'There's a poor fellow: come now, there's a good chap.' I thought it would be easy."

"Was it?"

"The moment he saw me in armour, and with a sword, he came straight at me like a tiger. I never saw such an attack. I tried to parry a bit, and I dare say I would have killed him in self–defence, if he had given me a chance. But the next thing I knew was that I was sitting on the ground, and my nose and ears were bleeding. He had given me a buffet, you know, which troubled my brains."

"Goodness," said King Pelles.

"The next thing he did was to throw away his sword and rush straight into the pavilion. My poor wife was there, in bed, with no clothes on. But he just jumped straight into bed with her, snatched the coverlet, rolled himself up in it, and went fast asleep."

"Must have been a married man," said King Pelles.

"The wife gave some frightful shrieks, hopped out of bed on the other side, jumped into her smock, and came running out to me. I was still a bit astonied, lying on the ground, so she thought I was dead. I can tell you we had a fine to–do."

"Did he sleep right through it?"

"He slept like a log. We managed to pull ourselves together eventually, and the wife put one of my gauntlets down my neck to stop the nosebleed, and then we talked it over. My dwarf, who is a splendid little chap, said we ought not to do him any harm, because he was touched by God. As a matter of fact, it was the dwarf who suggested that he might be Sir Lancelot. There was a good deal of talk about the Lancelot mystery that year."

Sir Bliant paused to take another bite.

"In the end," he said, "we took him to Castle Bliant in a horse litter, bed and all. He never stirred. When we got him there, we tied his hands and feet against the hour when he would wake up. I am sorry about it now, but we could not chance it according to what we knew at the time. We kept him in a comfortable room, with clean clothes, and the wife gave him a lot of nourishing food, to build up his strength, but we thought it best to keep him handcuffed all the same. We kept him for a year and a half."

"How did he get away?"

"I was coming to that. It is the plum of the story. One afternoon I was out in the forest for half an hour's questing, when I was set upon by two knights from behind."

"Two knights?" asked the King. "From behind?"

"Yes. Two of them, and from behind. It was Sir Bruce Saunce Pité and a friend of his."

King Pelles thumped his knee.

"That man," he exclaimed, "is a public menace. I can't think why somebody doesn't do away with him."

"The trouble is to catch the fellow. However, I was telling you about the Wild Man. Sir Bruce and the other one had me at a considerable disadvantage, as you will admit, and I regret to say that I was compelled to run away."

Sir Bliant stopped and gazed into the fire. Then he cheered up.

"Ah, well," he said, "we can't all be heroes, can we?"

"Not all," said King Pelles.

"I was sore wounded," said Sir Bliant, discovering a formula, "and I felt myself faint."

"Quite."

"These two came galloping with me all the way to the Castle, one on either side, and they kept hitting me all the time. I don't know to this day how I got away with my life."

"It was written in the Stones," said the King.

"We rode past the barbican loopholes, hell–for–leather, and it was there that the Wild Man must have seen us. We kept him in the barbican chamber, you know. Well, he saw us at all events, and we found out afterwards that he broke his fetters with his bare hands. They were iron fetters, and he had them on his ankles also. He wounded himself dreadfully doing it. Then he came hurling out of the postern, with his hands all bloody and the chains flying about him, and he pulled Bruce's ally out of the saddle, and took his sword from him, and walloped Bruce on the head so that he knocked him noseling, clean off his horse. The second knight tried to stab the Wild Man from behind—he was absolutely unarmed—but I cut off the fellow's hand at the wrist, just as he stabbed. Then the both of them caught their horses, and rode away for all they were fit. They rode more than a pace, I can tell you."

"That was Bruce all over."

"My brother was staying with me that year. I said to him: 'Why ever have we kept this dear fellow chained up?' I was ashamed when I saw his wounded hands. 'He is happy and gracious,' I said, 'and now he has saved my life. We must never chain him up again, but give him his freedom and do everything we can for him.' You know, Pelles, I liked that Wild Man. He was gentle and grateful, and he used to call me Lord. It is a dreadful thing to think that he might have been the great Dulac, and us keeping him tied up and letting him call me Lord so humbly."

"What happened in the end?"

"He stayed quietly for several months. Then the boar hounds came to the castle, and one of the followers left his horse and spear by a tree. The Wild Man took them and rode away. It was as if he were excited by gentlemanly pursuits, you know—as if a suit of armour, or a fight, or a hunt, stirred something in his poor head. They made him want to join in."

"Poor boy," said the King. "Poor, poor boy! It might well have been Sir Lancelot. He is known to have been killed by a boar last Christmas."

"I should like to know that story."

"If your man was Lancelot, he rode straightaway after the boar they were hunting. It was a famous boar which had troubled the hounds for several years, and that was why the field was not on foot. Lancelot was the only man up at the kill, and the boar slew his horse. It gave him a dreadful wound in the thigh, riving him to the hough bone, before he cut off its head. He killed it near a hermitage, with one blow. The hermit came out, but Lancelot was so mad with his pain and everything that he threw his sword at the man. I heard this from a knight who was actually there. He said there was no doubt about its being Sir Lancelot—he was ugly and all that—and he said that he and the hermit carried him into the hermitage after he had fainted. He said that nobody could possibly have recovered from the wound, and that, in any case, he saw him die. What made him most certain, he said, about the Wild Man being a great knight, was that when he was standing in his death agony beside the dead boar, he spoke to the hermit as 'Fellow'. So you see, there may have been a touch of sanity at the end."

"Poor Lancelot," said Sir Bliant.

"God be good to him," said King Pelles.

"Amen."

"Amen," repeated Sir Bliant, looking into the fire. Then he stood up and shook his shoulders.

"I shall have to be going," he said. "How is your daughter? I forgot to ask."

King Pelles sighed, and stood up also.

"She spends her time at the convent," he said. "I believe she is going to be received next year. However, we are to be allowed to see her next Saturday, when she comes home on a short visit."

CHAPTER XX

After Sir Bliant had ridden away, King Pelles stumped upstairs to do some biblical genealogy. He was puzzled about the Lancelot affair, and interested in it on account of his grandson Galahad. All of us have been driven nearly mad by our wives and sweethearts, but King Pelles was aware that there is a tough streak in human nature which generally prevents us from being quite driven. He thought it eccentric of Lancelot, to say the least, to lose his reason over a lover's tiff—and he wanted to find out, by looking up the Ban genealogy, whether there had been a streak of lunacy in the family which could account for it. If there were, it might descend on Galahad. The child might have to be sent to the hospital of Bethlehem, which later ages were to call Bedlam. There had been enough trouble without that.

"Ban's father," said King Pelles to himself, polishing his spectacles and blowing dust off numerous works of Heraldry, Genealogy, Nigromancy, and Mystical Mathematics, "was King Lancelot of Benwick, who married the King of Ireland's daughter. King Lancelot's father, in his turn, was Jonas, who married the daughter of Manuel of Gaul. Now who was the father of Jonas?"

When one comes to think of it, there may have been a weak link in Lancelot's mind. This may have been the cupboard skeleton we noticed, ten years ago, at the back of the small boy's head as he turned the kettle–hat to and fro, in the Armoury of Benwick Castle.

"Nacien," said King Pelles. "Drat this Nacien. There seem to be two of him."

He had got back, through Lisais, Hellias le Grose, Nacien the Hermit—from whom Lancelot probably inherited his visionary tendency—and Nappus, to a second Nacien who, if he existed, would quite upset the King's theory that Lancelot was but the eighth degree from Our Lord. As a matter of fact, nearly all hermits seemed to be called Nacien in those days.

"Drat him," repeated the King, and he glanced out of the window to see what the noise was about in the street outside the castle.

A Wild Man—there seemed to be a lot of them about this morning—was being run through Corbin by the villagers who had once gone out to welcome Lancelot. He was naked, as thin as a ghost, and he ran along with his hands over his head, to protect it. The small boys running all round him were throwing turfs at him. He stopped every now and then, and caught one of the boys and threw him over the hedge. This only made the boys throw stones. King Pelles could clearly see the blood running over his high cheek–bones, and the sunken cheeks, and the hunted eyes, and the blue shadows between his ribs. He could also see that the man was making for the castle.

In the castle yard, when King Pelles had gone dot–and–carry downstairs, there was quite a crowd of castle folk standing round the Wild Man in admiration. They had lowered the portcullis, to keep the village boys out, and they were disposed to treat the fugitive with kindness.

"Look at his wounds," said one of the squires. "Look at that great scar there. Perhaps he was a knight errant before he went mad, and so we ought to give him courtesy."

The Wild Man stood in the middle of the ring, while the ladies giggled and the pages pointed. He hung his head and stood motionless, without speaking, waiting for what was to be done to him next.

"Perhaps he is Sir Lancelot."

There was a great laugh at this.

"No, but seriously. It was never exactly proved that Lancelot is dead."

King Pelles went right up to the Wild Man and looked into his face. He had to stoop sideways to do this.

"Are you Sir Lancelot?" he asked.

The emaciated, dirty, bearded face: its eyes never even blinked.

"Are you?" repeated the King.

But there was no answer from the dummy.

"He is deaf and dumb," said the King. "We will keep him as a jester. He looks funny enough, I must say. Somebody get the man some clothes— you know, comic clothes—and put him to sleep in the pigeon house. Give him some clean straw."

The dummy suddenly lifted both its hands and let out a roar, which made everybody start back. The King dropped his spectacles. Then it lowered its hands again and stood sheepishly, so that the people gave a nervous giggle.

"Better lock him in," said the King wisely. "Safety first. And do not hand him his food—throw it to him. Can't be too careful."

So Sir Lancelot was led away to the pigeon house, to be King Pelles' fool —and there he was locked in, and fed by throwing, and lodged on clean straw.

When the King's nephew, a boy called Castor, came to be knighted on the following Saturday—this was the ceremony which Elaine was coming home to attend—there was gaiety in the castle. The King, who was addicted to festivals and ceremonials of all sorts, celebrated the occasion royally, by presenting a new gown to every man on the estate. He also celebrated it, regrettably, by making too generous a use of the cellars over which Dame Brisen's husband presided.

"Wossle," cried the King.

"Drink hail," replied Sir Castor, who was on his best behaviour.

"Everybody gotter gown?" shouted the King.

"Yes, thank you, Your Majesty," replied the attendants.

"Sure?"

"Quite sure, Your Majesty."

"Thas alri, then. Goo' ole gown!"

And the King wrapped himself in his own gown with great affection. He was a different man on occasions like this.

"Everybody wants to thank Your Majesty very much for his generous present."

"Notter tall."

"Three cheers for King Pelles!"

"Hurrah, hurrah, hurrah!"

"Warrabout the fool?" inquired the King suddenly. "Fool gotter gown? Where's the pore fool?"

There was a silence at this, for nobody had remembered to put a gown aside for Sir Lancelot.

"Notter gown? Nottergotter gown?" cried the King. "Fesha fool at once."

Sir Lancelot was fetched from the pigeon house, for the royal favour. He stood still in the torchlight with some straws in his beard, a pitiful figure in his jester's patch–work.

"Pore fool," said the King sadly. "Pore fool. Here, have mine."

And, in spite of all remonstrances and advices to the contrary, King Pelles struggled out of his costly robe, which he popped over Lancelot's head.

"Lettim loose," cried the King. "Givim holly–holly day. Karnkeepamanlocktupforever."

Sir Lancelot, standing upright in the grand dress, looked strangely stately in the Great Hall. If only his beard had been trimmed—our clean–shaven generation has forgotten what a difference the trimming of a beard can make—if only he had not starved away to a skeleton in the cell of the poor hermit after the boar hunt—if only he had not been rumoured to be dead—but, even as it was, a sort of awe came into the Hall. The King did not notice it. With measured tread Sir Lancelot walked back to his pigeon loft, and the house carls made an avenue for him as he went.

CHAPTER XXI

Elaine had done the ungraceful thing as usual. Guenever, in similar circumstances, would have been sure to grow pale and interesting—but Elaine had only grown plump. She walked in the castle garden with her companions, dressed in the white clothes of a novice, and there was a clumsy action in her walk. Galahad, now three years old, walked with her, holding hands.

It was not that Elaine was going to be a nun because she was desperate. She was not going to spend the rest of her life acting the cinema nun. A woman can forget a lot of love in two years—or at any rate she can pack it away, and grow accustomed to it, and hardly remember it more than a business–man might remember an occasion when, by ill–luck, he failed to make an investment which would have made him a millionaire.

Elaine was going to leave her son and become the bride of Christ, because she saw that this was the only thing to do. It was not a dramatic thing, and perhaps it was not very reverent—but she knew that she would never again love any human person as she had loved her dead knight. So she was giving in. She could not tack against the wind any longer.

She was not moping for Lancelot, nor did she weep for him on her pillow. She hardly ever thought of him. He had worn a place for himself in some corner of her heart, as a sea shell, always boring against the rock, might do. The making of the place had been her pain. But now the shell was safely in the rock. It was lodged, and ground no longer. Elaine, walking in the garden with her girls, thought only about the ceremony at which Sir Castor had been knighted, and whether there would be enough cakes for the feast, and that Galahad's stockings needed mending.

One of the girls who had been playing a kind of ball game to keep warm—the same game as Nausicaa was playing when Ulysses arrived—came running back to Elaine from the shrubbery by the well. Her ball had taken her in that direction.

"There is a Man," she whispered, much as if it had been a rattlesnake.

"There is a Man, sleeping by the well!"

Elaine was interested—not because it was a man, nor because the girl was frightened, but because it was unusual to sleep out of doors in January.

"Hush, then," said Elaine. "We will go and see."

The plump novice in the white clothes who tiptoed over to Lancelot, the homely girl going composedly towards him with a round face which had stubbornly refused to accept the noble traces of grief, the young matron who had been thinking about Galahad's mending—this person was not conscious of vulnerability or needs. She went over calmly and innocently, busy about quite different concerns, like the thoughtless rabbit who goes hop–and–nibble along the accustomed path. But the wire loop tightens suddenly.

Elaine recognized Lancelot in two heartbeats. The first beat was a rising one which faltered at the top. The second one caught up with it, picked its momentum from the crest of the wave, and both came down together like a rearing horse that falls.

Lancelot was stretched out in his knightly gown. Sir Bliant, in remarking that gentlemanly things seemed to stir something in his head, had noticed truly. Moved by the gown, by some strange memory of miniver and colour, the poor Wild Man had gone from the King's table to the well. There, alone in the darkness, without a mirror, he had washed his face. He had swilled out his eye sockets with bony knuckles. With a currycomb and a pair of shears from the stables he had tried to arrange his hair.

Elaine sent her women away. She gave Galahad's hand to one of them, and he went without protest. He was a mysterious child.

Elaine knelt down beside Sir Lancelot and looked at him. She did not touch him or cry. She lifted her hand to stroke his thin one, but thought better of it. She squatted on her hams. Then, after a long time, she did begin to cry—but it was for Lancelot, for his tired eyes smoothed in sleep, and for the white scars on his hands.

"Father," said Elaine, "if you don't help me now, nobody ever can."

"What is it, my dear?" asked the King. "I have a headache."

Elaine paid no attention.

"Father, I have found Sir Lancelot."

"Who?"

"Sir Lancelot."

"Nonsense," said the King. "Lancelot was killed by a boar."

"He is asleep in the garden."

The King suddenly pulled himself out of his chair of state.

"I knew it all along," he said. "Only I was too stupid to know. It is the Wild Man. Obviously."

He reeled a little and put his hand to his head.

"Leave this to me," said the King. "You let me deal. I know exactly what to do. Butler! Brisen! Where the devil has everybody gone to? Hi! Hi! Oh, there you are. Now, butler, you go and fetch your wife, Dame Brisen, and get two other men that we can trust. Let me see. Get Humbert and Gurth. Where did you say he was?"

"Asleep by the well," said Elaine quickly.

"Quite. So everybody must be told to keep out of the rose garden. Do you hear, butler? All people are to avoid, that none may be in the way where the King will come. And get a sheet. A strong sheet. We shall have to carry him in it, by the four corners. And get the tower room ready. Tell Brisen to air the bedclothes. Better have a feather bed. Light a fire, and fetch the doctor. Tell him to look up Madness in *Bartholomeus Anglicus*. Oh, and you had better get some jellies made, and things like that. In the heaviness of his sleep we shall have to put fresh garments on him."

When Lancelot came to himself in the clean bed, he groaned. He opened his eyes and looked at King Pelles. Next he looked at Elaine. He continued to look at them for some time, and made speaking movements with his monkey lips. Then he went to sleep again.

The next time he woke they could see that his eyes were clear. But he was evidently in a pitiful state of mind. He was relying on them to save him.

The third time he woke, he said: "O Lord Jesus, how did I get here?"

They said the usual things about resting now, and not talking till he was stronger, and so forth. The doctor waved his hand to the Royal Orchestra, who immediately struck up with *Jesu Christes Milde Moder*—since Dr. Bartholomew's book had recommended that madmen should be gladded with instruments. Everybody watched hopefully, to see the effect, but Lancelot grabbed the King's hand and cried in anguish: "For God's sake, my lord, tell me how I came here?"

Elaine put her hand on his forehead and made him lie down.

"You came like a madman," she said, "and nobody knew who you were. You have been having a breakdown."

Lancelot turned his puzzled eyes on her, and smiled nervously.

"I have been making a fool of myself," he said.

Later he asked: "Did many people see me while I was mad?"

Chapter XXII

Lancelot's body revenged itself on his mind. He lay in bed for a fortnight in the airy bedroom with an ache in every bone, while Elaine kept herself outside the room. She had him at her mercy, and could have nursed him day and night. But there was something in her heart—either decency, or pride, or generosity, or humility, or the determination not to be a cannibal —which spared him. She visited him not more than once a day, and thrust nothing on him.

One day he stopped her as she was going out. He was sitting up in a day–gown, and his hands lay still in his lap.

"Elaine," he said, "I suppose I ought to be making plans."

She waited for her sentence.

"I cannot stay here for ever," he said.

"You know you will be welcome as long as you like."

"I cannot go back to court."

Elaine remarked, with hesitation: "My father would give you a castle, if you liked, and we—could live there together."

He looked at her, and looked away.

"Or you could have the castle."

Lancelot took her hand and said: "Elaine, I don't know what to say. I can't very well say anything."

"I know you don't love me."

"Do you think we should be happy, then?"

"I only know when I shall be unhappy."

"I don't want you to be unhappy. But there are different ways of being that. Don't you think it might turn out that you would be more unhappy if we lived together?"

"I should be the happiest woman in the world."

"Look, Elaine, our only hope is to speak plainly, even if it sounds horrible. You know that I don't love you, and that I do love the Queen. It is an accident which has happened and it can't be changed. Things do happen like that: I can't alter it. And you have trapped me twice. If it had not been for you, I should still be at court. Do you think we could ever be happy, living together, like that?"

"You were my man," said Elaine proudly, "before you were ever the Queen's."

He passed a hand over his eyes.

"Do you want to have a husband on those terms?"

"There is Galahad," said Elaine.

They sat side by side, looking into the fire. She did not cry or bid for pity —and he knew she was sparing him these things.

He said, with difficulty: "I will stay with you, Elaine, if you want me to. I don't understand why you should want it. I am fond of you, very fond of you. I don't know why, after what has happened. I don't want you to be hurt. But, Elaine—I can't marry you."

"I don't mind."

"It is because—it is because marriage is a contract. I—I have always been proud of my Word. And if I do not—and if I have not that feeling for you —hang it, Elaine, I am under no obligation to marry you, when it was you who tricked me."

"No obligation."

"Obligation!" exclaimed Lancelot, with a wry face. He threw the word into the fire as if it had a bad taste. "I must be sure that you understand, and that I am not cheating you. I will not marry you, because I do not love you.

I did not start this, and I can't give you my freedom: I can't promise to stay with you for ever. I don't want you to accept these terms, Elaine: they are humiliating ones. They are dictated by the circumstances. If I were to say anything else, it would be lies, and things would be worse—"

He broke off and hid his head in his hands.

"I don't understand," he said. "I am trying to do my best."

Elaine said: "Under any terms, you are my good and gracious lord."

King Pelles gave them a castle which was already known to Sir Lancelot. The King's tenant, Sir Bliant, had to move out to make room for them—which he did the more readily when he knew that he was obliging the Wild Man who had saved his life.

"Is he Sir Lancelot?" asked Bliant.

"No," said King Pelles. "He is a French knight who calls himself the Chevalier Mal Fet. I told you I was right about Sir Lancelot being dead."

It had been arranged that Lancelot was to live incognito—because, if it were allowed to get about that he was still living and lodged at Bliant Castle, there would only be a hue–and–cry for him from the court.

Bliant Castle had such a fine moat that it was practically an island. The only way to get to it was by boat, from a barbican on the land side, and the castle itself was surrounded by a magic fence of iron, probably a sort of cheval de frise. Ten knights were appointed to serve Lancelot there, and twenty ladies to serve Elaine.

She was wild with joy.

"We will call it the Joyous Island," she said. "We shall be so happy there. And, Lance"—he flinched when she called him by the pet name—"I want you to have your hobbies. We must have tournaments, and hawking, and plenty of things to do. You must invite people to stay, so that we can have company. I promise I won't be jealous of you, Lance, and I won't try to live in your pocket. Don't you think we might have a happy time if we are careful? Don't you think the Joyous Isle would be a lovely name?"

Lancelot cleared his throat and said: "Yes, it would be an excellent one."

"You must have a new shield made for you, so that you can go on with your tournaments without being recognized. What sort of blazon will you have?"

"Anything," said Lancelot. "We can arrange that later."

"The Chevalier Mal Fet. What a romantic name! What does it mean?"

"You could make it mean several things. The Ugly Knight would be one meaning, or the Knight Who Has Done Wrong."

He did not tell her that it could also mean the Ill–Starred Knight—the Knight with a Curse on Him.

"I don't think you are ugly—or wrong."

Lancelot pulled himself together. He knew that it would be most unfair to stay with Elaine if he were going to mope about it, or to do the Grand Renunciation—but, on the other hand, it was empty work to pretend.

"That is because you are a darling," he said. He kissed her quickly and clumsily, to cover the crack in the word. But Elaine noticed it.

"You will be able to attend to Galahad's education personally," she said. "You will be able to teach him all your tricks, so that he grows up to be the greatest knight in the world."

He kissed her again. She had said, "If we are careful," and she was trying to be careful. He felt pity for her trying, and gratitude for the decency of her mind. He was like a distracted man doing two things at once, one of them important and the other unimportant. He felt a duty to the unimportant one. But it is always embarrassing to be loved. And he did not like to accept Elaine's humility because of his opinion of himself.

The morning when they were to set out for Bliant arrived, and the newly–made knight, Sir Castor, stopped Lancelot in the Hall. He was only seventeen.

"I know you are calling yourself the Ill–Made Knight," said Sir Castor, "but I think you are Sir Lancelot. Are you?"

Lancelot took the boy by the arm.

"Sir Castor," he said, "do you think that is a knightly question? Suppose I were Sir Lancelot, and was only calling myself the Chevalier Mal Fet— don't you think I might have some reasons for doing that, reasons which a gentleman of lineage ought to respect?"

Sir Castor blushed very much and knelt on one knee.

"I won't tell anybody," he said. Nor did he.

CHAPTER XXIII

The spring came slowly, the new menage settled down, and Elaine arranged a tournament for her cavalier. There was to be a prize of a fair maid and a jerfalcon.

Five hundred knights came from all parts of the kingdom to compete in the tournament—but the Chevalier Mal Fet knocked down anybody who would stand up to him, with a kind of absent–minded ferocity, and the thing was a failure. The knights went away puzzled and frightened. Not a single person had been killed—he spared everybody indifferently as soon as he had knocked them down—and, by the Chevalier at any rate, not a single word had been spoken. The defeated knights, jogging home with their bruises, missed the conviviality which usually happened on tournament evenings, wondered who the taciturn champion could be, and talked superstitiously among themselves. Elaine, smiling bravely until the last of them had gone, went up to her room and cried. Then she dried her eyes and set out to find her lord. He had vanished as soon as the fighting was over, for he had got into the habit of going away by himself at sunset every evening—she did not know where.

She found him on the battlements, in a blaze of gold. Their shadows, and the shadow of the tower on which they stood, and all the spectres of the burning trees, stretched over the parkland in broad strips of indigo. He was looking towards Camelot with desperate eyes. His new shield, with the blazon of his incognito, was propped in front of him. The cognizance was of a silver woman on a sable field, with a knight kneeling at her feet.

In her simplicity, Elaine had been delighted by the compliment on the shield. She had never been clever. Now she realized, for the first time, that the silver woman was crowned. She stood helplessly, wondering what she could do—but there was nothing she could do. Her weapons were blunt ones, of soft metal. She could only use patience and hope and self–restraint, poor tools when matched against the heart–felt mania of love to which the ancient race was martyred.

One morning they were sitting on a green bank at the edge of the lake.

Elaine was doing embroidery, while Lancelot watched his son. Galahad, a priggish, mute little boy, was playing some private game with his dolls— to which he remained attached long after most boys would have taken to soldiers. Lancelot had carved two knights in armour for him out of wood. They were mounted on wheeled horses, from which they were detachable, and they held their spears in fewter. By pulling the horses towards each other, with strings tied to the platform on which they stood, the knights could be made to tilt. They could be made to knock each other out of the saddle. Galahad did not care for them at all, but played with a rag doll which he called the Holy Holy.

"Gwyneth will ruin that sparrow hawk," remarked Lancelot.

They could see one of the castle gentlewomen coming towards them at a great pace, with the sparrow hawk on her fist. Her haste had excited the hawk, which was bating continuously—but Gwyneth paid no attention to it, beyond giving it an occasional angry shake.

"What is the matter, Gwyneth?"

"Oh, my lady, there are two knights waiting beyond the water, and they say they have come to tilt with the Chevalier."

"Tell them to go away," said Lancelot. "Say I am not at home."

"But, sir, the porter has told them the way to the boat, and they are coming over one at a time. They say they won't both come, but the second will come if you beat the first. He is in the boat already."

He got up and dusted his knees.

"Tell him to wait in the tilt yard," he said. "I will be twenty minutes."

The tilt yard was a long, sanded passage between the walls, with a tower at each end. It had galleries looking down on it from the walls, like a racquets court, and was open to the sky. Elaine and the domestics sat in these galleries to watch, and the two knights fought beneath them for a long time. The tilting was even—each of them had a fall—and the sword–play lasted for two hours. At the end of this time, the strange knight cried: "Stop!"

Lancelot stopped at once, as if he were a farm labourer who had been given permission to knock off for his dinner. He stuck his sword in the ground, as if it were a pitchfork, and stood patiently. He had, indeed, only been working with the quiet patience of a farm hand. He had not been trying to hurt his opponent.

"Who are you?" asked the stranger. "Please tell me your name? I have never met a man like you."

Lancelot suddenly lifted both gauntlets to his helm, as if he were trying to bury in them the face which was already hidden, and said miserably: "I am Sir Lancelot Dulac."

"What!"

"I am Lancelot, Degalis."

Degalis threw his sword against the stone wall with a clang, and began running back towards the tower by the moat. His iron feet threw echoes down the yard. He unlaced and tossed away his helm as he ran. When he had reached the portcullis of the gatehouse, he put his hands to his mouth and shouted with all his might:

"Ector! Ector! It is Lancelot! Come over!"

Immediately he was running back towards his friend.

"Lancelot! My dear, dear fellow! I was sure it was you, I was sure it was you!"

He began fumbling with the laces, trying to get the helm off with clumsy fingers. He snatched off his own gauntlet and hurled them, too, with a clash against the wall. He could hardly wait to see Sir Lancelot's face. Lancelot stood still, like a tired child being undressed.

"But what have you been doing? Why are you here? It was feared that you were dead."

The helm came off, and went to join the rest of the discards.

"Lancelot!"

"Did you say that Ector was with you?"

"Yes, it is your brother Ector. We have been looking for you for two years. Oh, Lancelot, I am glad to see you!"

"You must come in," he said, "and refresh yourselves."

"But what have you been doing all this time? Where have you been hidden? The Queen sent out three knights to search for you at the beginning. In the end there were twenty–three of us. It must have cost her twenty thousand pounds."

"I have been here and there."

"Even the Orkney faction helped. Sir Gawaine is one of the searchers."

By this time Sir Ector had arrived in the boat—Sir Ector Demaris, not King Arthur's guardian—and the portcullis had been raised for him. He ran for the Chevalier, as if he were to tackle him at football.

"Brother!"

Elaine had come down from her gallery and was waiting at the end of the tilt yard. She was now to welcome, as she knew well, the people who were to break her heart. She did not interfere with their greetings, but watched them like a child who had been left out of a game. She stood still, gathering her forces. All her powers, all the frontier guards of her spirit, were being called in and concentrated at the citadel of her heart.

"This is Elaine."

They turned to her and began to bow.

"You are welcome to Bliant Castle."

CHAPTER XXIV

"I can't leave Elaine," he said.

Ector Damaris said: "Why not? You don't love her. You are under no obligation to her. You are only making yourselves miserable by staying together."

"I am under an obligation to her. I can't explain it, but I am."

"The Queen," said Degalis, "is desperate. She has spent a fortune looking for you."

"I can't help that."

"It is no good sulking," said Ector. "It seems to me that you are sulking. If the Queen is sorry for what she has done, whatever it was, you ought to behave generously and forgive her."

"I have nothing to forgive the Queen."

"That is just what I say. You ought to go back to court and follow your career. For one thing, you owe it to Arthur: don't forget that you are one of his sworn knights. He has been needing you badly."

"Needing me?"

"There is the usual trouble with the Orkneys."

"What have the Orkneys been doing? Oh, Degalis, you don't know how it does my heart good to hear the old names. Tell me all the gossip. Has Kay been making a fool of himself lately? Is Dinadan still laughing? What is the news about Tristram and King Mark?"

"If you are so keen about the news, you ought to come back to court."

"I have told you I can't."

"Lancelot, you are not looking at this realistically. Do you seriously think you can stay here incognito with this wench, and still be yourself? Do you think you can beat five hundred knights in a tournament without being recognized?"

"The moment we heard about the tournament," said Ector, "we came at once. Degalis said: 'That is Lancelot, or I'm a Dutchman.'"

"It would mean," said Degalis, "if you insist on staying here, that you would have to give up arms altogether. One more fight, and you would be known all over the country. For that matter, I think you are known already."

"Staying with Elaine would mean giving up everything. It would mean absolute retirement—no quests, no tournaments, no honour, no love: and you might even have to stay indoors all day. Yours is not an easy face to forget, you know."

"Whatever it means, Elaine is kind and good. Ector, when people trust you and depend on you, you can't hurt them. You could not treat a dog so."

"People don't marry dogs, however."

"Damn it, this girl loves me."

"So does the Queen."

Lancelot turned the cap round in his hands.

"The last time I saw the Queen," he said, "she told me never to come near her again."

"But she has spent twenty thousand pounds looking for you."

He waited for some time and then asked, in a voice which sounded rough: "Is she well?"

"She is absolutely wretched."

Ector said: "She knows it was her fault. She cried a great deal, and Bors told her she was a fool, but she didn't argue with him. Arthur is wretched too, because the whole Table is upside down."

Lancelot threw his cap on the ground and stood up.

"I told Elaine," he said, "that I would not promise to stay with her: so I must."

"Do you love her?" asked Degalis, cutting to the root.

"Yes, I do. She has been good to me. I am fond of her."

At their looks, he changed the word.

"I love her," he said defiantly.

The knights had been staying for a week, and Lancelot, listening hungrily to their Table news, was weakening every day. Elaine, sitting at the high table beside her lord at dinner, lived in a flow of conversation about people whose names she had never heard and about events which she could not understand. There was nothing to do except to offer second helpings, which Ector would accept without interrupting the anecdote of the moment. They leaned across her and talked and laughed, and Elaine busily laughed too. Every day Lancelot went to his turret at sunset—she had tiptoed away when she first found him there, and he did not know it was a discovered rendezvous.

"Lancelot," she said one morning, "there is a man waiting on the other side of the moat, with a horse and armour."

"A knight?"

"No. He looks like a squire."

"I wonder who it can be this time. Tell the porter to fetch him across."

"The porter says he won't come across. He says he will wait there for Sir Lancelot."

"I will go and see."

Elaine detained him as he went down to the boat.

"Lancelot," she said, "what do you want me to do with Galahad, if you should go away?"

"Go away? Who says I am going away?"

"Nobody has said so, but I want to know."

"I don't understand what you are talking about."

"I want to know how Galahad is to be brought up."

"Well, I suppose in the usual way. He will learn to be a good knight, I hope. But the whole question is imaginary."

"That is what I wanted to know."

She detained him once more, however.

"Lancelot, will you tell me one other thing? If you should go away, if you should have to leave me—would you be coming back?"

"I have told you that I am not going away."

She was trying the meaning of her words, as she made them, like a man walking slowly over a bog and feeling in front of him as he went.

"It would help me to go on with Galahad—it would help me to go on living—if I knew that it was for something—if I knew that one day—if I knew that you would be coming back."

"Elaine, I don't know why you are talking like this."

"I am not trying to stop you, Lance. Perhaps it will be best for you to go. Perhaps it is a thing which has to happen. Only, I wanted to know if I should see you again—because it is important to me."

He took her hands.

"If I go," he said, "I will come back."

The man on the other side of the moat was Uncle Dap. He was standing with Lancelot's old charger, now two years older, and all his accustomed armour neatly stowed on the saddle, as if for a kit inspection. Everything was correctly folded and strapped in the proper military place. The habergeon was rolled in a tight bundle. The helm, pauldrons, and vambraces were polished, literally by weeks of polishing, to that veneer or patina of light which is to be found only on things bought newly from the shop before they have been dulled by household cleaning. There was a smell of saddle soap, mixed with the unmistakable, personal smell of armour—as individual a smell as that which you get in the professional's shop on a golf course, and, to a knight, as exciting.

All Lancelot's muscles made an emphatic sortie towards the feeling of his own armour, which he had not seen since he left Camelot. His forefinger felt where the handle of his sword would use it for a fulcrum. His thumb knew the exact weight in ounces which it would have to exert on the near side of the fulcrum. The pad on the inside of his palm lusted for the gripe of the hilt. His whole arm remembered the balance of Joyeux and wanted to wag him in the air.

Uncle Dap looked older, and would not speak. He only held the bridle and displayed the gear, waiting for the knight to mount and ride. His stern eye, as fierce as a goshawk's, waited on his charge. He held out the great tilting helm silently, with its familiar panache of heron hackles and the silver thread.

Lancelot took the helm from Uncle Dap, with both hands, and turned it round. His hands knew the weight to expect—exactly twenty–two and a half pounds. He saw the superb polish, the fresh padding, and the new mantling set behind. It was of azure sarsenet, hand–embroidered in gold thread with the numerous small fleur–de–lis of ancient France. He knew at once whose fingers had done the embroidery. He lifted the helm to his nose and sniffed the mantling.

Immediately she was there—not the Guenever whom he had remembered on the battlements, but the real Jenny, in a different posture, with every lash of her eyelids and every pore of her skin and every note of her voice and every articulation of her smile.

He did not look back as he rode away from Bliant Castle—and Elaine, standing on the barbican tower, did not wave. She watched him going with a still–struck concentration, like somebody who, shipwrecked, gets as much fresh water into the little boat as possible. She had a few seconds left, to make her store of Lancelot that must last her through the years. There would be only this store, and their son, and a lot of gold. He had left her all his money, enough to bring a thousand pounds a year for life—in those days a huge sum.

CHAPTER XXV

Fifteen years after leaving Elaine, Lancelot was still at court. The King's relations with Guenever and her lover were much as they had always been. The great difference was that everybody was older. Lancelot's hair, which had already turned badger–grey when he first came back from his madness as a fellow of twenty–six, was quite white. Arthur's also was prematurely snowed—but both men's lips were red in their silky nests of beard. Guenever alone had contrived to keep the raven on her head. She looked a splendid figure when she was forty.

Another difference was that a new generation had come to court. In their own hearts the chief characters of the Round Table felt the ardent feelings which they had always felt—but now they were figures instead of people. They were surrounded by younger clients for whom Arthur was not the crusader of a future day, but the accepted conqueror of a past one—for whom Lancelot was the hero of a hundred victories, and Guenever the romantic mistress of a nation. To these young people, a sight of Arthur as he hunted in the greenwood was like seeing the idea of Royalty. They saw no man at all, but England. When Lancelot rode by, laughing at some private joke with the Queen, the commonalty were amazed that he could laugh. "Look," they would say to each other, "he is laughing, as if he were a vulgar person like ourselves. How condescending, how splendidly democratic of Sir Lancelot, to laugh, as if he were an ordinary man! Perhaps he eats and drinks as well, or even sleeps at night." But in their hearts the new generation was quite sure that the great Dulac did no such things.

Indeed, a lot of water had flowed under the bridges of Camelot in twenty–one years. They had been the years of building. When they began, they had been years of perrières and mangonels trundling along the rutty highways from one siege to another, to hurl destruction over castle walls—of movable wooden towers on wheels, going lumbering against recreant keeps, so that the archers, shooting down from the top of them, could throw death into treacherous strongholds—of companies of engineers marching along in clouds of summer dust, their picks and shovels on their shoulders, to undermine revolted bartizans so that the great stones caved and fell tottering. When Arthur had been unable to take a strong–arm castle by assault, he had caused tunnels to be dug under selected parts of the wall. These tunnels, being supported on beams of wood which could be burned away with fire at the proper moment, had collapsed, bringing the rubble–filled baileys down on top of them.

The early years had been times of battle, in which those who insisted on living by the sword had been made to die by it. They had been years lit by whole towersful of combatants roasting like so many Guy Fawkes—for the great objection to a pele tower as a stronghold was that it made a first–class chimney—years ringing with the sound of battle–axes thudding on battle–axe–proof doors—which were constructed by nailing the first ply of boards horizontally, and the second ply vertically, so that the wood could not be split along the grain—years illustrated by the shambling tumble of Norman giants—who were most conveniently dealt with by cutting off their legs first, so that you could get a fair reach at their heads—and by the flicker of swords round helmets or elbow–cops, a flickering which, in extreme cases, was attended by such a shower of sparks as to make the struggling knights seem perfectly incandescent.

Wherever you went, during the first years, every vista had been terminated by a marching column of mercenaries, robbing and pilling from the Marches—or by a knight of the new order exchanging buffets with a conservative baron whom he was trying to restrain from murdering serfs—or by a golden–haired maiden being rescued out of some lofty keep by means of leather ladders—or by Sir Bruce Saunce Pité riding a full wallop with Sir Lancelot coming deliverly after him—or by a few surgeons carefully ransacking the wounds of an unfortunate combatant, and making him eat onions or garlic, so that, by smelling at the wound, they could discover whether the intestines had been perforated or not. When they had examined the wounds they dressed them with the oily wool from the udders of sheep, which made a natural lanolin dressing. Here would be Sir Gawaine sitting on his antagonist's chest, and finishing him off, through the ventails of his helm, with the long sharp poinard called the Mercy of God. There would be a couple of knights who had suffocated themselves in their own helms during the course of a battle, a misfortune which frequently happened in those days of violent exercise and small vents. On one side would be a commodious gibbet set up by some old–fashioned princeling to hang King Arthur's knights and the common Saxons who trusted them—a gibbet perhaps nearly as sumptuous as that constructed at Montfaucon, which could support sixty bodies depending like drab fuchsias between its sixteen stone pillars. The humbler gallows had rungs on them, like the footholds on telegraph poles, so that the executioners could scramble up and down. On another side would be a demesne so hedged about with man–traps in its shrubberies that none dared walk within a mile of it. In front of you, there might be a daffish knight who had been caught in a buck–trap, which, swinging him into the air on the end of a stout branch released by the action of the trap, had left him dangling helplessly between heaven and earth. Behind you, there might be a savage tournament or faction fight going on, with all the heralds crying out, "*Laissez les aller*" to ranks of chivalry who were about to charge—a cry which was exactly equivalent to the shout, "They're off!" which is still to be heard at the Grand National today.

The World had been expected to end in the year one thousand, and, in the reaction which followed its reprieve, there had been a burst of lawlessness and brutality which had sickened Europe for centuries. It had been responsible for the doctrine of Might which was the Table's enemy. The fierce lords of the Strong Arm had hunted the wild woodlands—only, of course, there had always been exceptions like the good Sir Ector of Forest Sauvage—till John of Salisbury had been forced to advise his readers: "If one of these great and merciless hunters shall pass by your habitation, bring forth hastily all the refreshment you have in your house, or that you can readily buy, or borrow from your neighbour: that you may not be involved in ruin, or even accused of treason." Children, Duruy tells us, had been seen hanging in trees, by the sinews of their thighs. It had been no uncommon sight to see a man–at–arms whistling like a lobster, and looking like porridge, because they had emptied a bucket of boiling bran over his armour during a siege. Other spectacles even more dramatic have been mentioned by Chaucer: the smyler with the knyf under the cloke, the careyne in the bush with throte y–corve, or the colde deeth with mouth gaping upright. Everywhere it had been blood on steel, and smoke on sky, and power unbridled—and, in the general confusion of the times, Gawaine had at last contrived to murder our dear old friend King Pellinore, in revenge for the death of his own father, King Lot.

Such had been the England which Arthur had inherited, such the birthpangs of the civilization which he had sought to invent. Now, after twenty–one years of patient success, the land presented a different picture.

Where the black knights had hoved, all brim and furious by some ford, to take toll of anybody rash enough to pass that way, now any virgin could circumambulate the whole country, even with gold and ornaments upon her person, without the least fear of harm. Where once the horrible lepers —they called them Measles—had been accustomed to ramble through the woods in white cowls, ringing their doleful clappers if they wanted to give warning, or just pouncing on you without ringing them if they did not, now there were proper hospitals, governed by religious orders of knighthood, to look after those who had come back sick with leprosy from the Crusades. All the tyrannous giants were dead, all the dangerous dragons—some of which used to come down with a burrr like the peregrine's stoop—had been put out of action. Where the raiding parties had once streamed along the highways with fluttering pennoncels, now there were merry bands of pilgrims telling each other dirty stories on the way to Canterbury. Demure clerics, taking a day's outing to Our Lady of Walsingham, were singing *Alleluia Dulce Carmen*, while the less demure ones were warbling the great medieval drinking–song of their own composition: *Meum est propositum in taberna mori*. There were urbane abbots, titupping along on ambling palfreys, in furred hoods which were against the rules of their orders, and yeomen in smart tackle with hawks on their fists, and sturdy peasants quarrelling with their wives about new cloaks, and jolly parties going out to hunt without armour of any sort. Some were riding to fairs as great as that of Troyes, others to universities which rivalled Paris, where there were twenty thousand scholars whose ranks eventually provided seven popes. In the abbeys all the monks were illuminating the initial letters of their manuscripts with such a riot of invention that it was impossible to read the first page at all. Those who were not doing the chi– ro page were carefully copying out the Historia Francorum of Gregory of Tours, or the Legenda Aurea, or the Jeu d'Echecs Moralisé, or a Treatise of Hawkynge—that is, if they were not engaged upon the Ars Magna of the magician Lully, or the Speculum Majus by the greatest of all magicians. In the kitchens the famous cooks were preparing menus which included, for one course alone: ballock broth, caudle ferry, lampreys en galentine, oysters in civey, eels in sorré, baked trout, brawn in mustard, numbles of a hart, pigs farsed, cockintryce, goose in hoggepotte, venison in frumenty, hens in brewet, roast squirrels, haggis, capon–neck pudding, garbage, tripe, blaundesorye, caboges, buttered worts, apple mousse, gingerbread, fruit tart, blancmange, quinces in comfit, stilton cheese, and causs boby. In the dining halls the older gentlemen, who had spoiled their palates with drinking, were relishing those strange delicacies of the Middle Ages—the strong flavours of whale and porpoise. Their dainty ladies were putting roses and violets in their dishes—baked marigolds still make an excellent flavouring for bread–and–butter puddings—while the squires were showing their weakness for sheep's–milk cheese. In the nurseries all the little boys were moving heaven and earth to persuade their mothers to have hard pears for dinner, which were stewed in honey–syrup and vinegar, and eaten with whipped cream. The manners of the table, too, had reached a pitch of civilization far beyond our own. Now, instead of the plates made of bread, there were covered dishes, scented finger bowls, sumptuous table cloths, a plethora of napkins. The diners themselves were wearing chaplets of flowers and graceful draperies. The pages were serving the food with the formal movements of a ballet. Wine bottles were being placed on the tables, but ale, being less respectable, was being put beneath. The musicians, with strange orchestras of bells, large horns, harps, viols, zithers and organs, were playing as the people ate. Where once, before King Arthur had made his chivalry, the Knight of the Tower Landry had been compelled to warn his daughter against entering her own dining hall in the evening unaccompanied—for fear of what might happen in the dark corners—now there was music and light. In the smoky vaults, where once the grubby barons had gnawed their bones with bloody fingers, now there were people eating with clean fingers, which they had washed with herb–scented toilet soap out of wooden bowls. In the cellars of the monasteries the butlers were tapping new and old ale, mead, port, claree, dry sherry, hock, beer, metheglyn, perry, hippocras, and the best white whisky. In the law courts the judges were dispensing the King's new law, instead of the fierce law of Fort Mayne. In the cottages the good wives were making hot griddle bread enough to make your mouth water, and putting fine turf on their fires regardless of expense, and herding fat geese on the commons enough to support twenty families for twenty years. The Saxons and Normans of Arthur's accession had begun to think of themselves as Englishmen.

No wonder that the young, ambitious knights of Europe flocked to the great court. No wonder that they saw a king when they looked on Arthur, a conqueror when they looked on Lancelot.

One of the young men who came to court in those days was Gareth. Another was Mordred.

CHAPTER XXVI

"We don't see many arrows thrilling in people's hearts nowadays," remarked Lancelot one afternoon at the archery butts.

"Thrilling!" exclaimed Arthur. "What a splendid word to describe an arrow vibrating, just after it has hit!"

Lancelot said: "I heard it in a ballad."

They went away and sat in an arbour, from which they could watch the young people practising their shots.

"It is true," said the King gloomily. "We don't get much of the old fighting in these decadent days."

"Decadent!" protested his commander–in–chief. "What are you so gloomy about? I thought this was what you wanted?"

Arthur changed the subject.

"Gareth is shaping well," he said, watching the boy. "It's funny. He can't be many years younger than you are, yet one thinks of him as a child."

"Gareth is a dear."

The King put his hand on Lancelot's knee and squeezed it affectionately.

"Some people might say that you are the dear," he said, "so far as Gareth is concerned. It has come to be quite a legend how the boy arrived at court anonymously, so that his own brothers didn't recognize him, and how he worked in the kitchen, and got nicknamed Beaumains when Kay wanted to be nasty, and how you were the only person who was decent to him until he did his great adventure and became a knight."

"Well," said Lancelot defensively, "his brothers hadn't seen him for fifteen years. You can't blame Gawaine for that."

"I am not blaming anybody. I was just saying that it was nice of you to take notice of a kitchen page, and help him along, and knight him in the end. But then, you always were nice to people."

"It is strange how they come here," said his friend. "I suppose they can't keep away. Any boy with a bit of go in him feels that he has to come to Arthur's court, even if it is to work in the kitchen, because it is the centre of the new world. That is why Gareth ran away from his mother. She wouldn't let him come, so he ran away and came incognito."

"Nonsense. Morgause is a bad old woman—that's all you can say about her. She forbade him to come to court because she hated you, but he came for all that."

"Morgause is my half–sister, and I have hurt her badly. It can't be nice for a woman to have all her sons going away to serve the man she hates. Even Mordred, her last."

Lancelot looked uncomfortable. He had an instinctive dislike for Mordred, and did not like having it. He did not know about Arthur being Mordred's father—for that was a story which had been hushed up in the earliest days, before either he or Guenever came to court, just as Arthur's own birth had been. But he did feel that there was something strange between the young man and the King. He disliked Mordred irrationally, as a dog dislikes a cat —and he felt ashamed of the dislike, because it was a confused principle of his to help the younger knights.

"It must have hurt her worst of all when Mordred came," pursued the King. "Women are always fondest of their last babies."

"So far as I can learn, she was never particularly fond of any of them. If she was hurt by their coming to court, it was only because she hated you. Why does she?"

"It's a bad story. I would rather not talk about it.

"Morgause," added the King, "is a woman—is a woman of pronounced character."

Lancelot laughed rather sourly.

"She must be," he said, "from the way she is carrying on. I hear she is making a dead set at Pellinore's son Lamorak now, although she is a grandmother."

"Who told you?"

"It's all over the court."

Arthur got up and walked three steps in agitation.

"Good God!" he exclaimed. "And Lamorak's father killed her husband! And her son killed Lamorak's father! And Lamorak is hardly of age!"

He sat down and looked at Lancelot, as if he were afraid of what he might say next.

"All the same, that is what she is doing."

The King suddenly and vehemently asked: "Where is Gawaine? Where is Agravaine? Where is Mordred?"

"They are supposed to be on some quest or other."

"Not—not in the North?"

"I don't know."

"Where is Lamorak?"

"I think he is staying in Orkney."

"Lancelot, if you had only known my sister—if you had only known the Orkney clan at home. They are mad on their family. If Gawaine—if Lamorak—O my God, have mercy on my sins, and on the sins of other people, and on the tangle in this world!"

Lancelot looked at him in consternation.

"What are you afraid of?"

Arthur stood up for the second time, and began talking fast.

"I am afraid for my Table. I am afraid of what is going to happen. I am afraid it was all wrong."

"Nonsense."

"When I started the Table, it was to stop anarchy. It was a channel for brute force, so that the people who had to use force could be made to do it in a useful way. But the whole thing was a mistake. No, don't interrupt me. It was a mistake because the Table itself was founded on force. Right must be established by right: it can't be established by Force Majeur. But that is what I have been trying to do. Now my sins are coming home to roost. Lancelot, I am afraid I have sown the whirlwind, and I shall reap the storm."

"I don't understand what you are talking about."

"Here comes Gareth," said the King calmly, suddenly, and as if everything were over. "I think you will understand in a minute."

While they had been talking, a messenger in leather leggings had arrived at the butts. The King had seen him out of the corner of his eye as he hastily sought Sir Gareth and handed him a letter. He had watched the boy reading the letter, once, twice, three times, and later as he spoke confusedly with the man. Now, after handing his bow to the messenger without noticing that he was doing so, Gareth was coming to them slowly.

"Gareth," said the King.

The young man knelt down and took the King's hand. He held it as if it were a banister or a life–line. He looked at Arthur with dull eyes, and did not cry.

"My mother is dead," said Gareth.

"Who killed her?" asked the King, as if it were the natural question.

"My brother Agravaine."

"What!"

The exclamation was from Lancelot.

"My brother has killed our mother, because he found her sleeping with a man."

"Keep quiet, Lancelot, please," said the King. Then to Gareth: "What did they do to Sir Lamorak?"

But Gareth had not finished the first part of his story.

"Agravaine cut off her head," he said. "Like the unicorn."

"The unicorn?"

"Please, Lancelot."

"He killed our mother in her blood."

"I am sorry."

"I always knew he would," said Gareth.

"Are you sure the news is true?"

"It is true. It is true. It was Agravaine who killed the unicorn."

"Was Lamorak the unicorn?" asked the King gently. He did not know what his nephew was talking about, but he was anxious to help. "Is Lamorak dead?"

"Oh, Uncle! It says that Agravaine found her naked in a bed with Sir Lamorak, and he cut off her head. Now they have hunted Lamorak down as well."

Lancelot was less patient than the King, because he knew fewer of the sorrows which had happened in the early days.

"Who were they?" he asked.

"Mordred, Agravaine, and Gawaine."

"So it comes to this," said Sir Lancelot, "that your three brothers have first murdered King Pellinore—who would not willingly have hurt a fly— murdered him because he killed their father by accident in a tournament—

then murdered their own mother in bed—and finally butchered Pellinore's young son Lamorak, for being seduced by their mother, who was three times as old as he was. I suppose they set upon him all against one?"

Gareth held the King's hand tighter, and began to droop his head.

"They surrounded him," he said numbly, "and Mordred stabbed him in the back."

CHAPTER XXVII

Gawaine and Mordred came straight to Camelot from their foray among the Old Ones, but Agravaine did not come with them. They had quarrelled as soon as Lamorak was dead, or rather, as soon as they had found time to realize what had happened. The murder of Queen Morgause had not been done on purpose. Agravaine had done it on the spur of the moment—in his outraged passion, he said—but they knew by instinct that it was from jealousy. So they had raised the old charge against him, that he was only a fat bully whose noblest employment was the killing of defenceless people or women, and they had left him, weeping, after a furious scene. Gawaine, who now remembered all his adoration for their peculiar mother—an adoration which the queen–witch had wished on each of her sons—rode to the King's court in gloomy penitence. He knew that Arthur would be furious about the way in which young Lamorak had been killed, for the boy had been the third best knight of the Table, and yet he was not ashamed of having killed him. To his mind Lamorak deserved death, like a felon, because he and his father had injured the Orkney clan. He knew that the whole court would look at him sideways on account of his mother's murder, and how the old talk would be revived about that woman whom he had slain himself in temper, when he was young. Even this did not dismay him much. But he was penitent and miserable because his own dear Orkney mother was gone—he was only beginning to realize how it had happened—because he had hurt Arthur's ideal, and because he was generous in his own heart. He hoped that the King would hang him, or send him into exile, or punish him severely. He went into the royal chamber with a sulky shame.

Mordred walked into the room behind Gawaine, as if nothing had happened. He was a thin wisp of a fellow, so fair–haired that he was almost an albino: and his bright eyes were so blue, so palely azure in their faded depths, that you could not see into them. He was clean–shaven. It seemed that there was no part of him which you could catch hold of, neither his hair, nor his eyes, nor his whiskers. Even the colour had been washed out of him, it seemed, so as to leave no handle. Only, in the skeletal, pink face, the brilliant eyes had crow's–feet round them—a twinkle which you could assume to be of humour, if you liked, or else of irony, or merely of screwing up those sky–blue pupils so as to look far and deep. He walked with an upright carriage, both ingratiating and defiant— but one shoulder was higher than the other. He had been born slightly crooked—a clumsy delivery by the midwife—like Richard III.

Arthur was waiting for them, with Guenever and Lancelot on either hand.

The burly, red–haired Gawaine knelt down clumsily on one knee. He did not look at the King, but spoke to the floor.

"Pardon."

"Pardon," said Mordred also—but he, kneeling beside his half–brother, looked the King between the eyes. He had a non–committal voice, beautifully modulated—its words might have meant the opposite of what they said.

"You are pardoned," said Arthur. "Go away."

"Go?" asked Gawaine. He was not sure whether he was being banished.

"Yes, go. We can meet at dinner. But go, now. Leave me, please."

Gawaine said roughly: "The half of yon was done by sore ill fortune."

This time Arthur's voice was neither tired nor miserable.

"Go!"

He stamped his foot like a war–horse, pointing to the door as if he would throw them out of it. His eyes flashed from his face, like a sudden flame of green ash, so that even Mordred got up quickly. Gawaine was startled and stumbled out of the door in confusion, but the crooked man recollected himself before he left. He made a play–actor's bow, a low, luxurious simulacrum of humility—then, straightening himself up, he looked the King in the eye, and smiled, and went.

Arthur sat down, trembling. Lancelot and Guenever looked at each other over his head. They would have liked to ask why he was going to forgive his nephews, or to protest that it was impossible to pardon matricides without damaging the Round Table. But they had never seen Arthur in his royal rage before. They felt that there was something in it which they did not understand, so they held their peace.

Presently the King said: "I was trying to tell you something, Lance, before this happened."

"Yes."

"You two have always listened to me about my Table. I want you to understand."

"We will do our best."

"Long ago, when I had my Merlyn to help, he tried to teach me to think. He knew he would have to leave in the end, so he forced me to think for myself. Don't ever let anybody teach you to think, Lance: it is the curse of the world."

The King sat looking at his fingers, and they waited while the old thoughts ran sideways across his hands like crabs.

"Merlyn," he said, "approved of the Round Table. Evidently it was a good thing at the time. It must have been a step. Now we must think of making the next one."

Guenever said: "I don't see what is wrong with the Round Table, just because the Orkney faction chooses to get murderous."

"I was explaining to Lance. The idea of our Table was that Right was to be the important thing, not Might. Unfortunately we have tried to establish Right by Might, and you can't do that."

"I don't see why you can't do it."

"I tried to dig a channel for Might, so that it would flow usefully. The idea was that all the people who enjoyed fighting should be headed off, so that they fought for justice, and I hoped that this would solve the problem. It has not."

"Why not?"

"Simply because we have got justice. We have achieved what we were fighting for, and now we still have the fighters on our hands. Don't you see what has happened? We have run out of things to fight for, so all the fighters of the Table are going to rot. Look at Gawaine and his brothers. While there were still giants and dragons and wicked knights of the old brigade, we could keep them occupied: we could keep them in order. But now that the ends have been achieved, there is nothing for them to use their might on. So they use it on Pellinore and Lamorak and my sister— God be good to them. The first sign of the fester was when our chivalry turned into Games–Mania—all that nonsense about who had the best tilting average and so forth. This is the second sign, when murder begins again. That is why I say that dear Merlyn would want me to start another thinking, now, if only he were here to help."

"It is something like idleness and luxury unmanning us—the strings have gone slack and out of tune."

"No: it is not that at all. It is simply that I have kept a rod in pickle for my own back. I ought to have rooted Might out altogether, instead of trying to adapt it. Though I don't know how the rooting could have been done. Now the Might is left, with nothing to use it on, so it is working wicked channels for itself."

"You ought to punish it," said Lancelot. "When Sir Bedivere killed his wife you made him carry her head to the Pope. You ought to send Gawaine to the Pope now."

The King opened his hands and looked up for the first time.

"I am going to send you all to the Pope," he said.

"What!"

"Not exactly to the Pope. You see, the trouble is—as I see it—that we have used up the worldly objects for our Might—so there is nothing left but the spiritual ones. I was thinking about this all night. If I can't keep my fighters from wickedness by matching them against the world—because they have used up the world—then I must match them against the spirit."

Lancelot's eye caught fire, and he began to watch the other man attentively. At the same moment Guenever withdrew into herself. She glanced quickly at her lover, a covert glance, then gave a new, reserved attention to her husband.

"If something is not done," went on the King, "the whole Table will go to ruin. It is not only that feud and open manslaughter have started: there is the bold bawdry as well. Look at the Tristram business with King Mark's wife. People seem to be siding with Tristram. Morals are difficult things to talk about, but what has happened is that we have invented a moral sense, which is rotting now that we can't give it employment. And when a moral sense begins to rot it is worse than when you had none. I suppose that all endeavours which are directed to a purely worldly end, as my famous Civilization was, contain within themselves the germs of their own corruption."

"What is this about sending us to the Pope?"

"I was speaking metaphorically. What I mean is, that the ideal of my Round Table was a temporal ideal. If we are to save it, it must be made into a spiritual one. I forgot about God."

"Lancelot," said the Queen in a peculiar voice, "has never forgotten."

But her lover was too interested to notice her tone.

"What do you intend to do?" he asked.

"I thought we could start by trying to achieve something which would be helpful to the spirit, if you see what I mean. We have achieved the bodily things: peace and prosperity: now we lack work. If we invent another bodily employment, a temporal employment—mere empire building or something like that—we shall be faced by the same problem again, probably worse, as soon as it has been achieved. But why can't we pull our Table together by turning its energies to the spirit? You know what I mean by the spirit. If our Might was given a channel so that it worked for God, instead of for the rights of man, surely that would stop the rot, and be worth doing?"

"A Crusade!" exclaimed Lancelot. "You are going to send us to the rescue of the Holy Sepulchre!"

"We could try that," said the King. "I hadn't exactly thought of it, but it might be a good thing to try."

"Or we could look for relics," cried his commander, who was quite on fire. "If all the knights were looking for a piece of the True Cross, they might not even need to fight. I mean, if we were to go on a Crusade, we should still be using force: we should be putting the Might into a channel against the infidels. But if we really and truly banded the whole Table together to search for something which belonged to God himself, why, that would be infinitely worth doing—and, although we should be busy, there might be no need for fighting at all. If it comes to that, we needn't necessarily look for one thing alone. Why, if all our knights—one hundred and fifty men, all specialists in questing, like detectives—if all our knights were to turn their energies to the quest for things which belonged to God—why, we might find hundreds and hundreds of things which would be of huge value. The Round Table might have been positively invented and trained just for that object. We might find some new gospels, even. The whole of Christianity might be helped by what we did. Think of a hundred and fifty men all trained for the search! And it is not too late to try. The True Cross was found in 326, but the Holy Shroud was not discovered at Lirey until 1360! We might find the spear which killed Our Lord!"

"I was thinking of that."

"We must look for manuscripts particularly."

"Yes."

"We must fare forth everywhere, to the Holy Land, to every place! We shall be like my dear de Joinville!"

"Yes."

"I think," said Sir Lancelot, "this is the most splendid idea you have ever had!"

"I am afraid of it," said the King, and this time it was his voice which sounded strange. "I thought, in the night time, that perhaps it was aiming too high. If people reach perfection they vanish, you know. It may mean the end of the Table. Supposing somebody were to find God?"

But Lancelot's mind was not made for metaphysics. He did not notice the change in Arthur's voice. He began to hum to himself the great Crusader's hymn:

Lignum crucis,
Signum ducis,
Sequitur exercitus …

"We could search for the Holy Grail!" he cried triumphantly.

It was at this moment that a messenger arrived from King Pelles. Sir Lancelot was wanted, he said, to knight a young man at an abbey. He was a fine young fellow, seemly and demure as a dove. He had been educated in a convent. His name, said the messenger, was thought to be Galahad.

Queen Guenever stood up, and sat down. She opened her hands, and closed them again. She knew that Sir Lancelot was going to his son by another woman—but she hardly minded that.

Chapter XXVIII

If you want to read about the beginning of the Quest for the Grail, about the wonders of Galahad's arrival—Guenever, in a strange mixture of curiosity, envy and horror, made a half–hearted attempt to vamp him—and of the last supper at court, when the thunder came and the sunbeam and the covered vessel and the sweet smell through the Great Hall—if you want to read about these, you must seek them in Malory. That way of telling the story can only be done once. The material facts were that the knights of the Round Table set out in a body, soon after Pentecost, with the immediate object of finding the Holy Grail.

It was two years before Lancelot came back to court—and it was a lonely time for those at home. Slowly those knights who had survived began to trickle back in twos and threes, tired men bearing news of loss or rumours of success. They came limping on crutches, or leading spent horses which could carry them no longer, or, as one did who had lost a hand in battle, carrying the one hand in the other. All these men looked worn and confused. Their faces were fanatical, and they babbled of dreams. Ships which moved of their own power, silver tables on which strange Masses had been said, spears which flew through the air, visions of bulls and of thorn trees, demons in old tombs, kings and hermits who had been living for four hundred years—these figured in the rumours which filled the palace. A count taken by Sir Bedivere showed that half the knights were missing. They were presumed dead. But all the time Sir Lancelot did not come back.

The first reliable witness to return was Gawaine, who reached the court in a black temper, with his head bandaged. He was the only one of the Orkney clan who had refused to learn English correctly and spoke in a Northern accent—almost an assumed one. He still thought half in Gaelic. He was defiant of the Southerners, proud of his race.

"Blindness and Darkness on the Quest," said Gawaine. "If I was e'er upon a sleeveless errand, it was yon."

"What happened?"

Arthur and Guenever, like good children, sat with their hands in their laps to listen to the stories. Like children, they were alert and eager, sifting the truth as best they could.

"What happened, is it? Why, what happened was that I wasted eighteen months and mair forbye in seeking footless for adventure—and ended up half deid with what ye name concussion. May God presairve me from the Holy Grail, whatever."

"Tell us from the beginning."

"From the beginning?"

He was surprised at his uncle's interest.

"Tuts, there is thing–a–bit to tell."

"Tell it all the same."

"Fetch some drink for Sir Gawaine," said the Queen. "Sit down, my lord. You are welcome home. Make yourself easy and tell the story—if you are not too tired?"

"I am nae tired—but only for the ache within my heid. I can relate the tale. Thanks to you, I will take whisky, Ma'am. Let see, where did yon stour begin?"

The laird of the Orkneys sat down and tried to remember.

"When we left the castle of Vagon ... Ye mind we rode to Vagon in a body, the first day, and aye dispairsed next morn? When we left thence, I raid north–west. It didna signify which way. Lancelot gave all men the hint, the day before we scattered, that auld King Pelles mentioned him a sacred dish one time, in yin of his great castles. He didna cleave importance tae it, but told the people for its worth. The best half went in that deerection, but I didna fash masel'. North–west, I raid."

He took a good swallow.

"The first tracks e'er I happened on," he said, "were Galahad's. For a conceited, kindless carl, commend me to yon mannie.

"Yon laddie," continued Sir Gawaine, taking another gulp and warming to his work, "yon lily laddie is, without discussion, the utmost catamite which it had been my woe to smell the stink of through the world—he is."

"Did he knock you down?" asked the King.

"Na, na. 'Twas later. I crossed his tracks at the outsetting.

"Bred in a nunnery," he went on furiously, "amidst a paircel of auld hens! I have news at me about his pairsonal quest from various who have fronted him—the holy milksop with his hairt of a cold puttock.... But there, the chiel's an Englishman. He wad be cut, if he dared cross the Border.

"Unless he will have been cut already," he concluded, struck by the idea.

"What has Sir Galahad been doing wrong?"

"Thing a bit. The man's a vegetarian and teetotaller, and he makes believe he is a vairgin. But I encountered with Sir Melias—ye ken Sir Melias is sairely maimed? He telt me how yon Galahad behaved. By some cause Melias had taken to the carl, and asked permissions of the boy to go the one way with him. I canna fathom why he would be doing sic a thing, for the first one that had sought to go with Galahad was Uwaine. Sir Galahad refused it! Sir Uwaine wasna guid enough for him! Well, well, he condescended to let Melias go, however, and he knighted him to boot! My soul to the devil—to be knighted by a gomeril of eighteen! When he had knighted Melias, he quoth these verra words: 'Now, fair sir,' says he, 'sith ye be come of kings and queens, now look that knighthood be well set in you, for ye ought to be a mirror unto all chivalry!' What like do ye name it? Aye, a Southron snob. The next act was that they twa came their ways to an adventure by the crossroads, where Melias had a wish to ride toward the left. Galahad said: 'It were better ye rode not that way, for I deem I should better escape in that way than ye.' There was nae fause modesty abune the bonnie Galahad, ye see? Well, Melias went left for a' that—and he came by ill–luck stricken through the hauberk at the hands of some mysterious knight wha rode upon him, as Galahad foretold. He was like to die—the broken truncheon in his side. When the great Galahad found him wounded, what does my mannie say, but: 'Therefore it had been better to have ridden that other way!' A handsome chiel to say I–told–ye–so to one half deid! Nor did he give him aid."

"What happened to Sir Melias?"

"He said to Galahad: 'Sir, let death come when it pleaseth him.' He drew the truncheon forth himself. Melias is a bonnie knight, and there is gladness on me that I may tell you he is still on life."

Arthur said: "After all, Galahad is only a child! He has growing pains, perhaps. I don't think we ought to judge him unkindly for little faults of social intercourse."

"Did ye ken that he has aye attacked his father, and unhorsed him too? Do ye ken that he has let his father kneel before him, for to ask his blessing? Do ye ken that peoples have been asking for to die in Galahad's arms, and that he has been granting them to do so, as a favour?"

"Well, perhaps it was a favour."

"Diabhal!" exclaimed Gawaine, and he buried his nose in the beaker.

"You are not telling us about yourself."

"The first adventure which I suffered—indeed it wasna far from being the single one—fell at the Castle of Maidens. It were best not tell of yon, before the Queen."

Arthur said rather coldly: "My wife is not a baby or an imbecile, Sir Gawaine. Everybody knows about the custom of that Castle."

Guenever said politely: "They call it *droit de seigneur* in French."

"Well then, indeed, I came to the Castle of Maidens with Uwaine and Sir Gareth. It was kept by seven knights, whatever, who insisted on the custom. We found those seven outside the castle fully armed, and had braw fight with them, and slew them all. When all was done, 'twas manifest that Galahad had been before us. 'Twas he had driven them forth at first, without his killing e'er a one of them, and he himself was ben the castle at the very time. All we had done was play the butcher's part, in finishing what wasna rightly ours."

"Bad luck."

"Galahad rode his gait and wouldna speak with us. The meaning was that we were sinful—he was blessed. I dinna mind what happened after that."

"Did you ride on with Uwaine and Gareth?"

"Nay, we parted after Maiden Castle. I rode all airts until I found a hermitage, with its releegious man. Ye ken the sort, e wheen Salvationist. The first demand he made was: 'I would wit how it standeth betwixt your God and you?' I asked that he should gie me lodging for the nicht. Well, he was host and priest as well, so when he pressed me to confession, I couldna well refuse. He clattered waeful havers of the seven knights—they being the seven deadly sins, said he—and told me, calm as daylight, that I was but a murdering man masel'."

"Did he tell you," asked the King with interest, "that it was wrong to kill people for any reason, and especially when you were looking for the Grail?"

"My soul to the devil, he did so. He preached that Galahad had aye expelled the seven knights without a slaughter, and mentioned that the Holy Grail was nae for bloodshed."

"What else did he say?"

"I canna mind. When he had complimented me as I was telling ye, he counselled I should make a penance. Unless a body made his guid confession—and was absolvit fair—it would be bootless seeking for the Grail, says he. The chiel was daffish. An errant knight stands in a posture which should make the penance needless—as I shewed him—the like that manual labourers dinna fast in Lent. I gave the man the lie and took my way forthwith. I met with Aglovale and Griflet after that ... What then, what then? I rode with them four days, I mind ... Aye then we parted once again, and darkness on me if I didna ride till Michaelmas without adventure!

"Troth is," added Gawaine, "there are nae ventures to be found in England, these late days. The place is failed."

"Fetch Sir Gawaine another drink."

"When Michaelmas was gone and past, I met with Ector Demaris. He had been luckless like masel'! We rode to a wee chapel in the forest, and slept there with a dram inside us—and each man had the one same dream that night. It concairned a hand and arm, in samite, with a bridle and a candle in its gripe. A voice made known that we twa were in need of them. I encountered with a second priest thereafter, wha said the bridle was for continence and the candle was for faith—it seems that Ector and masel' were lacking these. Ye mind how any man may twist a dream. The next thing after was a piece of dour misfortune, the like of that which has been on me all the while. We came, the twa of us, upon my cousin Uwaine with his shield in cover—and didna recognize his blazon. Ector conceded me the first fall with my cousin, my ain kin. The spear went fair through Uwaine's chest. There will have been a weakness in his brigandine."

"Is Uwaine dead?"

"Aye, dead, man. It is the black ill–happening that was on me."

Arthur cleared his throat.

"I should have thought it was worse happening for Uwaine," he said, "God rest him. Perhaps it might not have been a bad thing if you had listened to that priest of yours at the beginning."

"I had nae wish to kill! He was own cousin to the Orkneys! And think ye that the southron prig, him of the white shield, had before refused to ride with him!"

"Do you mean Galahad? Was he bearing the vergescu?"

"Aye, Galahad. It wasna the vergescu. He had laid hold upon a shield in some place, which was to have belonged to Joseph Arimathea, so he said. The cognizance was argent, a tau cross gules. The argent was to signify the white of virgins, we were let to know, and the red cross was for the Grail … I am from my tale."

"You had just killed Uwaine," said Arthur patiently.

"Ector and I rode on to one more hermitage, and it was there the priest made known about the bridle in our dream. This priest was vegetarian, may I tell ye! He gave the auld tale about murder, hot and hot, and was for pressing our repentance. We made excuses, and we rode out gait."

"Did he tell you that the reason why neither of you had any luck was because you were only looking for slaughter?"

"Aye, did he. He said that Lancelot was better man than us because he rarely killed his adversary—and in parteecular by cause he didna in this quest. Also he said that many other knights—Ector himself met twenty—were in the same case with us from their sins. He said manslaughter was contrary to the quest. We juist made speech with him, and slipped away while he was talking yet."

"And then?"

"We came upon a castle then, Ector and I, a bonnie tournament was forward. We joined the attacking men—and had fine battle—and were at point to force our way inside—the tempers were a wee bit risen—when Galahad came up. God the Almighty knows what ill wind brought yon mannie. It seems he wasna for approving of such knights as fight for sport. He joined the ither side, and drove us forth the castle, and he gave me this."

Gawaine touched his bandage.

"Ector was not for fighting him," he explained. "They were related. But I fought none the less for that, and small thanks with it. He gave a blow which split my helm whatever, and broke the iron coif—aye, and it glanced off too, killing my horse. Yon was the end for me, by Christ. I was for bed during one month and more."

"And then you came home?"

"Aye, home."

"You certainly seem to have been unlucky," said the Queen.

"Unlucky!"

Gawaine looked into his empty beaker for a moment or two. Then he cheered up.

"I slew King Bagdemagus," he said. "Nae doot ye heard of yon. I missed to tell ye in my tale."

Arthur had been listening closely and turning over his own thoughts. Now he made a movement of impatience.

"Go to bed, Gawaine," he said. "You must be tired. Go to bed and think about it."

CHAPTER XXIX

The next person to get home was Sir Lionel, one of Lancelot's cousins. Lancelot had one brother called Ector, and two cousins called Lionel and Bors. Lionel was in a temper, rather like Gawaine, but the object of his annoyance was not Galahad. It was his own brother, Bors.

"Morals," said Lionel, "are a form of insanity. Give me a moral man who insists on doing the right thing all the time, and I will show you a tangle which an angel couldn't get out of."

The King and Queen were sitting side by side as usual, to hear the traveller's story. They had formed a habit of carrying the refreshments into the Great Hall with their own hands, as soon as any knight got back, so that they could hear the news while he ate. The light fell on the table between them—from a high stained window—so that their hands moved among plates and glasses which were rubies, emeralds or pools of flame. They were in a magic world of gems, a glade under trees whose leaves were jewels.

"Has Bors been going in for morals?"

"Bors always did," said Lionel, "curse him. Morals seem to run in my family. Lancelot is bad enough to begin with, but Bors beats him to a frazzle. Did you know that Bors has only once committed the sexual act?"

"Really."

"Yes, really. And, so far as this Quest for the Holy Grail is concerned, he seems to have been doing a sort of advanced course in Catholic dogma."

"Do you mean he is studying?"

Lionel relented a little. He was fond of his brother in his heart, but he had been through an experience which had embittered their relations. Now that he could talk about it, and had had time to think it over, he was beginning to see the other side of the quarrel.

"No," he said. "You mustn't take me seriously. Bors is a dear fellow and, if ever there is to be a saint in our family, it will be him. He isn't bright in the head, and he is a bit of a prig, but his guesses are sometimes pure gold. I believe God has been testing him, during this quest, and I'm not sure that he has not come out trumps. I tried to kill him."

"You had better begin your story at the beginning," said Arthur, "or we shan't understand how it goes along."

"My story is nothing. I have been footling about like Gawaine, being called a murderer by a few hermits. I'll tell you the story of Bors, because I come into it.

"God," began Lionel, "has been making a trial of Bors, I suppose. It is as if he was going to be priested, and they wanted to be sure if he was orthodox. Do you know, I think that where Gawaine and myself and Ector and all the rest of us went off the right line, was when we didn't go to confession at the beginning? Bors went, the first day, and he took a penance too. He promised to eat nothing but bread and water, and to wear a Garment, and to sleep on the floor. Of course he was not going to have anything to do with the ladies—but then, he only once had. That's his trouble. Well, the first thing that happened after putting his life in order was that he began having visions. He saw the pelican in her piety, and a swan and a raven and some rotten wood and some flowers. It all had to do with his theology, and he did explain it to me, but I can't remember. The next thing which happened was that a lady begged him to rescue her from a knight called Sir Pridam. He rescued the lady easily enough, and had an opportunity to kill Sir Pridam. Mark this. He told me the story after our battle, and he insisted that it was his first trial. He said that he felt like a show jumper, being put over bigger leaps each time, and he was afraid that if he ever bungled a leap he would be sent back to the stable. If he had killed Sir Pridam he would have been finished. They would have put him out to grass again, just as they did with Gawaine and the rest of us. He said that nobody told him these things—the leaps suddenly appeared in front of him, and it was as if there were somebody watching—somebody who would not help or hint, but who just watched to see if he would get over. Well, he didn't kill Pridam. He only squealed at him to give in and hit his face with the flat of the sword until he yielded. And that jump was safely done. Do you think there can have been something against killing people in this quest, King? You know, some sort of supernatural No?"

"I think you are a wise man, Lionel," said the King, "even if you did try to kill your brother. Go on with the story."

"Well, the next trial was directly about me. It was the reason why I tried to kill him. I'm sorry about it now. I have only just realized I'm sorry. At the time I didn't understand."

"What was the second trial?"

"Bors and I have always been fond of each other, as you know. This tiff is nothing. We have always loved each other in our way, and Bors was riding through the forest, when he came face to face with two things. One was me, bound naked on a hackney, with two knights riding on either side, and flogging me with thorns. The other was a virgin, riding more than a pace, with a knight galloping after her, to have her maidenhead. The two convoys were going in opposite directions, and Bors was alone."

"Come to think of it," remarked Sir Lionel ruefully, "I am unlucky about getting flogged with thorns. I got it from Sir Turquine once before."

"Which party did Bors choose?"

"Bors decided to rescue the maiden. When I eventually asked him what the devil he meant by deserting his own brother, at the time of our battle later on, he explained that he had thought I was inclined to be a dirty dog— though fond of me—while the maiden was a maiden after all. So he thought his duty was toward the better party. That was why I tried to kill him.

"But now," added Lionel, "I can see his point. I can see it was his second trial, and a difficult decision it must have been to make."

"Poor Bors. I hope he was not too much of a prig about it?"

"He was humble. These trials just used to loom up in front of the old gossip, and he would make a wild guess, generally thinking that he had guessed wrong—and in the end he would come out bewildered, and find that he had guessed right. He sweated along, doing the best he could."

"What was the third trial?"

"They got worse as they went. In the third trial a man came to him dressed as a priest, and told him that there was a lady in a castle nearby who was doomed to death unless Bors made love to her. This supposed priest pointed out that he had already sacrificed the life of his own brother—that was me—by wrongly choosing to help the maiden, and that if he did not sin with the new lady now, he would have a second life on his conscience. I ought to have mentioned that the two knights left me for dead, and Bors found me apparently dead, and he had taken my body to an abbey for burial. Of course, I recovered later.

"Well, the lady appeared in the castle—as stated by the feigned priest—and she confirmed the story. She said that there was a magic which would make her die for love, unless my brother was good to her. Bors now realized that he must either commit mortal sin and save the lady, or refuse to commit it and let her die. He told me afterwards that he remembered some bits out of the penny catechism, and a sermon which was once given when there was a mission at Camelot. He decided that he was not responsible for the lady's actions, while he was responsible for his own. So he refused the lady."

Guenever giggled.

"That was not the end of it. The lady was dazzlingly beautiful, and she climbed to the highest keep of her castle, with twelve lovely gentlewomen, and she said that if Bors would not stop being so pure, they would all jump off together. She said she would force them to do so. She said that he only had to have one night with her—and why need it not be fun?—for the gentlewomen to be saved. All twelve of them shouted out to Bors, and begged him for mercy, and wept for dole.

"I can tell you my brother was in a quandary. The poor things were so frightened and so pretty, and he only had to stop being obstinate to save their lives."

"What did he do?"

"He let them jump."

"Shame!" cried the Queen.

"Oh, they were only a collection of fiends, of course. The whole tower turned up–so–down and vanished immediately, and it turned out that they had been fiends all the time, including the priest."

"I suppose the moral is," said Arthur, "that you must not commit mortal sin, even if twelve lives depend upon it. Dogmatically speaking, I believe that is sound."

"I don't know what the dogma is, but I know it nearly turned my brother's hair grey."

"And a good right it had to. What was the fourth trial, if there was one?"

"The fourth one was me, and it was the last hurdle. I revived at the abbey where he had left me to be buried, and, when I was well enough, I rode to seek him out. I am sorry about it now—by the way, I shall have to ask your pardon for some of the things I did—but, when you come to think of it, it does seem a bit steep to be left by your own brother to be beaten to death. What with taking one's meals off the mantelpiece, and not understanding at the time about the things which were happening to Bors, and knowing that, just before I lost consciousness, I had seen him leave me to my fate—well, I admit that I was in a bitter frame of mind. In fact, I was murderous.

"I found Bors at a chapel in the forest, and I told him at once that I was going to kill him. I said: 'I shall do to thee as a felon or a traitor, for ye be the untruest knight that ever came out of so worthy an house.' Bors refused to fight. I said: 'If you don't fight, I shall kill you as you stand.' Bors said that he couldn't fight his own brother, of all people. He said that he was not even allowed to kill ordinary chaps on the Grail Quest, so how could he kill his brother? I said: 'I do not care what you are allowed to do, or not allowed to do. If you like to defend yourself, I shall fight you: if not, I shall kill you anyway.' I was furious. Bors just knelt down and asked for mercy.

"I can see now," he went on, "that it was right enough for Bors to do as he did. He was after the Grail, he was in the anti–homicide squadron, and I was his brother. Also it was brave of him. But I couldn't see it at the time. I simply thought he was being obstinate, and I knocked him feet–upwards as he knelt. Then I drew my sword to cut off his head."

Lionel sat in silence for a minute, looking at the plate in front of him, where there was a bright pool of ruby from the stained glass, shaped like an egg.

"You know," he said, "it's all very well to take up with morals and dogmas, so long as there is only yourself in it: but what are you to do when other people join the muddle? I suppose it was clear enough for Bors to kneel down and let me kill him, but the next thing was that a hermit came rushing out of the chapel and threw himself across my brother's body. He said he was going to prevent me at all costs from becoming a fratricide. I killed the hermit."

"Killed a defenceless man?"

"I am desperately sorry, King, but it is true. Don't forget that I was in a frightful rage, and the fellow prevented me from getting at Bors, and I am a plain man of my hands. They were baffling me with a sort of moral weapon, and I used my own weapon against it. I felt that Bors was standing up to me in an unfair way, and that this hermit was helping him. I felt he was setting his will against mine. If he wanted to save the hermit, let him stop being obstinate and get up and fight. If you see what I mean, I felt that the hermit was his business, not mine.

"I'm afraid that I was simply in a passion," admitted Lionel after a bit. "You know how you get. I wanted to fight, and I was going to have it. I had said I would kill him if not, and I was going to kill him. You know how it is. It is like the sulks."

There was an uncomfortable silence.

"I had better finish my story," he said awkwardly.

"Go on."

"Well, Bors let me kill the hermit. He just lay on the ground and asked for love. I was more maddened than ever, by this time, partly by shame, and I raised my sword to cut off my brother's head there and then—when Sir Golgrevance of Gore turned up. He put himself between us and said fie on me for trying to shed my father's blood. That was the last straw, with all the hermit's blood round my feet, so I just went for Colgrevance instead. And in a few minutes I had him on the run."

"What did Bors do?"

"Poor Bors. What his feelings were at that moment, I don't like to think. There he was at his fence again, you see, and he only had to refuse it to save another life. He had wasted the hermit's, apparently through obstinacy, and now I was going to kill the innocent Golgrevance, who had tried to help him. Colgrevance kept sobbing out to him, too, saying: 'Get up and help, man. Why are you letting me be killed for you?'"

"Passive resistance," said Arthur with intense interest. "It is a new weapon. But it seems difficult to use. Go on, please."

"Well, I killed Colgrevance in fair fight. I am sorry, but I did. Then I came back to Bors, to finish the matter. He held his shield over his head, but would not struggle."

"What happened?"

"God came," said the boy solemnly. "He came between us, and dazzled us, and made our shields burn."

There was a long pause while Arthur digested the first tidings of certain things which he had hoped or feared.

"You see," said Lionel, "Bors prayed."

"And God came?"

"I don't know exactly what happened, but the sun was flaming on our shields. Something happened. We suddenly stopped fighting, and began to laugh. I saw that Bors was an idiot, and he kissed me and we made it up. Then he told me his story, as I have told you, and sailed away in a magic ship, covered in white samite. Bors will find the Grail, if anybody does find it, and that is the end of my story."

They sat silent, finding it difficult to talk about spiritual matters, until finally Sir Lionel spoke for the last time.

"It is all very well for Bors," he said complainingly, "but what about the hermit? What about Sir Colgrevance? Why didn't God save them?"

"Dogmas are difficult things," said Arthur.

Guenever said: "We don't know what their past history was. The killing didn't do any harm to their souls. Perhaps it even helped their souls, to die like that. Perhaps God gave them this good death because it was the best thing for them."

CHAPTER XXX

The third important arrival was Sir Aglovale, who came rather late in the afternoon, when the rubies had left the table and climbed the wall. He was a lad of less than twenty summers, with a fine noble face and a sense of humour. He was still in mourning for his Father, King Pellinore—and he signified this by wearing a black sash on his shield arm. At least, they thought it was for King Pellinore. As a matter of fact, his mother had died as well since they last saw him. He was also bringing news of the death of a sister—for nearly all of Pellinore's family had been unfortunate.

"Is Gawaine here?" asked Aglovale. "Where are Mordred and Agravaine?"

He glanced about him, as if he might actually find them in the Hall. Above his head, the coloured beam of light fell upon a small and primitive piece of tapestry—a picture of some knights in chain mail, with nose guards on their painted helmets, chasing a boar.

Arthur said: "Aglovale, they are here. My happiness is in your hands."

"I see."

"Are you going to kill them?"

"I came to kill Gawaine first. It seems queer, after looking for the Holy Grail."

"Aglovale, you have every right to try for revenge against the Orkneys, and I will not stop you if you do try. But I want you to know what you are doing. Your father killed their father and your brother slept with their mother. No, don't explain about it—let me remind you of the facts. Then the Orkneys killed your father and brother. Now you are going to kill some of the Orkneys, and Gawaine's sons will kill your sons, and so we shall go on. That is the law of the North.

"But, Aglovale, I am trying to make a new law in Britain, by which people don't have to go on shedding young blood for ever. Have you thought that it may be uphill work for me? There is a saying that two wrongs don't make a right, and I am fond of this saying. Don't apply it to yourself—apply it to me. I could have punished the Orkneys for murdering your brother. I could have cut their heads off. Would you have liked me to do that?"

"Yes."

"Perhaps I ought to have."

Arthur looked at his hands, as he often did when he was in trouble.

Then he said: "It is a pity you never had the opportunity of seeing the Orkneys at home. They didn't have a happy family life like yours."

Aglovale said: "Do you think my family life is very happy now? Do you know that my mother died a few months ago? Father used to call her Piggy."

"Aglovale, I am sorry. We had not heard."

"People used to laugh at my father, King. I know he was not a formidable character. But he must have made a fairly good husband, mustn't he, for my mother to die of loneliness because he had gone? Mother was not an introspective person, King, but she faded away after the Orkneys had killed father and Lamorak. Now she is in the same grave."

"You must do what you think right, Aglovale. I know you are a true Pellinore, and will do that. I won't ask any favours for myself. But will you let me mention three things? The first is that your father was the first knight I ever fell in love with: yet I didn't punish Gawaine. The second is that all the Orkneys adored their mother. She made them love her too much, but she only loved herself. And the third thing—oh, Aglovale, listen to this one—is that a king can only work with his best tools."

"I'm afraid I don't follow the third point."

"Do you think," asked Arthur, "that feuds are good things? Are they making for happiness in your two families?"

"Not exactly."

"If I want to stop the feud law, do you think it would be any good my appealing to Gawaine, and to people like him?"

"I see."

"What good would it have done if I had executed all the Orkney family? We should only have had three knights less to work with. And their lives have been unhappy, Aglovale. So, you see, my hope is with you."

"I must think it over."

"Do. Don't decide anything quickly. Don't consider me. Just do what you think right, because you are a Pellinore—and then I know all will turn out for the best. Now tell me about your Grail adventures, and forget about the Orkneys for one evening."

Aglovale heaved a sigh, and said: "So far as I am concerned, there have not been any Grail adventures. But it has cost me a sister. Perhaps a brother as well."

"Is your sister dead? My poor boy, I thought she was safe in a covent."

"They have found her dead in a sort of boat."

"Dead in a boat!"

"Yes, a magic boat. She had a long letter in her hands, all about the Grail Quest and about my brother Percy."

"Are we hurting you by asking questions?"

"No. I like to talk about it. I still have Dornar left, and it seems that Percy has been distinguishing himself."

"What has Sir Percivale been doing?"

"Perhaps I had better tell you what the letter said, from the start.

"As you know," began Sir Aglovale, "Percy was the one in our family who took after Daddy most. He was gentle and humble, and a bit vague. He was shy too. When he met Bors in this magic boat of theirs, he was abashed of him, it says in the letter. He was a maiden knight, like Galahad, you see. I used often to think, when I saw them together, that he and Daddy made a good pair. They were both fond of animals, for one thing, and they knew how to get on with them. There was Daddy's Questing Beast, and now Percy seems to have been befriending lions mainly, since he went away. Also Percy was benevolent and simple. One day, when they were trying to pull a blessed sword out of a scabbard—I mean the three of them in the holy boat—Percy was given the first pull. He did not succeed, of course—all that sort of thing was reserved for Galahad—but when he had failed he just looked round proudly and said: 'By my faith, now I have failed!' However, I am getting ahead of my story.

"It says in the letter that the first adventure Percy had, after leaving Vagon, was to ride off with Sir Lancelot until they met Sir Galahad. They jousted with him, and Galahad gave them both a fall. Then Percy left Lancelot, and went to a hermitage, where he was confessed. The hermit advised him to follow Galahad to Goothe or Carbonek, and never to fight him. As a matter of fact, Percy had been seized by a sort of enthusiastic hero worship for Galahad, so the advice suited him. He rode on to Carbonek, where he heard the abbey clock smite as he was pricking through the forest—and it was there that he came across King Evelake, who was about four hundred years old. I had better leave out about Evelake, for I don't quite understand it. I think the old man couldn't die until the Holy Grail had been found, or something like that. But King Pelles is mixed up with it too, and all that part of the letter is a bit difficult to follow. Anyway, Percy had a fight with eight knights and twenty men–at–arms, who set on him at Carbonek, and he was rescued in the nick of time by Galahad himself. Unfortunately his horse was killed, and Galahad rode away again without even passing the time of day.

"You know," said Lionel, pausing, "it may be all very well to be holy and invincible, and I don't hold it against Galahad for being a virgin, but don't you think that people might be a little human? I don't want to be catty, but that young man makes my hair go the wrong way. Why couldn't he say Good–morning or something, instead of rescuing a fellow and then riding away in silence with that white nose of his in the air?"

Arthur made no comment, and the young man resumed his story.

"Percy was trying to join up with Galahad, according to instructions, and Galahad had ridden off, so the poor old fellow just went running after him shouting out, 'I say!' He had some dreadful troubles trying to borrow horses from people, and finally ended up on a groom's hackney, cantering after Galahad as fast as it could go. But a knight turned up and knocked him off his hackney—I'm afraid our family was never exactly in the heroic style—and there he was on foot again, with Galahad no nearer. Well, a lady appeared at this point—they found out afterwards that she was a fairy, and not a very nice one at that—and asked him fiercely what he was trying to do. Percy said: 'I do neither good nor great ill, what?' So the lady lent him a black horse which turned out to be a fiend, and it vanished in dramatic circumstances when Percy luckily crossed himself that evening. He was in a sort of desert by that time, where he proceeded to make friends with a lion by rescuing it from a serpent. Percy was always keen on our Dumb Friends, as I said.

"The next thing that happened was that a perfectly delicious gentlewoman turned up, with full camping equipment, and invited Percy to dinner. He was hungry—what with the desert and so forth—and he had never been accustomed to drinking wine, so he had a terrific party. I'm afraid he got a bit huffed, and the upshot was that he laughed too much and got excited, and asked the lady—well, you know. The lady was agreeable, and it was just going to come off nicely, when Percy luckily noticed the cross on the pommel of his sword, which was lying on the ground. He blessed himself again, and the lady's pavilion turned up–so–down, and off she went in a ship, roaring and yelling, and the water burned after her.

"Percy was so ashamed of himself, and had such a headache next morning, that he stuck his sword into his own thigh as a punishment. After that, the holy boat turned up, with Bors inside it, and the two of them sailed away together, wherever it would take them."

Guenever said: "If that holy boat was intended to convey people to the Grail, I can perfectly well understand how Bors was in it. We know that he had been through some dreadful tests. But why Sir Percivale? I don't mean to be rude, Sir Aglovale, but your brother does not seem to have *done* much."

"He had preserved his integrity," said Arthur. "He was as clean as Bors—indeed, he was cleaner. He was perfectly innocent. God says something about suffering little children to come unto Him."

"But such a muddle!"

Arthur was annoyed.

"If God is supposed to be merciful," he retorted, "I don't see why He shouldn't allow people to stumble into heaven, just as well as climb there. Go on with your letter, Sir Aglovale."

"It is at this point that my sister comes into it. She was a nun, you know, and, when they first cut off her hair, there was a vision to say that it ought to be kept in a box. My sister was a learned woman, who had a vocation to pursue religious studies. Just about the time when Percy and Bors entered the boat, a new vision came to the convent which told her to do certain things. The first was to look for Sir Galahad.

"Galahad was spending a night in a hermitage near Carbonek, after knocking out Sir Gawaine, when my sister found him. She made him get up and arm himself, and together they rode off to the Collibe Sea, where, beyond a strong castle, they found the blessed barge with Bors and Percy waiting. They all sailed away together, until they came to a swallow of the sea, between two high rocks—and there a second barge was waiting. There was some reticence about entering the new boat, because it had a scroll on it which warned people off unless they were in perfect faith—but Galahad stepped aboard as usual, with his insufferable self–confidence. They followed him and found a rich bed with a crown of silk on it and a part–drawn sword. It was King David's sword. There were also three magic spindles, made out of the Eden tree, and two inferior swords for Percy and Bors. Naturally the main sword was for Galahad. The pommel was of marvellous stone, the scales of the haft were of the ribs of two beasts called Calidone and Ertanax, the scabbard was of serpent's skin, and one side of the sword was as red as blood. But the girdle was only plain hemp.

"My sister set to work with the spindles, and made a new girdle out of her own hair, which she had brought in the box according to instructions. She explained to them about the history of the sword, which she knew from her studies, and how the spindles had come to be made of wood which was coloured all through the grain, and finally the sword was put on Galahad. She was a virgin, and she fixed it on a virgin, with her own hair. Then they returned to their first vessel and sailed away toward Carlisle.

"On the way to Carlisle they rescued an old gentleman who was being kept prisoner by some wicked men in his castle. They killed a lot of these men in the fight, and Bors and Percy were upset about it, but Galahad said it was perfectly all right killing people who had not been christened—and it turned out that these had not been. So the old man of the castle asked permission to die in Galahad's arms, and Galahad condescendingly granted it.

"When they got to Carlisle, there was another castle which belonged to a lady who had the measle. The doctors told her that the only cure was to bathe in a dish filled with blood from a clean virgin of royal lineage. Everybody who went that way was forced to be bled by the people of the castle, and the description fitted my sister. The three knights fought all day to save her, but in the evening the reason for the custom was explained to them, and my sister said: 'Better is one harm than two.' She consented to be bled, stopped the fighting, and the next morning they did it. She blessed the surgeons, arranged for her body to be floated off in the holy boat with this letter in her hand, and then she died under the operation."

Sir Aglovale came back to the King, as he was going up to bed after the usual condolences and exclamations had been made. The Hall was dark, and the jewels of light had gone.

"By the way," he said shyly. "Will you ask the Orkney faction to have dinner with me tomorrow?"

Arthur looked at him closely through the looming twilight—then began an enormous smile. He kissed Aglovale, with a tear which ran into one corner of his smile. He said: "Now I have got a new Pellinore to love."

Chapter XXXI

Still there was no news of the great Dulac. He had become a magical name which gave warmth to all hearts, particularly women's, in whatever place he was. He had become a *maestro* himself—was regarded as he had once regarded Uncle Dap. If you have learned to fly, or been taught by a great musician or fencer, you have only to remember that teacher, to know how the people of Camelot had come to think of Lancelot. They would have died for him—for his mastery. And he was lost.

The survivors trickled in—Palomides, now christened and bored to death with the Questing Beast and aged by his long poetic rivalry with Sir Tristram for the love of La Beale Isoud—Sir Grummore Grummursum, as bald as an egg now, nearly eighty, afflicted by gout, but still bravely questin'—Kay, keen–eyed and sarcastic—Sir Dinadan making jokes about his own defeats, although he was so tired he could barely keep his lids apart—even old Sir Ector of the Forest Sauvage, eighty–five years old and tottering.

They brought with them broken arms and rumours. One said that Galahad, Bors, the other Ector and a nun had been present at a miraculous Mass. It had been celebrated by a lamb, served by a man, a lion, an eagle, and an ox. After the Mass, the celebrant had passed out through a stained–glass lamb in one of the church windows, without breaking the glass, thus signifying the immaculate conception. Another told how pitilessly Galahad had dealt with a fiend in a tomb, how he had cooled the well of lust, and how the castle of the leprous lady had finally been tumbled down.

These people, with their rusty armour and hewn shields, had seen Lancelot here and there. They spoke of a harnessed ugly man, praying at a wayside cross—of a worn face asleep in the moonlight on its shield. They spoke also of unbelievable things—of Lancelot unhorsed, defeated, kneeling after he had been knocked down.

Arthur asked questions, sent messengers, remembered his captain in his prayers. Guenever, in a dangerous frame of mind, began walking on the edge of a verbal precipice. At any moment she might say or do something which would be a compromise upon herself and upon her lover. Mordred and Agravaine, who had been among the first to retire from the Quest, watched and waited with bright eyes. They were as motionless as Lord Burleigh is said to have been at Queen Elizabeth's councils, or as a sleek cat who faces the mousehole secretly—a presence, a concentration.

The rumours began to be of Lancelot's death. He had been killed by a black knight at a ford—he had jousted with his own son, who had broken his neck—he had gone mad again, after being beaten by his son, and was riding overthwart and endlong—his armour had been stolen by a mysterious knight, and he had been eaten by a beast—he had fought against two hundred and fifty knights, been taken captive, and hanged like a dog. A strong faction believed and hinted that he had been murdered, sleeping, by the Orkneys, and had been buried under a pile of leaves.

The faint tail of knighthood straggled in by twos and threes, then one at a time, then with intervals of days between the solitary riders. The list of dead and missing, kept by Sir Bedivere, began to settle down into a list of dead, as the missing either returned exhausted or were confirmed dead by reliable report. An obituary tinge began to be present in the whispers about Lancelot. He was loved by nearly everybody, so that the speakers did not like to do more than whisper of his death, for fear that if they spoke of it aloud they would make it true. But they whispered about his goodness and remarkable visage: about such–and–such a blow which he had once given to so–and–so: about the grace of his leg–glides. A few obscure pages and kitchenmaids, who remembered vividly a smile or a tip at Christmas, went to sleep with damp pillows, although they knew that the great captain could not have been expected even to remember their names. Kay startled everybody by declaring with a sniff that he himself had always been a mean blackguard, and then went quickly out of the room blowing his nose. In all the court a tension grew, and a feeling of doom.

Lancelot came back out of a rainstorm, wet and small. He was leading an old barrel of a white mare, without a trot left in her. The black autumn clouds were behind them, and her hollow ribs stood out like flake–white against their indigo. A magic, a mind–reading, an intuition must have taken place—for all the palace battlements and turrets, and the drawbridge of the Great Gate, were thronged with people waiting, and watching, and pointing in silence, before ever he appeared. When the tiny figure could be seen, threading wearily through the far trees of the chase, a murmuration went up among the people. It was Lancelot in a scarlet gown beside the white. He was safe. Everything was known about all his adventures, before anything had been spoken. Arthur ran about like a madman, telling everybody to go in, to leave the battlements, to give the man a chance. By the time the figure arrived, there was nobody to hurt him. Only, the Great Gate stood open and Uncle Dap was there, bent and white-headed, to receive his horse. Hundreds of eyes, glancing from behind curtains, saw the spent man hand the reins to his squire—saw him standing with bowed head, which he had never raised—saw him turn and pace toward his own apartment, and vanish in the darkness of the turret stair.

Two hours later Uncle Dap presented himself in the King's chamber. He had been undressing Lancelot and putting him to bed. Under the scarlet gown, he said, there had been a fair white garment—under that, a horrible shirt of hair. Sir Lancelot had sent him with a message. He was very tired, and begged the King's pardon. He would wait on him tomorrow. Meanwhile, so that there should be no delay about the important news, Uncle Dap was to tell the King that the Holy Grail had been found. Galahad, Percivale and Bors had found it, and with it, and with the body of Percivale's sister, they had arrived at Sarras in Babylon. The Grail could not be brought to Camelot. Bors would be coming home eventually, but the others were never to return.

Chapter XXXII

Guenever had overdressed for the occasion. She had put on a make–up which she did not need, and put it on badly. She was forty–two.

When Lancelot saw her waiting for him at the table, with Arthur beside her, the heart–sack broke in his wame, and the love inside it ran about his veins. It was his old love for a girl of twenty, standing proudly by her throne with the present of captives about her—but now the same girl was standing in other surroundings, the surroundings of bad make–up and loud silks, by which she was trying to defy the invincible doom of human destiny. He saw her as the passionate spirit of innocent youth, now beleaguered by the trick which is played on youth—the trick of treachery in the body, which turns flesh into green bones. Her stupid finery was not vulgar to him, but touching. The girl was still there, still appealing from behind the breaking barricade of rouge. She had made the brave protest: I will not be vanquished. Under the clumsy coquetry, the undignified clothes, there was the human cry for help. The young eyes were puzzled, saying: It is I, inside here—what have they done to me? I will not submit. Some part of her spirit knew that the powder was making a guy of her, and hated it, and tried to hold her lover with the eyes alone. They said: Don't look at all this. Look at me. I am still here, in the eyes. Look at me, here in the prison, and help me out. Another part said: I am not old, it is illusion. I am beautifully made–up. See, I will perform the movements of youth. I will defy the enormous army of age.

Lancelot saw one soul alone, a condemned and innocent child, holding her indefensible position with the contemptible arms of hair dye and orange silk, with which she had—with what fears?—hoped to please him. He saw

The impassioned, pigmy fist
Clenched cloudward and defiant,
The pride that would prevail, the doomed protagonist
Grappling the ghostly giant.

Arthur said: "Are you rested now? How are you feeling?"

"We are so glad to see you," said Guenever, "so glad to have you back."

They, on their side, saw a man of serenity—the kind of sage that Kipling described in Kim. They saw their new Lancelot as a silence and perception. He had come from the height of his spirit.

Lancelot said: "I'm quite rested now, thank you. I expect you want to know about the Grail."

The King said: "It has been selfish of me, I'm afraid. I have kept everybody out. We will have it written down and put in almeries at Salisbury. But we did want to hear it from you first, Lance, without interruptions."

"Are you sure you won't be too tired to tell?"

Lancelot smiled and took their hands.

"There isn't much to tell," he said. "After all, I didn't find the Grail myself."

"Sit down and break your fast. You can talk when you have eaten. You are much thinner."

"Would you like a glass of hippocras, or some perry?"

"I am not drinking at present," he said, "thank you."

While he was eating, the King and Queen sat on either side and watched. Before he knew that he wanted the salt—just as his fingers were beginning to reach for it—they handed it to him. He laughed at their serious faces, which made him feel uncomfortable, and pretended to asperge Arthur with his cup of water to make them smile.

"Do you want a relic?" he asked. "You could have my boots if you like. They are quite worn out."

"Lancelot, it is not a thing to joke about. I believe you have seen the Holy Grail yourself."

"Even if I have seen it, I don't need to be handed the salt."

But they still looked at him.

Lancelot said: "Please understand. It is Galahad and the others who were allowed the Grail. I was not allowed it. So it will be wrong and you will hurt me, if you make a fuss about it. How many of the knights got back?"

"Half," said Arthur. "We have heard their stories."

"I expect you know more about it than I do."

"We only know that the homicides and those who didn't confess were turned back; and you say that Galahad, Bors, and Percivale were allowed. I am told that Galahad and Percivale were virgins; and Bors, although he was not quite a virgin, turned out to be a first–class theologian. I suppose Bors passed for his dogma, and Percivale for his innocence. I know hardly anything about Galahad, except that everybody dislikes him."

"Dislikes him?"

"They complain about his being inhuman."

Lancelot considered his cup.

"He is inhuman," he said at last. "But why should he be human? Are angels supposed to be human?"

"I don't quite follow."

"Do you think that if the Archangel Michael were to come here this minute, he would say: 'What charming weather we are having today! Won't you have a glass of whisky?'"

"I suppose not."

"Arthur, you mustn't feel that I am rude when I say this. You must remember that I have been away in strange and desert places, sometimes quite alone, sometimes in a boat with nobody but God and the whistling sea. Do you know, since I have been back with people, I have felt I was going mad? Not from the sea, but from the people. All my gains are slipping away, with the people round me. A lot of the things which you and Jenny say, even, seem to me to be needless: strange noises: empty. You know what I mean. 'How are you?'—'Do sit down.'—'What nice weather we are having!' What does it matter? People talk far too much. Where I have been, and where Galahad is, it is a waste of time to have 'manners.' Manners are only needed between people, to keep their empty affairs in working order. Manners makyth man, you know, not God. So you can understand how Galahad may have seemed inhuman, and mannerless, and so on, to the people who were buzzing and clacking about him. He was far away in his spirit, living on desert islands, in silence, with eternity."

"I see."

"Please don't think me rude to say these things. I am trying to explain a feeling. If you had ever been to Patrick's Purgatory, you would know what I mean. People seem ridiculous when you come out."

"I see exactly. I understand about Galahad too."

"He was a lovely person really. I spent a long time in a boat with him, and I know. But this did not mean that we always had to be offering each other the best seat in the boat."

"It was my worldly knights who disliked him most. I see. However, we are waiting to hear your story, Lance, not Galahad's."

"Yes, Lance; tell us how you got on, and leave out about the angels."

"As I was never allowed to meet any angels," said Sir Lancelot with a smile, "it's the best thing I can do."

"Go on."

"When I left Vagon," began the commander–in–chief, "I had a shrewd idea that the best place to search would be the castle of King Pelles—"

He stopped, for Guenever had made a sudden move.

"I didn't go to the castle," he said gently, "because I had an accident. Something happened to me which was outside my own plans, and after that I went where I was taken."

"What was the accident?"

"It was not an accident really. It was the first stroke of a correction which I have had, and for which I am thankful. Do you know, I shall be talking about God a great deal, and this is a word which offends unholy people just as badly as words like 'damn' and so on offend the holy ones. What shall we have to do about it?"

"Just assume that we are the holy ones," said the King, "and go on about your accident."

"I was riding with Sir Percivale, when we came across my son. He unhorsed me at the first tilt—my son did."

"A surprise attack," said Arthur quickly.

"It was a fair tilt."

"Naturally you would not want to beat your son."

"I did want to beat him."

Guenever said: "Everybody has to be unlucky sometimes."

"I rode at Galahad with all the skill I could manage, and he gave me the finest fall I ever had.

"Indeed," added Lancelot, with one of his gaping grins, "I might say that he gave me one of the only falls I ever had. The first thing I can remember feeling, when I was lying on the ground, was pure astonishment. It was only later that it turned to something else."

"What did you do?"

"I was lying on the ground, and Galahad was standing his horse beside me without saying a word, when a woman came up who was a recluse in a hermitage where we had been fighting. She made a curtsy and said: 'God be with thee, best knight of the world'."

Lancelot looked on the table, and moved his hand in a gesture to stroke the cloth. Then he cleared his throat and said: "I looked up, to see who was talking to me."

The King and Queen waited.

Lancelot cleared his throat again: "I am trying to tell you about my spirit, if you see what I mean, not about my adventures. So I can't be modest about it. I am a bad man, I know, but I was always good with arms. It was a consolation to me in my badness, sometimes, to think—to know that I was the best knight of the world."

"And so?"

"Well, the lady was not talking to me."

They digested the position in silence, watching a flutter which had developed on the right side of his mouth.

"Galahad?"

"Yes," said Sir Lancelot. "The lady was looking past me at my son Galahad, and he cantered away as soon as she had spoken. Soon afterwards the lady went away as well."

"What a disgusting thing to say!" exclaimed the King. "What a dirty, deliberate outrage! She ought to have been whipped."

"It was true."

"But to come and say it in front of you on purpose!" cried Guenever. "Besides, after a single fall—"

"She said what God told her to say. You see, she was a holy woman. But I couldn't understand it at the time—

"I am much holier now," he added apologetically, "but at the time I couldn't bear it. I felt as if my prop had been taken from me, and I knew that she only said the simple truth. I felt as if she had broken the last piece of my heart. So I rode away from Percivale to be by myself, like an animal, with my hurt. Percivale suggested something to do, but I only said: 'Do as ye list.' I rode away with heavy cheer, overthwart and endlong, to find a place where I could split my heart alone. I rode to a chapel eventually, feeling as if I might be going mad again. You see, Arthur, I had a lot of troubles on my mind which being a famous fighter seemed to make up for, a little, and when that was gone it felt as if there was nothing left to me."

"There was everything left. You are still the finest fighter in the world."

"The funny thing was that the chapel had no door. I don't know whether it was my sins, or my resentment at being broken, but I couldn't get in. I slept on my shield outside, and there was a dream of a knight who came and took away my helm and my sword and my horse. I tried to wake up, but I couldn't. All my knightly things were being taken away from me, but I could not wake, because my heart was full of bitter thoughts. A voice said that I was never more to have worship—but I only rebelled against the voice, and so, when I woke, the things were gone.

"Arthur, if I don't make you understand about that night, you will never understand the rest. I had spent all my childhood, when I might have been chasing butterflies, learning to be your best knight. Afterwards I was wicked, but I had one thing. I used to feel so proud, inside myself, because I knew that I was supposed to be top of the averages. It was a base feeling, I know. But I had nothing else to be proud of. First my Word and my miracles had gone, and now, on the night I am telling you about, this was gone too. When I woke up and found that my arms were taken, I walked about in agony. It was disgusting, but I cried and cursed. That was the time when they began to break me."

"My poor Lance."

"It was the best thing that ever happened. In the morning, do you know, I heard the little fowls singing—and that cheered me up. Funny to be comforted by a lot of birds. I never had time for bird's–nesting when I was small. You would have known what kind of birds they were, Arthur—but I couldn't tell. There was one very small one, which cocked its tail in the air and looked at me. It was about as big as the rowel of a spur."

"Perhaps it was a wren."

"Well, then, it was a wren. Will you show me one tomorrow? The thing which these birds made me see, because my black heart could not see it alone, was that if I was to be punished, it was because of my own nature. What happened to the birds was according to the nature of birds. They made me see that the world was beautiful if you were beautiful, and that you couldn't get unless you gave. And you had to give without wanting to get. So I accepted that beating from Galahad, and the taking away of my armour; and in a blessed moment, I went to find a confessor so that I would not be wicked any more."

"All the knights," said Arthur, "who got to the Grail had the sense to be confessed first."

"I had always made bad confessions before that. I have lived nearly all my life in mortal sin. But this time I confessed everything."

"Everything?" asked the Queen.

"Everything. You see, Arthur, I have had a sin on my conscience all my life, which I thought I could not tell to people, because—"

"There is no need to tell it to us," said the Queen, "if it hurts you. After all, we are not your confessors. It was enough to tell the priest."

"Leave her in peace," agreed the King. "At any rate she bore a fine son, who seems to have achieved the Grail."

He was alluding to Elaine.

Lancelot looked with sudden misery from one to the other, and clenched his fists. All three stopped breathing.

"I confessed, then," he said eventually, and they breathed again—but his voice was leaden. "I was given a penance." He paused, still doubtful, half recognizing the moment as a cross–road of his life. Now was the time, they all knew, if there ever was to be a time, when he ought to have had it out with his friend and king—yet Guenever was thwarting him. It was her secret too.

"The penance was to wear the hair shirt of a certain dead religious that we knew of," he went on at last, defeated. "I was to take no meat or wine, and to hear Mass daily. So I left the priest's house after three days, and rode back to a cross near the place where I had lost my arms. The priest had loaned me some to go on with. Well, I slept at the cross that night, and had another dream—and in the morning, the knight who had stolen my armour came back. I jousted with him and retrieved the armour. Wasn't that strange?"

"I suppose you were in a state of grace now, after your good confession, so you could be trusted with your might."

"That was what I thought, but you will see about it presently. I thought, now that I had got my sin off my chest, I would be allowed to be the best knight in the world once more. I rode away very happy, trying to sing a bit, until I came to a fair plain with a castle and pavilions and everything—and there was a tournament of five hundred knights in black and white. The white knights were winning, so I thought I would join with the black. I thought I would do a great exploit of rescue for the weaker party, now that I was forgiven." He stopped, and closed his eyes. "But the white knights," he added, opening them, "took me prisoner quite soon."

"You mean you were beaten again?"

"I was beaten and disgraced. I thought I was more sinful than ever. When they had set me loose, I rode and cursed just as I had done on the first evening, and, when the night came, I lay down under an apple tree and actually cried myself to sleep."

"But this is heresy," exclaimed the Queen, who was a good theologian, like most women. "If you were clean confessed, and had done penance and been absolved—"

"I had done penance for one sin," said Lancelot. "But I had forgotten about another one. In the night I had a new dream, of an old man who came to me and said: 'Ah, Lancelot of evil faith and poor belief, why is thy will turned so lightly toward thy deadly sin?' Jenny, I have all my life been in another sin, the worst of all. It was pride that made me try to be the best knight in the world. Pride made me show off and help the weaker party of the tournament. You could call it vainglory. Just because I had confessed about—about the woman, that did not make me into a good man."

"So you were beaten."

"Yes, I was beaten. And next morning I went to another hermit to be confessed again. This time I made a thorough job of it. I was told that it was not enough, in the Quest for the Grail, to be continent and to refrain from killing people. All boasting and pride of the world had to be left behind, for God did not like such deeds in his Quest. I had to renounce all earthly glory. And I did renounce it, and was absolved."

"What happened next?"

"I rode to the water of Mortoise, where a black knight came to joust with me. He knocked me down as well."

"A third defeat!"

Guenever cried: "But if you really were absolved this time!"

Lancelot put his hand over hers, and smiled.

"If a boy steals sweets," he said, "and his parents punish him, he may be very sorry and good afterwards. But that doesn't entitle him to steal more sweets, does it? Nor does it mean that he must be given sweets. God was not punishing me by letting the black knight knock me down—he was only withholding the special gift of victory which it had always been within his power to bestow."

"But, my poor Lance, to have given up your glory and not to get anything back! When you were a sinful man you were always victorious, so why should you always be beaten when you were heavenly? And why are you always hurt by the things you love? What did you do?"

"I knelt down in the water of Mortoise, Jenny, where he had knocked me —and I thanked God for the adventure."

Chapter XXXIII

Arthur could not stand much more of this.

"It is disgusting," he exclaimed indignantly. "I don't like to listen to it. Why should a good, kind, dear person be tortured like that? It makes me feel ashamed inside, even to hear of it. What—"

"Hush," said Sir Lancelot. "I am very glad that I gave up love and glory. And, what is more, I was practically forced to do it. God did not take such pains for Gawaine or Lionel, did he?"

"Bah!" said King Arthur, in the tone which Gawaine had used before him.

Lancelot laughed.

"Well," he said, "that's a convincing remark. But perhaps you had better hear the end of the story.

"I lay down by the water of Mortoise that evening, and a dream came which told me to go in a ship. The ship was there when I woke up, sure enough; and when I went inside it there was the most lovely smell and feeling and food to eat and—well, whatever, you can think of. I was 'fulfilled with all things that I thought on or desired'. I know I can't explain to you about the ship at this hour, because, for one thing, it is fading from me now that I am with people. But you mustn't think just of incense in the ship, or precious cloths on it. There were these, but they were not the loveliness. You must think of a tar smell too, and the colours of the sea. Sometimes it was quite green, like thick glass, and you could see the bottom. Sometimes it was all in big, slow terraces, and the water fowl who were flying along the top vanished in the hollows. When it was stormy, the huge fangs of the breakers gnawed at the rocky islands. They made white fangs on the cliffs, not as they burst up, but as the water streamed down. At night, when it was calm, you could see the stars reflected on the wet sands. There were two stars quite close together. The sands were all ribbed, like the roof of your mouth. And there was the smell of seaweed, the noise of the lonely wind. There were islands with little birds on them like rabbits, but their noses were rainbows. The winter was the best thing, because then there were the geese on the islands—long smoke lines of them singing like hounds in the cold streak of morning.

"It is no good being indignant about what God did to me at the beginning, Arthur, for he gave me far more in return. I said: 'Fair Sweet Father Jesu Christ, I wot not in what joy I am, for this joy passeth all earthly joys that ever I was in.'

"A strange feature about the ship was that there was a dead woman in it. She had a letter in her hand which told me how the others had been getting on. It was stranger still that I was not frightened of her for being dead. She had such a calm face that she was company for me. We felt a sort of communion together in the ship and in the sea. I don't know what I was fed on.

"When I had been in this ship with the dead lady for a month, Galahad was brought to us. He gave me his blessing, and let me kiss his sword."

Arthur was as red as a turkey cock.

"Did you ask for his blessing?" he demanded.

"Of course."

"Well!" said Arthur.

"We sailed in the holy ship for six months together. I got to know my son very well in that time, and he seemed to care for me. Quite often, he said the most courteous things. We had adventures with animals on the out islands all that time. There were sea weasels which whistled beautifully, and Galahad showed me cranes flying along the water, with their shadows flying under them, upside down. He told me that the fishing people call a cormorant the Old Black Hag, and that ravens live as long as men. They went cronk, cronk, high in the air, and came tumbling down for fun. One day we saw a pair of choughs: they were beautiful! And the seals! They came along beside the music of the ship, and talked like men.

"One Monday we came to a forest land. A white knight rode down to the shore and told Galahad to come out of the boat. I knew that he was being taken away to find the Holy Grail, so I was sad that I couldn't go too. Do you remember, when you were little, how children used to pick up sides for a game and perhaps you wouldn't be picked at all? It felt like that, but worse. I asked Galahad to pray for me. I asked him to pray God to hold me in his service. Then we kissed each other and said good–bye."

Guenever complained: "If you were in a state of grace, I can't understand why you should have been left."

"It is difficult," said Lancelot.

He opened his hands and looked between them on the table.

"Perhaps my intentions were bad," he said at length. "Perhaps, inside myself, unconsciously, you could say, I had not a proper purpose of amendment...."

The Queen was subtly radiant as she listened.

"Nonsense," she whispered, meaning the opposite. She pressed his hand warmly, and Lancelot took it away.

"When I prayed to be *held*," he said, "perhaps it was because..."

"It seems to me," said Arthur, "that you are allowing yourself the luxury of a needlessly tender conscience."

"Perhaps. At all events, I was not picked."

He sat, watching the sea heaving between his hands, and hearing the wooden clatter of gannets on an island cliff.

"The ship took me out to sea again," he said at length, "on a big wind. I did not sleep very much, and I prayed a great deal. I asked that, in spite of not being picked, I might be allowed to get some tidings of the Sangreal."

In the silence which fell on the room, they pursued their separate thoughts. Arthur's were of the pitiful spectacle—the show of an earthly, sinful man, but the best of them, plodding along behind these three supernatural virgins; his doomed, courageous, vain toil.

"Funny," said Lancelot, "how the people who can't pray say that prayers are not answered, however much the people who can pray say they are.

My ship took me at midnight, in a great gale, to the back side of Carbonek Castle. Strange, also, that it should have been the very place I was heading for when I started.

"The moment the ship came alongside, I knew that I was to be granted a part of my desire. I couldn't see it all, of course, because I was not a Galahad or Bors. But they were very kind to me. They went out of their way to be kind.

"It was black as death behind the castle. I put on my armour and went up. There were two lions at the entry of the stairs, who tried to bar my way. I drew my sword to fight them, but a hand struck me on the arm. It was silly of me, of course, to trust in my sword, when I could have trusted in God. So I blessed myself with my numb arm and went in, and the lions didn't hurt me. All the doors were open except the last one, and there I kneeled down. When I prayed, it opened.

"Arthur, this must seem untrue as I tell it. I don't know a way of putting it in words. Behind the last door there was a chapel. They were at Mass.

"Oh, Jenny, the beautiful chapel with all its lights and everything! You would say: 'The flowers and the candles.' But it was not these. Perhaps there were none.

"It was, oh, the shout of it—the power and the glory. It seized on all my senses to drag me in.

"But I couldn't go in, Arthur and Jenny—there was a sword to stop me. Galahad was inside, and Bors, and Percivale. There were nine other knights, from France and Danemark and Ireland: and the lady from my ship was there as well. The Grail was there, Arthur, on a silver table, and other things! But I was forbidden to go in, for all my yearning at the door. I don't know who the priest was. It may have been Joseph of Arimathea, it may have been—oh, well. I did go in to help him—in spite of the sword— because he was carrying what was too heavy to be carried. I only wanted to help, Arthur, as God was my witness. But a breath smote my face at the last door like a blast from a furnace, and there I fell down dumb."

Chapter XXXIV

In the dark chamber there was a coming and going of maids. The cans and pails rattled on the stairway, and there was much steam. When the maids trod in the puddles on the floor, they made a slashing noise, and from the next room there was whispering mixed with the secret noise of silk.

The Queen had climbed the six steps of the wooden ladder which led to her bath, and now she was sitting on the plank inside it, with her head showing over the top. The bath was like a large beer barrel, and her head was wrapped in a white turban. She was naked, except for a pearl necklace. There was a mirror—it had been very expensive—in one corner, and a little table in another one held the scents and oils. Instead of a powder puff, there was a chamois leather bag with powdered chalk in it, scented with attar of roses from the crusades. All over the floor between the puddles, there was a confusion of linen towels for drying her, and of jewellery boxes, brocades, garments, garters, shifts, which had been brought from the other room for her to choose. There were some condemned head–dresses lying in disgrace—strange shapes of starch like candle extinguishers, and meringues, and the double horns of cows. The hair nets which kept them together were strung with pearls, and the kerchiefs were of Eastern silk. One of the ladies–in–waiting was standing in front of the Queen's tub, holding an embroidered mantle for inspection. It was charged with the impaled arms of her husband and of her father: the dragon rampant of England and the six charming lioncels passant regardant of King Leodegrance, who bore lions on account of his name. This mantle had a heavy silk tassel, like a curtain cord, to join it across her breast. The silk bordure was furred with countervair, silver and blue.

Guenever had lost her raddled look, and sat accepting the clothes which were recommended for her, without fuss. The ladies–in–waiting had a happy air. For more than a year they had waited on a Queen who was petulant, cruel, contradictory, miserable. Now she was pleased with anything, and did not hunt them. They were all quite sure that Lancelot must have become her lover again. This was not the case.

Guenever looked upon the six lioncels passant regardant—they were marching along with red tongues and claws, winking pertly over their backsides and waving their flame–tipped tails. She nodded her head with a contented, sleepy look, and the lady–in–waiting carried it to the dressing–room with a curtsy. The Queen watched her go.

You could pretend that Guenever was a sort of man–eating lioncelle herself, or that she was one of those selfish women who insist on ruling everywhere. In fact, this is what she did seem to be, to a superficial inspection. She was beautiful, sanguine, hot–tempered, demanding, impulsive, acquisitive, charming—she had all the proper qualities for a man–eater. But the rock on which these easy explanations founder, is that she was not promiscuous. There was never anybody in her life except Lancelot and Arthur. She never ate anybody except these. And even these she did not eat in the full sense of the word. People who have been digested by a man–eating lioncelle tend to become nonentities—to live no life except within the vitals of the devourer. Yet both Arthur and Lancelot, the people whom she apparently devoured, lived full lives, and accomplished things of their own.

One explanation of Guenever, for what it is worth, is that she was what they used to call a "real" person. She was not the kind who can be fitted away safely under some label or other, as "loyal" or "disloyal" or "self–sacrificing" or "jealous". Sometimes she was loyal and sometimes she was disloyal. She behaved like herself. And there must have been something in this self, some sincerity of heart, or she would not have held two people like Arthur and Lancelot. Like likes like, they say—and at least they are certain that her men were generous. She must have been generous too. It is difficult to write about a real person.

She lived in warlike times, when the lives of young people were as short as those of airmen in the twentieth century. In such times, the elderly moralists are content to relax their moral laws a little, in return for being defended. The condemned pilots, with their lust for the life and love which is probably to be lost so soon, touch the hearts of young women, or possibly call up an answering bravado. Generosity, courage, honesty, pity, the faculty to look short life in the face—certainly comradeship and tenderness—these qualities may explain why Guenever took Lancelot as well as Arthur. It was courage more than anything else—the courage to take and give from the heart, while there was time. Poets are always urging women to have this kind of courage. She gathered her rose–buds while she might, and the striking thing was that she only gathered two of them, which she kept always, and that those two were the best.

Guenever's central tragedy was that she was childless. Arthur had two illegitimate children, and Lancelot had Galahad. But Guenever—and she was the one of the three who most ought to have had children, and who would have been best with children, and whom God had seemingly made for breeding lovely children—she was the one who was left an empty vessel, a shore without a sea. This was what broke her when she came to the age at which her sea must finally dry. It is what turned her for a little time into a raving woman, though that time was still in the future. It may be one of the explanations of her double love—perhaps she loved Arthur as a father, and Lancelot because of the son she could not have.

People are easily dazzled by Round Tables and feats of arms. You read of Lancelot in some noble achievement, and, when he comes home to his mistress, you feel resentment at her because she cuts across the achievement, or spoils it. Yet Guenever could not search for the Grail. She could not vanish into the English forest for a year's adventure with the spear. It was her part to sit at home, though passionate, though real and hungry in her fierce and tender heart. For her there were no recognized diversions except what is comparable to the ladies' bridge party of today. She could hawk with a merlin, or play blind man's buff, or pince–merille. These were the amusements of grown–up women in her time. But the great hawks, the hounds, heraldry, tournaments—these were for Lancelot. For her, unless she felt like a little spinning or embroidery, there was no occupation—except Lancelot.

So we must imagine the Queen as a woman who had been robbed of her central attribute. As she grew to her difficult age, she did strange things. She was even to be suspected of poisoning a knight. She even became unpopular. But unpopularity is often a compliment—and Guenever, though she lived tempestuously and finally died in an unreconciled sort of way—she was not cut out for religion, as Lancelot was—was never insignificant. She did what women do, on the whole right royally, and at the moment, in the tub with the lioncels before her, she was busy doing it.

When a man had practically seen God, however human he might be, you could not immediately expect him as a lover. When the man was Lancelot, who was mad on God in any case, you had to be both sanguine and cruel to expect him like that at all. But women are cruel in this way. They do not accept excuses.

Guenever knew that Lancelot would come back to her. She had known it from the moment when he had prayed to be "held." The knowledge had revived her like a watered flower too long left unwatered. It had swept away the rouge and bedizening silks which had moved his pity when he first came back. Now it only remained for her to accomplish the reunion smoothly and fully. There was no hurry.

Lancelot, who did not know that he was to betray his much–loved God again for the sake of the Queen, was made happy by her attitude—though it surprised him. He had feared some terrible scene of jealousy or recrimination. He had wondered how he would be able to explain to the tortured child, imprisoned in the painted eyes, that he could not come to her—that he had a sweeter necessity, however much her pain. He had been afraid that she would attack him, would lay her poor snares before him— snares which would be all the more pitifully beguiling because of their poverty. He had really not known how he was to face the pity.

Instead, Guenever had bloomed and lost her paints. She had made no assault, no recrimination. She had smiled with real joy. Women, he had told himself wisely, were unpredictable. He had even been able to discuss the matter with her, in complete frankness, and she had agreed with what he said.

Guenever, sitting in the bath and looking sightlessly upon the lioncels, had a sleepy look of secret happiness when she remembered their conversation. She saw the charming, ugly face, talking so seriously about the interests of its honest heart. She loved these interests—loved the old soldier to follow so faithfully his innocent love of God. She knew it was doomed to failure.

Lancelot had said, apologizing and begging her not to think him offensive, (1) that they could not very well go back to the old way, after the Grail; (2) that, had it not been for their guilty love, he might have been allowed to achieve the Grail; (3) that it would be dangerous in any case, because the Orkney faction was beginning to watch them unpleasantly, particularly Agravaine and Mordred; and (4) that it would be a great shame to themselves and also to Arthur. He numbered the points carefully.

At other times he tried to explain to her, in confused words and at great length, about his discovery of God. He thought that if he could convert

Guenever to God, this would solve the moral problem. If they could go to God together, he would not be deserting his mistress or sacrificing her happiness to his own.

The Queen smiled outright. He was a darling. She had agreed with every word he said—was a regular convert already!

Then she lifted one white arm out of the bath, and reached for a scrubbing brush on an ivory handle.

CHAPTER XXXV

It was all very well at the first flush of his return. Queens may see further ahead than common men, but there seems to be a limit to their vision. It was fine to wait with a warm feeling while Lancelot kept faith with his divinity for a week or for a month. But, when the months began to grow to a year, then it was a different matter. Perhaps he would relapse in the end —perhaps. But a woman could wait too long for victory—she could be too old to enjoy it. It could be senseless to go on waiting for a joy, when joy was on the doorstep, and Time hurried by.

Guenever grew slowly, not less blooming, but angrier. A storm gathered in her deep breasts, as the months of holiness added together. Holiness? Selfishness, she cried to herself—selfish to abandon another soul so as to save your own. The story of Bors, allowing the twelve supposed gentlewomen to be hurled from the castle turret rather than save them by committing a mortal sin, had shocked her to the heart. Now Lancelot was doing the same thing. It was well for him, with his chivalry and mysticism and all the compensations of the male world, to make the grand renunciation. But it took two to make a renunciation, just as it took two to make love, or to make a quarrel. She was not an insensate piece of property, to be taken up or laid down at his convenience. You could not give up a human heart as you could give up drinking. The drink was yours, and you could give it up: but your lover's soul was not your own: it was not at your disposal; you had a duty towards it.

Lancelot saw these things as clearly as the bold Guenever—and, as their relations gradually worsened, he was hard put to it to keep his mind. It was for him the same as it had been for Bors, when the unarmed hermit interfered. So far as he himself was concerned, he had every right to insist on yielding to the God he loved, as Bors had yielded to Lionel. But when Guenever threw herself across him, as the hermit had thrown himself across Bors, had he the right to sacrifice his old love as the hermit had been sacrificed? Lancelot, like the Queen, was shocked by the solutions of Bors. The hearts of these two lovers were instinctively too generous to fit with dogma. Generosity is the eighth deadly sin.

It came to a head one morning, while they were singing together, alone in the solar. A musical instrument called a regal stood on the table between them. It looked like two large bibles. Guenever had sung a little piece by French Mary, and Lancelot was plodding his way through another by the hunchback of Arras, when the Queen put her right hand on all the notes which she could cover, and pressed both bibles with her left. The regal gave a dreadful sneer, and died.

"Why did you do that?"

"You had better go," she said. "Go away. Start a quest. Can't you see that you are wearing me out?"

Lancelot took a deep breath and said: "Yes, I do see it, every day."

"Then you had better go. No, I am not making a scene. I don't want to quarrel about it, and I don't want to alter your mind. But I think it would be kinder if you went."

"It sounds as if I were hurting you on purpose."

"No. It is not your fault. But I would just like you to go, Lance, so as to give me a rest. For a little while. We needn't fight about it."

"If you want me to go, I will, of course."

"I do want you to."

"Perhaps it would be better."

"Lance, I want you to realize that I am not trying to trick you into anything, or to force you. It is only that I think it would be good for us to be parted for a month or two, as friends. It is only that."

"I know you would never try to trick me, Jenny. And I feel muddled too. I was hoping that you would understand about it. About what has happened to me. It would have been easy if you had been on that boat as well, or felt it yourself. But I can't make you feel it, because you were not there, and so it is difficult for me. I feel as if I were sacrificing you, or us if you like, to a new sort of love…

"And besides," he said, turning away, "it is not as if—as if I didn't want my old love too."

After he had stood in silence for a minute, looking out of the window with his hands unnaturally still at his sides, he added in a harsh voice, without turning round: "If you like, we will start again."

When he swung round from the window, the room was empty. After dinner he asked for the Queen at her door, but received only a verbal message begging him to do as she had asked. He packed his scanty traps, not understanding what had happened, but feeling that he had escaped calamity by a hairbreadth. He said good–bye to his bent old squire, who was now far too ancient to go with him in any case, and rode from Camelot next morning.

Chapter XXXVI

If the maids–in–waiting were pleased by the Queen's supposed renewal of intrigue, there were others at court who were not. Or, if they were pleased, it was a cruel and waiting pleasure. The tone of the court had changed for the fourth time.

There had been the first feeling, a companionship of youth under which Arthur had launched his grand crusade—the second, of chivalrous rivalry growing staler every year in the greatest court of Europe, until it had nearly turned to feud and competition. Then the enthusiasm of the Grail had burned the bad gasses of the air into a short–lived beauty. Now the maturest or the saddest phase had come, in which enthusiasms had been used up for good, and only our famous seventh sense was left to be practised. The court had "knowledge of the world" now: it had the fruits of achievement, civilization, savoir–vivre, gossip, fashion, malice, and the broad mind of scandal.

Half the knights had been killed—the best half. What Arthur had feared from the start of the Grail Quest had come to pass. If you achieve perfection, you die. There had been nothing left for Galahad to ask of God, except death. The best knights had gone to perfection, leaving the worst to hold their sieges. A leaven of love was left, it is true—Lancelot, Gareth, Aglovale and a few old dodderers like Sir Grummore and Sir Palomides: but the tone was set elsewhere. It came from the surly angers of Gawaine, the fripperies of Mordred, and the sarcasms of Agravaine. Tristram had done no good to it in Cornwall. A magic cloak had gone the rounds, which only a faithful wife could wear—or perhaps it was a magic horn which only a faithful wife could drink from. A canting shield had been presented with a voiceless snigger, a shield whose blazon was a hint to cuckolds. Marital fidelity had become "news." Clothes had become fantastic. The long toes of Agravaine's slippers were secured by gold chains to garters below his knee, and, as for Mordred's toes, their chains were secured to a belt round his waist. The surcoats, which had originally served as covering to armour, were long behind and high in front. You could hardly walk for fear of tripping over your sleeves. Ladies were compelled to shave their foreheads and to show no hair, if they wanted to be in the mode, while, so far as their sleeves were concerned, they had to tie knots in them to keep them off the floor. Gentlemen showed their legs to an equally startling extent. Their clothes were parti–coloured. Sometimes one leg was red and the other was green. And they did not wear their slittered mantle, their gaycoat graceless, from a sense of exuberance. Mordred wore his ridiculous shoes contemptuously: they were a satire on himself. The court was modern.

So there were eyes on Guenever now—not the eyes of strong suspicion or of warm connivance, but the bored looks of calculation and the cold ones of society. At the mouse–hole the sleek cats were still.

Mordred and Agravaine thought Arthur hypocritical—as all decent men must be, if you assume that decency can't exist. They found Guenever barbarous.

La Beale Isoud, they said, had made a cuckold of King Mark in a civilized way. She had done it with an air, publicly, fashionably, in the best taste. Everybody had been able to rub it into the King, and to enjoy the fun. She had shown a perfect flair for dress, for comic hats which made her look like a tipsy heifer. She had spent millions of Mark's money on peacock tongues for dinner.

Guenever, on the other hand, dressed like a gipsy, entertained like a lodging–house keeper, and kept her lover a secret. On top of this, she was a nuisance. She had no sense of style. She was growing old ungracefully, and she cried or made scenes like a fishwife. It was said that she had sent Lancelot away after a terrible quarrel, during which she had accused him of loving other women. She was supposed to have cried out: "I see and feel daily that thy love beginneth to slake." Mordred said, in his equivocal, musical voice, that he could understand a fishwife, but not a fish mistress. The epigram was widely reported.

Arthur, reserved and unhappy in the new atmosphere which had begun to pull away from him instead of with him, moved about the palace in his plain dress, trying to be polite. The Queen, more aggressive—she had been a bold girl as he first remembered her, with dark hair and red lips, tossing her head—went out to meet the situation, and tried to deal with it by entertaining and by pretending to be fashionable herself. She fell back on the paints and finery which she had left when Lancelot returned. She began to behave as if she were a little mad. All glorious reigns have these blank patches, during which the Crown is unpopular.

Trouble came suddenly, while Lancelot was away. The feeling of danger, which had hung in the air since the Grail, suddenly crystallized upon a dinner party given by the Queen.

It seems that Gawaine was fond of fruit. He liked apples and pears best— and the poor Queen, anxious to be successful in her new line as a fashionable entertainer, took particular care to have nice apples when she gave a dinner for twenty–four knights, at which Gawaine was to be present. She knew that the Cornwall and Orkney faction had always been the menace to her husband's hopes—and Gawaine was now the head of the clan. She hoped that the dinner would be a success, that it would help in the new atmosphere, that it would be a sophisticated dinner. She was trying to placate her critics by being a courteous hostess like La Beale Isoud.

Unfortunately there were other people who knew of Gawaine's weakness for apples, and bad blood over the Pellinore murders still existed. Arthur had managed to wean Sir Aglovale from his revenge, it is true, and the old feud seemed to have healed over. But there was a knight called Sir Pinel, who was a distant relative of the Pellinores, and he considered that revenge was necessary. Sir Pinel poisoned the apples.

Poison is a bad weapon. It went astray in this case, as it often does, and an Irish knight called Patrick ate the apple which was intended for Gawaine.

You can imagine the situation: the pale knights starting to their feet in the candlelight, the ineffectual attempts at aid, and their supposing eyes turning upon one another with ashamed suspicion. Everybody knew of Gawaine's foible. His family had never been favourites with the now unpopular Queen. She herself had given the dinner. And Pinel was not in a position to explain. Somebody in that room had murdered Sir Patrick in mistake for Gawaine, and until the murderer was discovered they would all be under the same suspicion. Sir Mador de la Porte—more pompous than the rest, or more malevolent, or more of a stickler—ended by voicing the thought which was in every mind. He accused the Queen of treason.

Nowadays, when a point of justice is obscure and difficult, each side hires lawyers to argue it out. In those days the upper classes hired champions to fight it out—which came to the same thing. Sir Mador decided to save himself the expense of a champion by fighting his own case, and he insisted that Guenever must brief a champion for her defence. Arthur, whose whole philosophy of royalty hinged on justice instead of power, could do nothing to save his wife. If Mador demanded the Court of Honour, he must have it. And Arthur could not fight in his wife's quarrel, just as married people are not allowed to give evidence against each other today.

Here was a pretty state of affairs. Suspicion and rumour and counter–recrimination had obscured the issue almost before it started. The Pellinore feud, the old Pendragon–Cornwall feud, the Lancelot entanglement, and then the sudden death of a person not apparently concerned with any of them—all these mixed themselves together into a fume of venom which coiled about the Queen. If Lancelot had been there, he would have fought as her champion. But she had sent him away—nobody knew where, some thought to his parents in France. Perhaps, if he had been known to be on hand, Sir Mador might have swallowed his accusation.

It seems kinder not to dwell on the days before the trial by battle—not to describe the distracted woman kneeling to Sir Bors, who had never liked her before, and who now, just back from his virginal achievement of the Grail, liked her still less. She begged him to fight for her if Lancelot could not be found. She had to beg for it, poor creature, because the feeling at court had come to such a pitch that nobody would accept her brief. The Queen of England was unable to command a champion.

The night before the battle was the worst. All night, neither she nor Arthur slept. He firmly believed her innocence, but he could not interfere with justice. She, pathetically and repeatedly asserting this innocence, although she was in the entanglement which the other trouble had brought her to, knew that the next night might see her burned to death. Together they saw the tragedy and humiliation of their Table, from which no man was willing to save them—knew that the Queen of it was called, by common breath, a destroyer of good knights. In the bitter darkness Arthur suddenly cried despairingly: "What aileth you, that ye cannot keep Sir Lancelot on your side?" And so it went on until the morning.

CHAPTER XXXVII

Sir Bors the misogynist had reluctantly consented to fight for the Queen, if nobody else could be found. He had explained that it was irregular to do so, because he himself had been present at the dinner—but, when discovered by Arthur with the Queen kneeling at his feet, he had blushed, raised her, and consented. Then he had vanished for a day or two, because the trial was not to take place for a fortnight.

A meadow at Westminster had been prepared for the combat. A barricade of strong logs, like a corral for horses, had been erected round the wide square—which had no barrier down the middle. For an ordinary joust there would have been a barrier: but in this case the fight was to be à outrance, which meant that it might end with swords on foot, and so the barrier was left out. A pavilion had been erected for the King on one side, and another one for the Constable on the other. The barricades and the pavilions were decorated with cloth. There was a curtained gateway at each end, like the dramatic hole through which the circus people ride into their arena. In one corner of the corral, visible for all to see, was a great bundle of faggots with an iron stake in the middle, which would not burn or melt. This was for the Queen, if the law went against her. Before Arthur had started his life's work, a man accusing the Queen of anything would have been executed out of hand. Now, because of his own work, he must be ready to burn his wife.

For a new idea had begun to form in the King's mind. The efforts to dig a channel for Might had failed, even when it was turned to the spirit, and now he was feeling his way towards abolishing it. He had decided not to truckle with Might any more—to cut it out, root and branch, by establishing another standard altogether. He was groping towards Right as a criterion of its own—towards Justice as an abstract thing which did not lean upon power. In a few years he would be inventing Civil Law.

It was a cold day. The cloths strained against the scaffolding of barricade and pavilion, and the pennons lay taut on the wind. In the corner the executioner blew on his nails, standing close to the brazier from which he would take the fire for his bigger blaze. The heralds in the Constable's pavilion moistened their lips, which the breeze was cracking, before lifting their trumpets for a fanfare. Guenever, sitting between guards under the Constable's ward, had to ask for a shawl. The people noticed that she was thinner. It was the bleak face of middle age, waiting intent and stoical between the beefy faces of the soldiers.

Naturally it was Lancelot who rescued her. Bors had managed to find him at an abbey, during his two days' absence, and now he came back in the nick of time to fight Sir Mador for the Queen. Nobody who knew him would have expected him to do anything else, whether he had been sent away in disgrace or not—but, as it was thought that he had left the country, his return did have a dramatic quality.

Sir Mador came from his recess at the south end of the lists, and proclaimed the accusation while his herald blew. Sir Bors came from the northern hole to parley with the King and with the Constable—a long, indistinct argument or explanation which the people could not catch on account of the wind. The spectators became restive, wondering what the hitch was, and why the trial by battle did not proceed in the usual way. Then, after several journeys from King's pavilion to Constable's, and vice versa, Sir Bors returned to his own hole. There was an uncomfortable pause, during which a black lap dog with a pug nose escaped into the lists and scampered about on some errand best known to itself. One of the kings–of–arms caught it and tied it with his guige, for which the people gave him an ironic cheer. Then there was silence, except for the vendors who were crying nuts and gingerbread.

Lancelot rode out from the north exit, marked with the Bors escutcheon— and immediately everybody in the amphitheatre knew that it was he, although he was disguised. The silence was as if everybody had caught their breath simultaneously.

He had not come back out of condescension to the Queen. The cruel explanation that he had "given her up" so as to save his soul, and that he had now returned from a sense of dramatic magnanimity, was not the true one. It was more complicated.

This knight's trouble from his childhood—which he never completely grew out of—was that for him God was a real person. He was not an abstraction who punished you if you were wicked or rewarded you if you were good, but a real person like Guenever, or like Arthur, or like anybody else. Of course he felt that God was better than Guenever or Arthur, but the point was that he was personal. Lancelot had a definite idea of what he looked like, and how he felt—and he was somehow in love with this Person.

The Ill–Made Knight was not involved in an Eternal Triangle. It was an Eternal Quadrangle, which was eternal as well as quadrangular. He had not given up his mistress because he was afraid of being punished by some sort of Holy Bogy, but he had been confronted by two people whom he loved. The one was Arthur's Queen, the other a wordless presence who had celebrated Mass at Castle Carbonek. Unfortunately, as so often happens in love affairs, the two objects of his affection were contradictory. It was almost as if he had been confronted with a choice between Jane and Janet —and as if he had gone to Janet, not because he was afraid that she would punish him if he stayed with Jane, but because he felt, with warmth and pity, that he loved her best. He may even have felt that God needed him more than Guenever did. This was the problem, an emotional rather than a moral one, which had taken him into retreat at his abbey, where he had hoped to feel things out.

Still, it would not be quite true to say that he had not come back from some motives of magnanimity. He was a magnanimous man. He was a maestro. Even if God's need for him was the greater in normal times, now it was obvious that his first love's need was pressing. Perhaps a man who had left Jane for Janet might have had enough warmth inside him to return for Jane, when she was in desperate need, and this warmth might be compared to pity or to magnanimity or to generosity—if it were not unfashionable and even a little disgusting to believe in these emotions nowadays. Lancelot, in any case, who was wrestling with his love for Guenever as well as with his love for God, came back to her side as soon as he knew that she was in trouble, and, when he saw her radiant face waiting for him under shameful durance, his heart did turn over inside its habergeon with some piercing emotion—call it love or pity, whichever you please.

Sir Mador de la Forte's heart turned over at the same time—but it was too late to draw back. His face went crimson inside its helm, where nobody could see it, and he felt a warm glow under the straw fillet which padded his skull. Then he went back to his own corner and spurred his horse.

There is something beautiful about the way in which a broken lance sails into the air. Down below it, on the ground, there is much bustle going on. The lazy motion with which the lance goes up, turning over silently and languidly as it goes, contrasts with this. It seems superior to earthly considerations and does not seem to be moving fast. The fast movement—which was, in this case, Sir Mador dismounting backwards and upside down—is going on underneath the lance, which performs its own independent pirouette in graceful detachment, and comes down elsewhere, when everybody has forgotten it. Sir Mador's lance came down on its point, by some ballistic freak, just behind the king–of–arms who was holding the black pug. When the latter turned round later on, and found it upright behind him, looking over his shoulder as it were, he gave a start.

Sir Lancelot dismounted, so as not to have the advantage of a horse. Sir Mador got up and began doing some wild swipes at the enemy with his sword. He was over–excited.

It took two knockouts to finish Sir Mador. The first time he was down, when Lancelot was coming towards him to accept his surrender, he became flustered and thrust at the towering man from below. It was a foul blow, for it went into the groin from underneath, just at the point where armour must necessarily be weakest. When Lancelot had withdrawn, to let Mador get up if he wanted to go on fighting, it was seen that the blood was streaming down his cuisses and greaves. There was something terrible about the patient way in which he withdrew, although he had been badly stabbed in the thigh. If he had lost his temper it would have been easier to bear.

The Queen's champion knocked Sir Mador down harder the second time. Then he jerked off his helm.

"All right," said Sir Mador. "I give in. I was wrong. Spare my life."

Lancelot did a nice thing. Most knights would have been satisfied with winning the Queen's case, and would have left it at that. But Lancelot had a sort of methodical consideration for people—he was sensitive to things which they might be feeling, or might be likely to feel.

"I will spare your life," he said, "only if you promise that nothing is to be written about this on Sir Patrick's grave. Nothing about the Queen."

"I promise," said Mador.

Then, while the defeated advocate was being carried away by some leeches, Lancelot went to the royal box. The Queen had been released immediately, and was there with Arthur.

Arthur said: "Take off your helm, stranger."

They felt a swelling of love when he took it off, and compassion to see the hideous, well–known face again, while he stood in front of them, bleeding hard.

Arthur came down from the box. He made Guenever get up, and took her hand, and led her down into the arena. He made a regular bow to Sir Lancelot, and pulled Guenever's hand so that she curtsied too. He did this in front of his people. He spoke in the old–fashioned talk, and said with a full voice: "Sir, grant mercy of your great travail that ye have had this day for me and for my Queen." Guenever, behind his smiling loving face, was sobbing as if her heart would burst.

CHAPTER XXXVIII

It so happened that the Patrick accusation was cleared up next day, when Nimue arrived with a second–sighted explanation. Merlyn, before letting her lock him up in the cave, had given the Matter of Britain into her hands. He had made her promise—it was all that he could do—that she would watch over Arthur herself, now that she knew his own magic. Then he had gone meekly to his imprisonment, casting a last, long, doting look upon her. Nimue, though scatterbrained and unpunctual, was a good girl in her way. She turned up a day late, told how the apple had come to be poisoned, and went back to her own concerns. Sir Pinel confirmed the statement by running away the same morning, leaving a written confession, and everybody had to admit that it was a lucky thing Sir Lancelot had been about.

It was not so lucky for the Queen. She was alive and saved, it was true—but the unbelievable happened. In spite of the tears, in spite of the fountain of feeling which had sprung between them once again, Lancelot persisted in remaining loyal to his Grail.

Well for him, she exclaimed—she was growing madder every day, and it hurt people to watch it—well for him to wrap himself in his new delight. He had a grand feeling, no doubt, a compensation of vigour and clarity and uplifting of the heart. Perhaps his famous God did give him something which she could not give. Perhaps he was happier with God, and would soon begin doing miracles left and right. But what about her? He was not considering what she got out of God. The position was exactly the same, she railed at him, as if he had left her for another woman. He had taken the best of her, and now that she was old and worthless he had gone elsewhere. He was behaving with the beastly selfishness of Man, taking all he could get from one quarter, and then, when that was used, going to another. He was a sneak–thief. And to think that she had believed in him! She did not love him any more now, would not let him come near her if he were to pray for it on bended knees. As a matter of fact, she had despised him even before the search for the Grail began—yes, despised him, and had determined to throw him over. He was not to think that he was deserting her: it was quite the contrary. She was tossing him away, like a dirty clout, because she felt nothing but contempt for him. For his poses and swelled head and meanness and childishness and conceit. For his futile little God, and his goody–goody lies. To tell him the truth, and really she felt no further interest in concealing it, there was a young knight at court who was already her lover: had been her lover long before the Grail! He was a much finer young man than Lancelot. What would she want with a sour husk when she had a rosy boy at her feet who worshipped her, yes, worshipped the ground she trod on? Lancelot had better return to Elaine, to the mother of his famous son. Perhaps they would be able to say their prayers together, one frump with the other frump, all night. They could talk about their baby, their Galahad, who had found the loathsome Grail, and they could laugh at her if they liked, yes, they were welcome to laugh at her, laughing because she had never managed to bear a son.

Then Guenever would begin the laughing—while always one part of her looked out from the eye windows, and hated the noise which she was making—and the tears would come after the laughter, and she would weep with all her heart.

A strange feature was that Arthur, who wanted to arrange a tournament in celebration of the Queen's acquittal, fixed upon a place near Corbin as the spot where the tournament was to be held. The place may have been Winchester or Brackley, where one of the four surviving English tilting grounds is to be found. It does not matter where it was—what does matter is that Corbin was the castle where the now childless Elaine lived out her lonely middle age.

"I suppose you will go to this tournament?" asked the Queen fiercely. "I suppose you will go to be near your trull?"

Lancelot said: "Jenny, couldn't you forgive her? She is probably ugly as well as miserable now. She never had much to fall back on."

"The generous Lancelot!"

"If you don't want me to go," he said, "I won't. You know I have never loved any human being except you."

"Only Arthur," said the Queen. "Only Elaine. Only God. Unless there are some others I haven't heard about."

Lancelot shrugged his shoulders—one of the stupidest things to do, when the other party wants to have a fight.

"Are you going?" he asked.

"I going? Am I to watch you flirting with that turnip? Certainly I shan't go, and I forbid you to go either."

"Very well," he said. "I will tell Arthur that I am ill. I could say that my wound has not healed yet."

He went to find the King.

Everybody had started for the tournament, and the court was empty, when Guenever changed her mind. Perhaps she had kept Lancelot behind so as to be alone with him, and, finding that it was no good being alone with him, had reversed her decision—but we do not know the reason.

"You had better go," she said. "If I keep you here you will say it was because I was jealous, and you will cast it in my teeth. Besides, there may be a scandal if you stay with me. And I don't want you. I don't want to see your face. Take it away. Go!"

"Jenny," he said reasonably, "I can't go now. There will be much more of a scandal if I do go after all, when I have said that my wound prevents me. They will think that we have had a quarrel."

"Let them think what they please. The only thing I tell you is that you are to go, before you drive me mad."

"Jenny," he said.

He felt that his heart was breaking in two pieces, and that the madness which she had given him once before might well be coming again. Perhaps she noticed this too. At all events, she suddenly relented in her manner. She saw him off to Corbin with a loving kiss.

"I promise I will come back," he had said, and now he was keeping his promise. It was unthinkable that he should go to the tournament without visiting Elaine. He had not only promised to return to her, but he was the repository of all the last messages of their only son, now dead or at least translated. The cruellest man could hardly have refused to visit her with such messages.

He would lodge at Corbin, tell her about Galahad, and fight in the tournament disguised. He would explain to Arthur that he had pleaded the wound so as to come unexpectedly, in disguise, because that was one of the new–fashioned things to do. This subterfuge would be assisted by the fact of his staying at Corbin castle, instead of at the actual place of the tournament. It would prevent any scandal about a last–minute quarrel with the Queen.

He was surprised to find, as he rode up the avenue to the moat, through the cheval de frise, that Elaine was waiting for him on the battlements, in the same attitude as that in which he had left her twenty years before. She met him at the Great Gate.

"I was waiting for you."

She was plump and dumpy now, rather like Queen Victoria, and she received him faithfully. He had said that he would come back and here he was. She had expected nothing else.

With her next words she stabbed him to the heart.

"You will be staying for good now," said she, hardly as a question. It was in this way that she had construed his answer when they parted all that time ago.

CHAPTER XXXIX

If people want to read about the Corbin tournament, Malory has it. He was a passionate follower of tournaments—like one of those old gentlemen who nowadays frequent the cricket pavilion at Lord's—and he may have had access to some ancient Wisden, or even to the score–books themselves. He reports the celebrated tournaments in full, with the score of each knight, and the name of the man who bowled him over, or how knocked out. But the accounts of old cricket matches are inclined to be boring for those who did not actually play in them, so we must leave it unreported. The only things which are apt to be dull in Malory are the detailed score–sheets, which he gives two or three times—and even they are not dull for anybody who knows the form of the various smaller knights. It is sufficient for our purposes to say that Lancelot hit the other side all round the field—his skill had come back to him since the Grail— and that he would have carried his sword after the innings of a lifetime, if the wound which he got from Sir Mador had not broken out afresh. It is strange that he should have played well on this occasion—for he was distracted by the triple misery of Guenever and God and Elaine—but great performances have been given by others in similar circumstances. Finally, when he had made thirty or forty in spite of the old wound (and, incidentally, he had knocked out Mordred and Agravaine), three knights set upon him at the same time, and the spear of one of them penetrated his defence. It broke, leaving the head of the spear in his side.

Lancelot withdrew from the field while he could still sit his horse, and galloped away, lolling in the saddle, to find a place where he could be alone. When he was badly hurt he had this instinct for solitude. To him, there was something private about death—so that, if he had to die, he tried to get a chance of doing it by himself. Only one knight went with him—he was too weak to shake him off—and it was this knight who helped him to draw the spearhead from his ribs, and who eased him when he finally fainted by "turning him into the wind." It was also this knight who brought the distracted Elaine to his bedside, after he had been put to bed.

The importance of the Winchester tournament did not lie in any particular feat of arms, nor even in Lancelot's grievous hurt—for he eventually recovered from it. Where it did touch the lives of our four friends was in a circumstance which remains to be told. For Lancelot, suddenly faced with the unlucky Elaine's unfounded conviction that he was going to stay with her for ever, had faltered in telling her the truth. Perhaps he was a weak man in most ways—weak to have taken Guenever from his best friend in the first place, weak to have tried to exchange his mistress for his God, and weakest of all to have helped Elaine by telling her he would come back. Now, in the face of the poor lady's simple hope, he had lacked the courage to break her illusion with an immediate blow.

One of the troubles in dealing with Elaine, in spite of her simplicity or ignorance, was that her nature was a sensitive one—more sensitive than Guenever's, in fact, although she lacked the power of that bold and extraverted queen. She had been sensitive enough not to overwhelm him with welcomes when he came home from his long absence: not to reproach him—she had never felt that she had reason to reproach him: and, above all, not to suffocate him with pity for herself. She had held her heart with a firm hand while they waited at Corbin for the tournament, carefully hiding the long years during which she had hoped for her lord, and her absolute loneliness now that their son was gone. Lancelot had known quite well what she was hiding. Uncertain and sensitive himself, he had forgotten about the way in which their peculiar relationship had started. He had begun to blame himself exclusively for Elaine's sorrows.

So, when she did make her small request, after having spared him so many tears and welcomes, what could he do but seek her pleasure? He had still to tell her that her unflinching hope was baseless. He was putting it off. Feeling like an executioner who knows that he must kill tomorrow, he had tried to give a little joy today.

"Lance," she had said before the tournament, asking her strange favour humbly and childishly, "now that we are together, you will wear my token at the fight?"

Now that we are together! And in her tone of voice he had read a picture of twenty years' desertion, realizing for the first time that during all that period she had been following his career of chivalry like a schoolchild doting on the batsman Hobbs. The poor bird had been picturing all the fights—almost certainly picturing them quite wrong: nourishing a starved heart on second–hand accounts in secret: wondering whose token was in the place of honour today. Perhaps she had been telling herself for twenty years that some day the great champion would fight under a favour of her own—one of those ridiculous ambitions with which the wretched soul consoles itself, for lack of decent fare.

"I never wear favours," he had said, truthfully.

She had not pleaded or complained, and she had truly tried to hide her disappointment.

"I will wear yours," he had said immediately. "I shall be proud to wear it. And, besides, it will help my disguise very much. Just because everybody knows that I don't wear favours, it will be a splendid disguise to wear one. How clever of you to think of it! And it will make me fight better. What is it to be?"

It was a scarlet sleeve embroidered with large pearls. You can do good embroidery in twenty years.

A fortnight after the Winchester tournament, while Elaine nursed her hero back to life, Guenever was having a scene with Sir Bors at court. Being a woman–hater, Bors always had instructive scenes with women. He said what he thought, and they said what they thought, and neither of them understood the other a bit.

"Ah, Sir Bors," said the Queen, having sent for him in great haste as soon as she heard about the red sleeve—Bors being one of Lancelot's closest relations. "Ah, Sir Bors, have ye heard say how falsely Sir Lancelot hath betrayed me?"

Bors noted that the Queen was "nigh out of her mind for wrath," blushed deeply, and said with exaggerated patience: "If anybody has been betrayed, it is Lancelot himself. He has been mortally wounded by three knights at once."

"And I am glad," cried the Queen, "glad to hear it! A good thing if he dies. He is a false traitor knight!"

Bors shrugged his shoulders and turned his back, as much as to say that he was not going to listen to talk like that. The whole of his back, as he went to the door, showed what he thought about women. The Queen rushed after him, to retain him by force if necessary. She was not going to be cheated of her scene as easily as that.

"Why should I not call him a traitor," she shouted, "when he bare the red sleeve upon his head at Winchester, at the great jousts?"

Bors, afraid that he was going to be physically assaulted, said: "I am sorry about the sleeve. If he had not worn it as a disguise, perhaps people would not have set upon him three to one."

"Fie on him," exclaimed the Queen. "He got a good thrashing anyway, in spite of all his pride and boasting. He was beaten in fair fight."

"No, he was not. It was three to one, and his old wound broke out too."

"Fie on him," repeated the Queen. "I heard Sir Gawaine say in front of the King that it was wonderful how much he loved Elaine."

"I can't stop Gawaine saying things," retorted Sir Bors hotly, desperately, pathetically, furiously, and with terror. Then he went out and slammed the door, leaving the honours about even.

At Corbin, Elaine and Lancelot were holding hands. He smiled feebly at her, and said in a pale voice: "Poor Elaine. You always seem to be nursing me back from something. You never seem to have me, except when I am only half alive."

"I have you for good now," she said radiantly.

"Elaine," he said, "I want to talk to you."

Chapter XL

When the Ill–Made Knight came back from Corbin, Guenever was still in a rage. For some reason she was determined to believe that Elaine had become his mistress again, possibly because this seemed to be the best way of hurting her lover. She claimed that he had only been pretending about his religious feelings—as was shown by his immediately going off with Elaine when he had the chance. This, she said, had been at the back of his mind all along. He was a sham, and a weak sham at that. They had hysterical scenes together, about his weakness and shamness, alternating with other scenes of a more affectionate kind, which were necessary to counter–balance the idea that she had been in love with a sham man all her life. She began to look healthier, even beautiful again, as a result of these quarrels. But two lines came between her eyebrows, and she had a frightening eye sometimes, which glittered like a diamond. Lancelot began to have a dogged look. They were drifting.

Elaine had been explained to, and it was Elaine who now struck the only strong blow of her life. She struck it unintentionally, by committing suicide.

A death–barge came down the river to the capital, since rivers were the highways of the day, and it was moored beneath the palace wall. She was in it—the plump partridge who had always been helpless. Probably people commit suicide through weakness, not through strength. Her gentle efforts to guide the hand of destiny, by decoying her master with feeble tricks or by reticent considerations—these had not been strong enough to be recognized in the despotism of life. Her son had gone, and her lover, and there was nothing left. Even the promise to return had failed her futile grasp. It had once been something to live for, a handrail—not a particularly sumptuous handrail, but sufficiently serviceable to keep her upright. She had been able to make do. Never having been a high–handed or demanding girl, she had been able to make a little go a long way. But now even the little was gone.

Everybody went down to see the barge. It was not a lily maid of Astolat they saw, but a middle–aged woman whose hands, in stiff–looking gloves, grasped a pair of beads obediently. Death had made her look older and different. The stern, grey face in the barge was evidently not Elaine—who had gone elsewhere, or vanished.

Even if Lancelot was a weak man, or a games–maniac, or that infuriating creation, a person who consistently tries to be decent, he does not seem to have had an easy time of it. With his inherited tendency to madness, and his fantastic face, the confusion of his loyalties and moral standards, it must have been difficult enough to keep the balance of life without the various blows which were given to him above the bargain. He could have supported even the extra blows if he had been blessed with a callous heart. But his heart had been made as a match for Elaine's, and now it was unable to bear the burden which hers had been forced to lay down. All the things which he might have done for the poor creature, but which it was now too late to do, and all the shameful questions about responsibility which go with the irrevocable, united in his mind.

"Why were you not kinder to her?" cried the Queen. "Why could you not have given her something to live for? You might have showed her some bounty and gentleness, which would have preserved her life."

Guenever, who did not yet realize that Elaine had come between them more effectively than ever, said this quite spontaneously, and she meant it. She was overwhelmed with pity for her rival in the barge.

CHAPTER XLI

The new kind of life went on at Camelot in spite of the suicide. Nobody could have called it a specially happy kind—but people are tenacious of life, and will go on living. It was not all of it a plot–like life: most of it was just story—one thing after the other—a chain of unnecessary accidents. One ridiculous accident which happened about this time is worth mentioning, not because it had any consequences or antecedents, but because it was somehow the sort of thing which happened to Lancelot. He behaved about it in his own way.

He was lying on his stomach in a wood one day, with what sad thoughts nobody knows, when a lady archer came by, who was hunting. It does not say whether she was a masculine sort of lady with a moustache and gentlemen's neckwear, or whether she was one of those scatterbrains from the film world who do archery because it is so cute. Anyway, she saw Lancelot, and she thought he was a rabbit. On the whole she must have been one of the masculine ladies, for, although it is a pretty trait to shoot at men in mistake for rabbits, it would have been unusual for a film star to hit the mark. Lancelot, bounding to his feet with about six inches of arrow embedded in his rump, behaved exactly like Colonel Bogey—driven into on the second tee at golf. He said passionately: "Lady or damsel, what that thou be, in an evil time bare ye a bow; the devil made you a shooter!"

In spite of the wound in his backside, Lancelot fought in the next tournament—an important one, because of several things which happened at it. The true tension at court—which was apparent to everybody except Lancelot, who was too innocent to be conscious of such things—began to show itself clearly at the Westminster jousts. For one thing, Arthur began to assert his position in their wretched triangle. He did this, poor fellow, by suddenly taking the opposite side to Lancelot in the *grand mêlée*. He set upon his best friend, and tried to hurt him, and lost his temper. He did nothing unknightly, and, as it happened, did no harm to Lancelot. But the strange turn of feeling was there all the same. Before and afterward they were friends. But just for that one moment of anger Arthur was the cuckold and Lancelot his betrayer. Such is the apparent explanation—an unconscious recognition of their relationship—but there may have been another thought behind it. It was a long time since Arthur had been the happy Wart, long since his home and his kingdom had been at their fortunate peak. Perhaps he was tired of the struggle, tired of the Orkney clique and the strange new fashions and the difficulties of love and modern justice. He may have fought against Lancelot in the hope of being killed by him—not a hope exactly, not a conscious attempt. This just and generous and kind–hearted man may have guessed unconsciously that the only solution for him and for his loved ones must lie in his own death—after which Lancelot could marry the Queen and be at peace with God—and he may have given Lancelot the chance of killing him in fair fight, because he himself was worn out. It may have been. At all events, nothing came of it. There was the blaze of temper, and then their love was fresh again.

Another important feature of the tournament was that Lancelot, with innocent idiocy, alienated the Orkneys finally and for good. He unhorsed the whole clan except Gareth, one after the other, and Mordred and Agravaine he unhorsed twice. Only a saint could have been fool enough to have saved their lives so often in rescues from Dolorous Towers and so on —but to cap it by knocking them down at will, at such a time, was the policy of a natural. Gawaine, it is true, was decent enough to refuse to have a hand in plots against Lancelot's life, and Gaheris was dull. But from this day on it was only a question of time, as between the fashionable party of Mordred and Agravaine and the safety of the commander–in–chief.

A third straw in the wind was that Gareth fought on Lancelot's side at Westminster. The peculiar cross–plays of sentiment were noticed by everybody—the King against his second self, and Gareth against his own brothers. With such an undertow there was evidently a storm to come. It came characteristically, from a quarter which nobody had suspected.

There was a cockney knight called Sir Meliagrance, who had never been happy at court. If he had lived in the earlier days, when a man was judged as a man, he might have got along well enough. Unfortunately he belonged to the later generation, of Mordred's fashions, and he was judged by the new standards. Everybody knew that Sir Meliagrance was not quite out of the top drawer. He knew it himself—the top drawer had been invented by Mordred—and the knowledge did not make him happy. Beside all this, Sir Meliagrance had a special cause for misery which had poisoned society for him. He was desperately, hopelessly—and had been ever since he could remember—in love with Guenever.

The news came while Arthur and Lancelot were at the nine–pin alley. They had got into the habit of going off to this unfashionable spot every day to cheer themselves with a little conversation.

Arthur was saying: "No, no, Lance. You never understood poor Tristram at all."

"He was a cad," said Lancelot obstinately.

They were talking in the past tense because Tristram had finally been murdered, while playing the harp to La Beale Isoud, by the exasperated King Mark.

"Even if he is dead," added the knight.

But the King shook his head vehemently.

"Not a cad," he said. "He was a buffoon, one of the great comic characters. He was always getting himself into extraordinary situations."

"A buffoon?"

"Absent–minded," said the King. "That is the great comic affliction. Look at his love–affairs."

"You mean Isoud White–Hands?"

"I firmly believe that Tristram got those two girls completely mixed up. He goes mad on La Beale Isoud, and then forgets all about her. One day he is getting into bed with the other Isoud when something about the action reminds him of something. It dawns on him that there are two Isouds, not one—and he is terribly upset about it. Here am I getting into bed with Isoud White–Hands, he says, when all the time I was in love with La Beale Isoud! Naturally he was upset. And then being nearly murdered in his bath by the Queen of Ireland. There was a light of high comedy about that young man, and you ought to forgive him for being a cad."

"I—" began Lancelot, but at that moment the messenger arrived.

He was a small, breathless boy with an arrow–slit in his jupon, under the right armpit. He held the rent together with his fingers and talked fast.

It was about the Queen, who had gone a–Maying—for it was the first of May. She had started early, as the custom was, intending to be back by ten o'clock, with all the dewy primroses and violets and hawthorn blooms and green–budding branches which it was proper to gather on such a morning. She had left her bodyguard behind—the Queen's knights, who all bore the vergescu as their badge of office—and had taken with her only ten knights in civilian clothes. They had been dressed in green, to celebrate the festival of spring. Agravaine was among them—he had attached himself to Guenever lately, to spy on her—and Lancelot had been left out on purpose.

Well, they had been riding home cheerfully, all chattering and bloomy and branchy, when Sir Meliagrance had leaped up at their feet, in an ambush. The top–drawer business had preyed on his mind till he had determined to be ungentlemanly in earnest, if everybody accused him of being so. He had known that the Queen's party was unarmed, and that Lancelot was not with them. He had brought a strong force of archers and men–at–arms to take her captive.

There had been a fight. The Queen's knights had defended her as best they could with swords and falchions, until they were all wounded, six of them seriously. Then Guenever had surrendered, to save their lives. She had made a bargain with Sir Meliagrance—whose heart was not really in the business of being a blackguard—that, if she called her defenders off, he must promise to take the wounded knights with her to his castle, and he must let them sleep in the anteroom of her chamber. Meliagrance, loving Guenever, flinching at his own half–hearted wickedness, and knowing the hopelessness of forcing his beloved against her will, had agreed to terms. The poor fellow had never been cut out to be a villain.

In the confusion of getting the sorry procession of hurt men slung across their horses, the Queen had kept her head. She had beckoned the little page, who had a fresh and fast pony, and she had secretly slipped him her ring, with a message for Lancelot. When he saw his opportunity, he was to gallop for his life—and he had done so, with the archers after him. Here was the ring.

Lancelot, half–way through the story, was already shouting for his armour. By the time it was told Arthur was kneeling at his feet, strapping on the greaves.

Chapter XLII

When the mounted archers rode back crestfallen, saying that they had been unable to shoot the boy, Sir Meliagrance knew what was going to happen. He was distracted with misery, not only because he knew that he had been acting unwisely and wickedly, but also because he was genuinely in love with the Queen. He still had a kick in him, however, and he saw that after having gone so far it was too late to retreat. Lancelot would be bound to come in answer to the message, and it was necessary to gain time. The castle was not ready for a siege—but, if it could be got ready, there would be a fair prospect of making terms with the besiegers, considering that the Queen would be inside. So Lancelot must be stopped at all costs, until the castle had been put in posture of defence. He guessed correctly that Lancelot would come riding helter–skelter to the Queen's aid, as soon as he could get himself armed. The best way of stopping him would be with a second ambush, at a narrow glade in the wood which he would have to ride through—a glade so narrow that archers would certainly be able to kill his horse, if not to pierce his armour. Since the Troubled Times, all roads had been cleared of undergrowth for the distance of a bowshot on either side—but this glade, on account of peculiarities in the terrain, had been overlooked. And a well–shot arrow at fair range could penetrate the best armour, as Meliagrance knew.

So the ambush was sent out post–haste, and everything within the castle was at sixes and sevens. Herdsmen were driving beasts into the keep—and all the beasts strayed, or got muddled with each other, or would not go through gates. Pump boys were feverishly bringing water to the great tubs —it was one of those futile castles, which appear to have originated in Ireland, whose bailey was without a well. Maids were running about on the verge of hysterics—for Sir Meliagrance, like many people out of the wrong drawer, was determined to receive his captive Queen in a way which would be above criticism. They were making boudoirs for her, and taking the tapestries out of his bachelor bedroom to go in hers, and polishing the silver, and sending to the nearest neighbours for the loan of gold plate. Guenever herself, ushered into a small waiting–room while the state apartments were made ready for her reception, added to the confusion by insisting on bandages and hot water and stretchers for her wounded men. Sir Meliagrance, running up and down stairs with cries of "Yes, Ma'am, in 'arf a minute" or "Marian, Marian, where the 'ell have you put the candles?" or "Murdoch, take them sheep out of the solar this instant," found time to lean his forehead against the cold stone of an embrasure, to clutch his bewildered heart, to curse his folly, and further to disarrange his already disordered plots.

The Queen was the first to get her affairs in order. She only had the bandaging to arrange, and naturally her wants were the earliest to be attended. She was sitting with her waiting–women at one of the windows of the castle, a sort of calm–centre in the middle of the whirlwind, when one of the girls called out that something was coming down the road.

"It is a cart," said the Queen. "It will be something to do with the provisions of the castle."

"There is a knight in the cart," said the girl, "a knight in armour. I suppose somebody is taking him away to be hanged."

In those days it was considered disgraceful to ride in a cart.

Later, they saw that there was a horse trotting behind the cart—which was coming at a great gallop—with its reins dangling in the dust. Later still they were horrified to see that all the entrails of the horse were dangling in the dust also. It was stuck full of arrows like a porcupine, and trotted along with a strange look of unconcernedness. Perhaps it was numbed by shock. It was Lancelot's horse, and Lancelot was in the cart, beating the cart–horse with his scabbard. He had fallen into the ambush as expected, had spent some time trying to get at his assailants—who had escaped the heavy dismounted iron man easily, by jumping over hedges and ditches—and then he had set out to walk the rest of the way, in spite of his armour. Meliagrance had counted on the impossibility of such a walk, for a man dressed in an equipment which may have weighed as much as himself— but he had not counted on the cart which Lancelot commandeered. A measure of the great man's anxiety about the Queen on this occasion is that he is said to have swum his horse across the Thames at the beginning of the ride, from Westminster Bridge to Lambeth, in spite of the fact that, if anything had gone wrong, his armour would certainly have drowned him.

"How dare you say it was a knight going to be hanged?" exclaimed the

Queen. "You are a hussy. How dare you compare Sir Lancelot to a felon?"

The wretched girl blushed and held her tongue, while Lancelot could be seen throwing his reins to the terrified carter, and storming up the drawbridge, shouting at the top of his voice.

Sir Meliagrance heard of the arrival just as Lancelot was bursting in at the Great Gate. A flustered porter, taken by surprise, tried to shut it in his face, but received a blow on the ear from the iron fist, which knocked him flat. The gate swung open, undefended. Lancelot was in one of his rare passions, possibly on account of the sufferings of his horse.

Meliagrance, who had been overseeing some men–at–arms while they broke up the wooden sheds on the Great Court as a precaution against Greek Fire, lost his nerve. He sprinted for the back stairs and was already kneeling at the Queen's feet, while Lancelot was raging round the Porter's lodge, demanding the Queen.

"What is the matter now?" asked Guenever, looking at the extraordinary, vulgar man who sprawled before her—a look, curiously enough, not without affection. After all, it is a compliment to be kidnapped for love, especially when all ends happily.

"I yield, I yield!" cried Sir Meliagrance. "Ow, I yield to you, dear Queen. Save me from that Sir Lancelot!"

Guenever was looking radiantly beautiful. It may have been the Maying, or the compliment which the cockney Knight had paid her, or some premonition such as comes to women before their joy. At any rate she was feeling happy, and she bore no grudge against her captor.

"Very well," she said, cheerfully and wisely. "The less noise there is about this, the better for my reputation. I will try to calm Sir Lancelot."

Sir Meliagrance positively whistled with relief, he sighed so hard.

"That's right," he said. "That's the old cock sparrer—ahem! ahem! Beg pardon, I'm sure. Will it please your gracious Majesty to stye the night at Meliagrance Castle, when you 'ave been and calmed Sir Lancelot, for the sike of your wounded knights?"

"I don't know," said the Queen.

"You could all go awai in the morning," urged Sir Meliagrance, "and we could sye no more abaht it. It would be more regular like. You could sye you was here on a visit."

"Very well," said the Queen, and she went down to Lancelot while Sir Meliagrance mopped his brow.

He was standing in the Inner Court, shouting for his enemy. When Guenever saw him, and he saw her, the old electric message went between their eyes before they spoke a word. It was as if Elaine and the whole Quest for the Grail had never been. So far as we can make it out, she had accepted her defeat. He must have seen in her eyes that she had given in to him, that she was prepared to leave him to be himself—to love his God, and to do whatever he pleased—so long as he was only Lancelot. She was serene and sane again. She had renounced her possessive madness and was joyful to see him living, whatever he did. They were young creatures—the same creatures whose eyes had met with the almost forgotten click of magnets in the smoky Hall of Camelot so long ago. And, in truly yielding, she had won the battle by mistake.

"What is all the fuss about?" asked the Queen.

They had a light, bantering tone. They were in love again.

"You may well ask."

Then he added in an angrier voice, and flushing: "He has shot my horse."

"Thank you for coming," said the Queen. Her voice was gentle. It was the first voice he remembered. "Thank you for coming so fast and so bravely. But he has given in, and we must forgive him."

"It was shameful to murder my poor horse."

"We have made it up."

"If I had known you were going to make it up," said Lancelot rather jealously, "I would not have nearly killed myself in coming."

The Queen took his bare hand. The gauntlet was off.

"Are you sorry," she asked, "because you have done so well?"

He was silent.

"I don't care about him," said the Queen, blushing. "I only thought it would be better not to have a scandal."

"I don't want a scandal any more than you do."

"You must do as you please," said the Queen. "Fight him if you like. You are the one to choose."

Lancelot looked at her.

"Madam," he said, "so ye be pleased, I care not. As for my part, ye shall soon please."

He always fell into the grandeur of the High Language, when he was moved.

CHAPTER XLIII

The wounded knights were laid on stretchers in the outer room. The inner room, where Guenever slept, had a window with iron bars. There was no glass.

Lancelot had noticed a ladder in the garden, which was long enough for his purpose—and, although they had made no assignation, the Queen was waiting. When she saw his crumpled face at the window, with the inquisitive nose against the stars, she did not think it was a gargoyle or a demon. She stood for a few heartbeats, feeling the wild blood surge in her neck, then went silently to the window—the silence of an accomplice.

Nobody knows what they said to each other. Malory says that "they made either to other their complaints of many divers things." Probably they agreed that it was impossible to love Arthur and also to deceive him. Probably Lancelot made her understand about his God at last, and she made him understand about her missing children. Probably they fully agreed to accept their guilty love as ended.

Later, Sir Lancelot whispered: "I wish I might come in."

"I would as fain."

"Would you, madam, with all your heart that I were with you?"

"Truly."

The last iron bar, as he broke it out, cut the brawn of his hand to the bone.

Later still, the whispers faltered, and there was silence in the darkness of the room.

Queen Guenever lay long in bed next morning. Sir Meliagrance, anxious to get the whole affair safely ended as soon as possible, fussed in the antechamber, wishing she were gone. For one thing, he was not anxious to prolong his own torture, by keeping the Queen under his roof, whom he loved and could not have.

At last, partly to hurry her off and partly out of a lover's uncontrollable curiosity, he went into the bedroom to wake her up—a proceeding which was possible in the days of the levee.

"Mercy," said Sir Meliagrance, "what ails you, Ma'am, to sleep so long?"

He was looking at his lost beauty in the bed, and pretending not to do so. The blood of Lancelot's cut hand was all over the sheets.

"Traitress!" cried Sir Meliagrance suddenly. "Traitress! You are a traitor to King Arthur!"

He was beside himself with rage and jealousy, believing himself deceived. He had been assuming, since his own enterprise had gone agley, that the Queen was a pure woman; and that he, in seeking to enjoy her, was in the wrong. Now he saw that all the time she had been cheating him, only pretending to be too virtuous to love him, and meanwhile sporting with her wounded knights under his very nose. He had jumped to the conclusion that the blood had come from a wounded knight—otherwise why should she have insisted on having them in the antechamber? The wildest envy was mixed with his rage. He never saw the bars of the window, which had been replaced as carefully as possible.

"Traitress! Traitress! I accuse you of high treason!"

The yells of Sir Meliagrance brought the hurt knights hobbling to the door —the commotion spread—tire–women and serving maids, pages, turf boys, a couple of grooms, all came with excitement to the scene.

"They are all false," cried Sir Meliagrance, "all or some. A wounded knight hath been here."

Guenever said, "That is untrue. They can prove it."

"It is a lie," the knights shouted. "Choose which of us you will fight. We will fight you."

"No, you won't," yelled Sir Meliagrance. "Away with your proud language. A wounded knight 'as been sleeping with 'er Majesty!"

And he kept on pointing to the blood, which was certainly good evidence, until Sir Lancelot arrived among the now sheepish bodyguard. Nobody noticed that his hand was in a glove.

"What is the matter?" asked Lancelot.

Meliagrance began telling him, wildly, gesticulating, seizing with excitement upon a fresh person to tell. He was like a man crazy with grief.

Lancelot said coldly: "May I remind you about your own conduct towards the Queen?"

"I don't know what you mean. I don't care. I know a knight was in this room last evening."

"Be careful what you say."

Lancelot looked at him hard, trying to warn him and to bring him to his senses. They both knew that this accusation must end in trial by combat, and Lancelot wanted to make him realize with whom he would have to fight. Sir Meliagrance did realize this eventually. He looked at Lancelot with unexpected dignity.

"And you be careful too, Sir Lancelot," he said quietly. "I know you are the best knight in the world, but be careful 'ow you fight in a wrong quarrel. God might strike a stroke for justice, Sir Lancelot, after all."

The Queen's true lover set his teeth.

"That must be left to God," he said.

Then he added, very meanly: "So far as I am concerned, I say plainly that none of these wounded knights was in the Queen's room. And if you want to fight about it, I will fight you."

Lancelot was, in the end, to fight for the Queen at the stake three times: first in the good quarrel of Sir Mador, second in this very doubtful quibble of words with Sir Meliagrance, and third in a quarrel which was wrong altogether—and each fight brought them nearer to destruction.

Sir Meliagrance threw down his glove. He was so certain of the truth of his assertion that he had become obstinate, as people do in violent arguments.

He was prepared to die rather than withdraw. Lancelot took the glove—what else could he do? Everybody began attending to the paraphernalia of a challenge, the usual sealing of the gages with signets and so on, and the fixing of the date. Sir Meliagrance grew quieter. Now that he was caught in the machinery of justice, he had time to reflect, and, as usual, his reflections went the opposite way. He was an inconsistent man.

"Sir Lancelot," he said, "now that we are fixed to have a fight, you won't do nothing treacherous to me meanwhile?"

"Of course not."

Lancelot looked at him in genuine amazement. His heart was like Arthur's. He was always getting himself into trouble—as, for instance, by unhorsing the Orkneys at Westminster—through underestimating the wickedness of the world.

"We will be friends till the battle?"

The old warrior felt his long–accustomed pang of shame. He was to fight this man for saying what was practically true.

"Yes," he said enthusiastically, "friends!"

He moved towards Meliagrance with an uprush of remorse.

"Then we will have peace for now," said Meliagrance in a pleased voice. "Everything above–board. Would you like to see my castle?"

"Indeed I should."

Meliagrance led him all over the castle, from room to room, until they came to a chamber with a trap–door. The board rolled and the trap opened. Lancelot fell sixty feet, landing on deep straw in a dungeon. Then Meliagrance ordered one of the horses to be hidden, and went back to the Queen to tell her that her champion had ridden ahead. Lancelot's well–known habit of abrupt departures lent colour to the story. It seemed to Meliagrance the best way of ensuring that God should not choose the wrong side of this quarrel—for Meliagrance was muddled with his standards too.

Chapter XLIV

The second trial by combat was as sensational as the Mador one had been. For one thing, Lancelot arrived, at the last moment, by a still narrower margin. They had waited for him, and given him up, and persuaded Sir Lavine to fight in his place. Sir Lavine was actually riding into the lists when the great man came at full gallop, on a white horse which belonged to Meliagrance. He had been held captive in the dungeon until that morning—when the girl who brought him his food had finally liberated him in the absence of her master, in exchange for a kiss. He had suffered some complicated scruples about this kiss: but had decided in the end that it was permissible.

Meliagrance went down at the first charge, and refused to get up.

"I yield," he said. "I'm a gonner."

"Get up, get up. You have not fought at all."

"I shan't," said Sir Meliagrance.

Lancelot stood over him in perplexity. He owed him a thrashing for the business of the horse, and for the treachery of the trap–door. But he knew that the man's accusation was essentially right, and he did not like the idea of killing him.

"Mercy," said Sir Meliagrance.

Lancelot turned his eyes sideways to the Queen's pavilion, where she sat under the Constable's ward. Nobody could see this look of inquiry because of the great helm.

Guenever saw it, however, or felt it in her heart. She turned her thumb down, over the edge of the box, and secretly jabbed it downward several times. Meliagrance, she thought, was a dangerous man to keep alive.

There was great silence in the arena, while everybody waited without breath, leaning forward and looking upon the combatants like a circle of vultures whose prey is not yet dead. Everybody was waiting for the *coup de grâce*, like the people at a Roman amphitheatre or at a Spanish bull–fight, and everybody was sure that Lancelot would give it. The accusation of Meliagrance had been, in their opinion, much more serious than the accusation of Mador—and they thought, like Guenever, that he deserved to perish. For in those days love was ruled by a different convention to ours. In those days it was chivalrous, adult, long, religious, almost platonic. It was not a matter about which you could make accusations lightly. It was not, as we take it to be nowadays, begun and ended in a long week–end.

The spectators saw Lancelot hesitating over the man, then heard his voice coming muffled by the helm. He was making proposals.

"I will give you odds," he was saying, "if you will get up and fight me properly, to the death. I will take off my helm and all the armour on the left side of my body, and I will fight without a shield, with my left hand tied behind my back. That will be fair, surely? Will you get up and fight me like that?"

A sort of high, hysterical squeal came from Sir Meliagrance, who could be seen crawling towards the King's box and making violent gestures.

"Don't forget what 'e said," he was shouting. "Everybody 'eard 'im. I accept 'is terms. Don't let 'im go back on 'em. No harmour for the left side, no shield or 'elm, and 'is left hand tied behind 'is back. Everybody 'eard! Everybody 'eard!"

The King cried, "Ho and abide!" The heralds and kings–at–arms came down the lists, and Meliagrance was silenced. Everybody felt shame on his behalf. In the distasteful stillness, while he muttered and insisted that the terms should be observed, reluctant hands disarmed Sir Lancelot and tied him. They felt they were helping at the execution of somebody whom they loved very much, for the odds were too heavy. When they had bound him and given him his sword, they patted him—pushing him forward towards Meliagrance with these rough pats, and turning away their faces.

There was a flash in the sandy lists, like a salmon jumping a weir. It was Lancelot showing his naked side to draw the blow. And, as the blow came, there was the click of changing forms—the same click as comes in the kaleidoscope when the image alters. The blow which Meliagrance was giving had changed to a blow which Lancelot was giving.

Sir Meliagrance was dragged out of the field by horses. His helm and head were in two pieces.

Chapter XLV

Well, that is the long story of how the foreigner from Benwick stole Queen Guenever's love, of how he left her for his God and finally returned in spite of the taboo. It is a story of love in the old days, when adults loved faithfully—not a story of the present, in which adolescents pursue the ignoble spasms of the cinematograph. These people had struggled for a quarter of a century to reach their understanding, and now their Indian Summer was before them. Lancelot had given his God to Guenever, and she had given him his freedom in exchange. Elaine, who had never been more than an incidental part of the muddle, had achieved a peace of her own. Arthur, whose corner of the triangle was the least fortunate from a personal point of view, was not entirely wretched. Merlyn had not intended him for private happiness. He had been made for royal joys, for the fortunes of a nation. These, for the time of their sunset, Lancelot's two sensational victories had restored. Fashion and modernity and the rot at the Table's heart were in hiding, and his great idea was on the move once more. He was inventing Law as Power. Nor had Arthur cause for private reproach. He had kept himself aloof from the pains of Guenever and Lancelot, unconsciously trusting them not to bring the matter to his consciousness, not from motives of fear or of weak connivance, but from the noblest of motives. The power had been in the King's hands. He had been in the position of a husband who could, by a single command, solve the problem of eternal triangles by reference to the headsman's block or to the stake. His wife and her lover had been at his mercy—and that was the reason, not any reason of cowardice, why his generous heart had been determined to remain unconscious.

The Indian Summer was within their grasp, gossip was silenced, discourtesy put down. The Orkney faction could only grumble, a distant and almost subterranean complaint. In the scriptoria of the abbeys, and in the castles of the great nobles, the harmless writers scribbled away at Missals and Treatises of Knighthood, while the limners illuminated the capital letters and carefully drew blazons of arms. The goldsmiths and silversmiths hammered away, with small hammers, at gold leaf. They twisted gold wire and inlaid interlacements of the wildest complexity on the crosiers of the bishops. Pretty ladies kept robins and sparrows for pets, or tried very hard to teach their magpies to talk. Housewives of a provident turn of mind filled their cupboards with treacle as a medicine for bad air, and with home–made plasters called Flos Unguentorum for the rheumatics and muskballs to smell. They provided against Lent by purchasing dates, and green ginger of almonds, and herrings at 4s. 6d. the horse–load. Falconers and austringers abused each other's hawks to their hearts' content. In the new law courts—for Fort Mayne was over—the lawyers were as busy as bees, issuing writs for attainder, chancery, chevisance, disseisin, distraint, distress, embracery, exigent, fieri facias, maintenance, replevin, right of way, oyer and terminer, scot and lot, Quorum bonorum, Sic et non, Pro et contra, Jus primae noctis, and Questio quid juris? Thieves—it is true—could be hanged for stealing goods to the value of one shilling—for the codification of Justice was still weak and muddled—but that was not so bad as it sounds, when you remember that for a shilling you could buy two geese, or four gallons of wine, or forty–eight loaves of bread—a troublesome load for a thief in any case. In the country lanes the mere lovers, who were not gentles, walked in the sunsets with their arms round each other's waists, so that they gave the impression of a capital X when seen from behind.

Arthur's Gramarye was at peace, and the joys of peace stretched before Lancelot and Guenever. But there was a fourth corner in the puzzle.

God was Lancelot's totem. He was the other person of their battle, and now He chose the final moment to step across the path. The small boy who looked in the kettle–hat, and who dreamed of well–water which always slipped away from his lips, had cherished an ambition to do some ordinary miracle. He had managed a sort of miracle, when he rescued Elaine from her tub by being the best knight in the world—before he was trapped by Elaine on that terrible evening so that he broke his taboo. For a quarter of a century he had remembered the night with grief, and it had been with him through all the searches for the Grail. Before it, he had thought himself a man of God. Since then, he had been a swindle. Now the time had finally come to a head, when he was to be forced to face his doom.

There was a knight from Hungary called Sir Urre, who had received wounds in a tournament seven years before. He had been fighting with a man called Sir Alphagus, whom he had killed after getting these wounds—three of them on the head, four on the body and on the left hand. The mother of the dead Alphagus had been a Spanish witch, and she had put an enchantment on Sir Urre of Hungary, so that none of the wounds could ever heal up. All the time they were to go on bleeding, turn about, until the best knight in the world had tended them and salved them with his hands.

Sir Urre of Hungary had long been carried from country to country—perhaps it was a sort of hemophilia—searching for the best knight who would be able to help him. At last he had braved the channel to reach this foreign, northern land. Everybody had told him, everywhere, that his only chance was Lancelot, and in the end he had come to seek.

Arthur, who always felt the best of everybody, was sure that Lance would be able to do it—but he thought it fair that every knight of the Table should have a try. There might be a hidden excellence lurking somewhere, as had happened before.

The court was at Carlisle at the time, for the feast of Pentecost, and it was arranged that everybody should meet in the town meadow. Sir Urre was carried there in a litter and laid on a cushion of gold cloth, for the attempt at healing to begin. A hundred and ten knights—forty were away on quests—stood round him in ordered ranks, in their best clothes, and there were carpets laid down, and pavilions set up for the great ladies to watch. Arthur loved his Lancelot so much that he wanted him to have a splendid setting, in which his crowning achievement could be done.

This is the end of the book of Sir Lancelot, and now we are to see him for the last time in it. He was hiding in the harness–room of the castle, whence he could spy the field. There were plenty of leather reins in the room, hanging orderly among the saddles and the bright bits. He had noticed that they were strong enough to bear his weight. He was waiting there, hidden, praying that somebody—Gareth perhaps?—would be able to do the miracle quickly: or, if not, that they would overlook him, that his absence would not be noticed.

Do you think it would be fine to be the best knight in the world? Think, then, also, how you would have to defend the title. Think of the tests, such repeated, remorseless, scandal–breathing tests, which day after day would be applied to you—until the last and certain day, when you would fail. Think also that you know of a good reason for your failure, which you have tried to hide, tried pathetically to hide and overlook, for five and twenty years. Think that you are now to go out, before the largest and most honourable gallery that can be assembled, to make a public demonstration of your sin. They are expecting you to succeed, and you are to fail: you are to publish the deceit which you have practised for a quarter of a century, and they will all immediately know the reason for it—that reason of shame which you have sought to conceal from your own mind, and which, when it has remembered itself in the silence of your empty chamber, has pricked you into a physical motion of your head to throw it off. Miracles, which you wanted to do so long ago, can only be done by the pure in heart. The people outside are waiting for you to do this miracle because you have traded on their belief that your heart was pure—and now, with treachery and adultery and murder wringing the heart like a cloth, you are to go out into the sunlight for the test of honour.

Lancelot stood in the harness–room as white as a sheet. Guenever was out there, he knew, and she was also pale. He twisted his fingers and looked at the strong reins, and prayed as best he could.

"Sir Servause le Breuse!" cried the heralds, and Sir Servause stepped forward—a knight far down the list of competitors. He was a shy man, interested only in natural history, who had never fought with anybody in his life. He went over to Sir Urre, who was groaning from all the handling, and he knelt down and did his best.

"Sir Ozanna le Cure Hardy!"

It went on like that down the full list of a hundred and ten, whose gorgeous names are given by Malory in their proper order, so that you almost see the fine cut of their heavy brigandines, the tinctures of their blazons, and the gay colour in each panache. Their feathered heads made them look like Indian braves. The plates of their sabatons clinked as they walked, giving the firm, exciting ring of spurs. They knelt down, and Sir Urre winced, and it was no good.

Lancelot did not hang himself with the reins. He had broken his taboo, deceived his friend, returned to Guenever, and murdered Sir Meliagrance in a wrong quarrel. Now he was ready to take his punishment. He went to the long avenue of knights who waited in the sun. By the very attempt to evade notice, he had brought on himself the conspicuous place of last. He walked down the curious ranks, ugly as ever, self–conscious, ashamed, a veteran going to be broken. Mordred and Agravaine moved forward.

When Lancelot was kneeling in front of Urre, he said to King Arthur: "Need I do this, after everybody has failed?"

"Of course you must do it. I command you."

"If you command me, I must. But it would be presumptuous to try—after everybody. Could I be let off?"

"You are taking it the wrong way," said the King. "Of course it is not presumptuous for you to try. If you can't do it, nobody can."

Sir Urre, who was weak by now, raised himself on an elbow.

"Please," he said. "I came for you to do it."

Lancelot had tears in his eyes.

"Oh, Sir Urre," he said, "if only I could help you, how willingly I would. But you don't understand, you don't understand."

"For God's sake," said Sir Urre.

Lancelot looked into the East, where he thought God lived, and said something in his mind. It was more or less like this: "I don't want glory, but please can you save our honesty? And if you will heal this knight for the knight's sake, please do." Then he asked Sir Urre to show him his head.

Guenever, who was watching from her pavilion like a hawk, saw the two men fumbling together. Then she saw a movement in the people near, and a mutter came, and yells. Gentlemen began throwing their caps about, and shouting, and shaking hands. Arthur was crying the same words again and again, holding gruff Gawaine by the elbow and putting them into his ear. "It shut like a box! It shut like a box!" Some elderly knights were dancing around, banging their shields together as if they were playing Pease Pudding Hot, and poking each other in the ribs. Many of the squires were laughing like madmen and slapping each other on the back. Sir Bors was kissing King Anguish of Ireland, who resented it. Sir Galahalt, the hault prince, had fallen over his scabbard. Generous Sir Belleus, who had borne no grudge for having his liver cut open on that distant evening beside the pavilion of red sendal, was making a horrible noise by blowing on a grass blade held edgewise between his thumbs. Sir Bedivere, frightfully repentant ever since his visit to the Pope, was rattling some holy bones which he had brought home as a souvenir of his pilgrimage: they had written on them in curly letters, "A Present from Rome." Sir Bliant, remembering his gentle Wild Man, was embracing Sir Castor, who had never forgotten the Chevalier's knightly rebuke. Kind and sensitive Aglovale, the forgiver of the Pellinore feud, was exchanging hearty thumps with the beautiful Gareth. Mordred and Agravaine scowled. Sir Mador, as red as a turkey cock, was making it up with Sir Pinel the poisoner, who had come back incognito. King Pelles was promising a new cloak all round, on him. The snow–haired Uncle Dap, so old as to be absolutely fabulous, was trying to jump over his walking–stick. The tents were being let down, the banners waved. The cheers which now began, round after round, were like drumfire or thunder, rolling round the turrets of Carlisle. All the field, and all the people in the field, and all the towers of the castle, seemed to be jumping up and down like the surface of a lake under rain.

In the middle, quite forgotten, her lover was kneeling by himself. This lonely and motionless figure knew a secret which was hidden from the others. The miracle was that he had been allowed to do a miracle. "And ever," says Malory, "Sir Lancelot wept, as he had been a child that had been beaten."

CPSIA information can be obtained
at www.ICGtesting.com
Printed in the USA
BVHW051243060223
657963BV00014B/1071

ISBN 9798688463026